the
year
i
left

Other Books by Christine Brae

the
year
i
left

CHRISTINE BRAE

The Year I Left

Edited by Jim Thomas (JimThomasEditor.com)

ISBN: 978-1-944109-90-5

VESUVIAN BOOKS

Published by Vesuvian Books
www.vesuvianbooks.com

Printed in the United States

10 9 8 7 6 5 4 3 2 1

For all of us who once suffered in silence. Come out into the light –
we deserve to live in the sunshine just like everyone else. CB

Table of Contents

Part I: MY FALL AND WINTER

"A thousand half loves must be forsaken to take one whole heart home."

Rumi

Chapter One

A Thousand Half Loves

Sometime in the late summer when the air began to tingle and the leaves started to fall, I opened my eyes one morning and my view of the world had changed.

Just like that. I can still see it in my head. The way I let it all unfold. It was a train wreck waiting to happen, and I let it.

I left for a business trip that morning with my house in total disarray. I had no good reason for refusing to take Charlie to his school bus, and despite having some time to change our dog's water bowl, I chose not to do it. There it lay, next to the unwashed food dish, crusted with the remains of last night's dinner. I figured Jack would get home from the gym and handle it all.

Piles of paper gathering dust on the floor and debit card receipts busting out of a little white box screamed for my attention. I ignored them. My home office, the place where I used to hide all day, was like a war zone.

And it wasn't like we had money issues. Paying our bills was the least of my worries. Jack had made a killing when his startup was bought out, and I was the head of client services at a global real-estate company.

I just stopped giving a damn. Nothing interested me. I was beset by indifference. I just couldn't keep up anymore. The sleepless nights, the exhaustion, the constant streaming in my head. Everything seemed so insignificant, so mundane. My successes, my accomplishments, they had lost all meaning.

All I wanted was a chance to get out of the house, to leave that life for the only thing I seemed to do well these days—work.

That was my morning.

And this was my afternoon.

I took a deep whiff of the cool sea air, filling my lungs to the brim with relief, grateful for the reprieve of being far from home. Our San Francisco sales office was located right by the Embarcadero, a quick walk from where I sat. The wharf was crowded that afternoon, something I hadn't expected in mid-September. Save for a few young students on field trips, there were tourists everywhere. The sun was so bright that the tips of the waves sparkled like diamonds. I don't know why I thought of gilded stones and shiny white pearls, but I did. I imagined them bobbing up and down in the water while I leaned on the wooden rail surrounding the deck.

Maybe it's because of my mother and my grandmother—they both loved pearls. Whenever Jack wanted to buy me jewelry, I begged him to stay away from those misshapen, ugly white things. They age you. Make you look old.

"Well, we are kind of old," he'd tease.

"You're old. Thirty-five is not that old," I'd snap back. Although it did feel old when you'd married at twenty-five and this was the only life you'd known.

"Hello?" A woman's voice coupled with a light touch of my shoulder filled me with a surge of energy. There she was, my friend Valerie, leaning in to give me a kiss on both cheeks, her long brown hair blowing in the wind, almond-shaped eyes squinting from the sun's glare.

"Hi, you!" I squealed before wrapping my arms around her and glancing around for another familiar face. "Dylan?" I asked.

"He had to take a call at the office. He'll meet us for dinner tonight."

She opened her purse and handed me what I'd been waiting for all morning. I leaned my head toward the flame and lit that glorious cigarette.

Birds gathered at our feet, dirty, bedraggled pigeons. I stiffened up and let out a shriek as one of them came too close. Valerie flapped her hands and stamped her feet. "Shoo," she mewed, sounding more sexy than scary.

"We can't stay here," I said. "There's too many of them." My fear of birds had started when I was only three years old. I think it's because I had broken out in hives the first time I'd touched feathers. After that, my older sister Trish would use a feather duster to scare me into submission while we were growing up.

When they all flew away, I calmed down somewhat. "Hey, before I forget, I got us a room at the Clift on Geary. It's by Union Square, so you know what that means?" I asked.

Val continued to stomp at the birds even after they had scurried off. She turned to face the ocean.

"So, yes?"

"Oh," she said. "Actually, I booked my own room so I can work late into the night."

"Huh."

I slipped past her and closer to the water. "Oh, God, that feels so good." I turned my head to the side to avoid blowing smoke in her face.

Valerie scrunched her nose in response. I watched her shift her weight from right leg to left, a familiar motion required by the stilettos she wore with every single outfit. As consultants who'd developed the sales tracking system for our company, we'd worked together for a year now. In the realm of professional relationships, I shouldn't have allowed our friendship to develop as it had—it went against my own advice to wait until the end of the project. But we'd hit it off so well, I convinced myself that being friends with a coworker was no one's business.

"Jack still does not know."

"Nope. They'd kill me. Charlie's on this health kick with soccer season starting and all."

Another deep, wonderful, invigorating drag. This time I made smoke circles.

Valerie laughed and shook her head. And while basking in the silence, all I could think about was that I was where I belonged. Far away from home where the air wasn't so suffocating and my indifference wasn't so evident.

I loved everything about Val. She spoke English with a thick French accent and lived in a messy apartment in Paris with shoes and purses lined up along the hallway and ashtrays on every single thing that would hold them up. To me, she epitomized independence.

We kept walking.

"Hey, look, churros!" I exclaimed. "I think I'm going to get one. Want one too?"

Valerie laughed and shook her head. "Go get your fix, I'm going to the restroom. See you by the fortune teller, over"—she pointed to the far left corner past the aquarium—"there. It's next to that oyster place we like."

"How 'bout right there." I pointed to the floating docks and the benches stacked with onlookers. "I want to send Charlie some pictures."

The sea lions at Pier 39 were especially boisterous that day, barking and grunting as they slid in and out of the water. I was minding my own business, enjoying my snack when Valerie emerged from the washroom with a phone to her ear. I licked the crusted sugar granules from the top of my lips and stood for a few minutes, mesmerized by the lolling movement of a frolicking mother and sea pup.

Just as I turned away from the landing, my vision was blocked by two giant orange feet that lay flat against my cheeks. A drooping, pointy beak brushed against my lips and snatched the churro right out of my mouth. A strong burst of air and a flapping of wings knocked me to the ground. I fell to my knees and stared out in front of me, stunned and flustered at the same time.

"Mommy, that seagull just stole the lady's food!" said a little girl in pigtails.

My biggest phobia had just been realized. Not only had gross webbed feet touch my face, I had been kissed by a bird.

"Miss, are you all right?"

I heard your voice for the first time. I heard it before I saw you in front of me, one knee up, the other on the ground to keep your balance. Your face was so close to mine, I thought for a moment you were someone I knew. And then I realized that you were a stranger, one with kind consoling eyes. I struggled to lift my knees up while you helped me keep my balance. You looked polished, business-like—your white shirt uncreased and tucked into gray dress pants.

Valerie came running, phone in hand, heels click-clacking. "Carin!" she yelled. "What happened?"

Her voice, familiar, woke me up. Slowly I pushed up with my hands, lifting myself off the ground. When you sprang to your feet and hoisted me up by the shoulders, I finally saw your face. You looked like winter. Dark and deep-set eyes whose gaze could cut through ice. With your brows furrowed and lips pursed, you looked genuinely worried. I noticed how thick your hair was—it blew in the wind and covered your face.

Soon enough, Valerie had reached us.

I turned to address her, ignoring the fact that you were still standing right in front of me. "I'm okay." Embarrassment began to set in. I straightened my shirt, patted down my hair, and directed a forced smile at both of you. Valerie took my hand and led me away.

"Miss?" you called to me. Softly at first and then louder. "Miss."

I didn't stop to look at you, kept on walking. "I'm okay, thank you!"

Chapter Two
Not Since You

Valerie slowed to a stop as soon as we were out of the crowds, far from Pier 39. I kept my eyes fixed on her feet. They made me nervous. I could just imagine those skinny stilettos getting stuck in one of those wooden slats and her falling flat on her face.

I grabbed her arm instinctively as if trying to fasten her to the ground.

"Who was that guy?" she asked.

I shook my head. "No idea."

"The way he helped you up, I thought he was a friend."

"Nope."

"He would make a nice friend, wouldn't he?" she said with a giggle.

I laughed too. "Valerie, the walking guy-dar."

"Well, are you saying it isn't true? The way those men all flock to you, the interesting experiences you have, even when you're not looking."

"It's all in your mind, my friend."

"Yes, I suppose the fact that the people at your office named you 'Legs Frost' is just a figment of my imagination," she quipped to get the last word. As always.

We found a bench directly facing the ocean, our view obscured by tourists hanging on to the railings for dear life. "Spaghetti," I muttered out loud, referring to the arms and legs twisted around the rails right in front of me.

These accidental thoughts did not discriminate. They never gave me a moment to myself.

Val's gentle nudge brought me back. "Spaghetti? You want Italian?"

She searched on Open Table, so focused on that little red app until she looked up at me with a smile.

"No, no!" I stressed. "I was thinking about something else."

"Oh." Val swiped her screen a few times. "Butterfly? I feel like Asian fusion tonight."

"I don't care," I responded. "I'm just happy I'm here. I needed a break."

"From what? You've got a pretty good life, from what I can see." She did this all the time—tried to make me see the good side of things. And I swear, I used to. I had been grateful once. These days I was impervious to the passion I used to have for life.

I agreed that nothing made sense when you looked at me from the outside. Everything was so in place, it was ridiculous. I had no secrets, no scandalous past. Just an ordinary life with ordinary joys and ordinary sorrows. At least that's how it looked to me.

That was all before I met you.

"If only you knew," I answered, looking away. I wondered whether she'd heard me. Our conversation was drowned out by the buzz of other chatter, exclamations, excited yelps and shrieks.

She looked at me, a smile breaking on her face. "It's your birthday! We have to do something special."

"Next week."

"Yeah but I won't be with you, so it's got to be tonight," she said, clutching her hands together. Valerie paused before placing a hand on my forearm. "So, Paris next month? I'll clean my apartment, I promise. We're going to see Imagine Dragons, right?"

"Does their tour take them somewhere else a few weeks later? Mid-

November, perhaps? Can't do it the week of Halloween—still deciding what to do for my mom's thing."

The atmosphere always turned awkward every time I mentioned my mother. I was ten years older than Val, and when my mother had died suddenly, the fragility of life, the vulnerability that often accompanied random tragedy smacked me in the face.

We stayed quiet for a while. The clouds rolled across the water and turned into a heavy mist of fog. Alcatraz faded in the distance.

"You miss her, I know."

I kept staring into the heavy gray haze. "If she were here, she'd know what to tell me. She always had the answers, you know?"

"I do." Valerie took my hand. I leaned my head on her shoulder. She played with her phone, swiped up and down before holding it up. "London, but it's the week of Thanksgiving!"

"So what? Let's do it then."

She glared at me. "Thanksgiving. Did you hear me?"

"Jack's with his family. I'm sure he'll manage."

"What about Charlie? Should we take him with us?"

"He'll be with his cousins. He won't even notice I'm gone."

Val knew not to go further. She shrugged and leaned back into the bench. "Were you able to find someone?" Her voice had turned into a whisper. "You know, to talk to about those night attacks?"

"Attacks?" I giggled. "You mean when the pillows come alive in the middle of the night and try to smother me?"

Valerie's face was always too kind; even when she tried to assume a dirty look. "You are just so funny. You know what I mean. Panic."

"Oh, those." I fidgeted with my front pockets, crossing my right leg over my left and then uncrossing it. I wished I'd never told her. When you open up to even your closest allies, they always turn your deepest darkest secrets against you. "They only last for about five minutes. Nothing I can't handle."

"Until you get some help." She grabbed my arm and shook it.

"Right?"

Right.

Nights out with Valerie were always eventful. I'd learned from my French friends that sometimes Americans were too uptight, too concerned with so much political correctness.

"Why are you Americans always so indecisive, so noncommittal?" she'd asked me once.

"What do you mean?"

"When I ask you, did you like it? Do you like them? You never say yes or no. You say, so-so, or yeah, it was okay, or not really. It's always gray with you. With us, it's either yes or no. Nothing in between."

Her European-ness rubbed off on me whenever we were together. There was a different feeling of boldness, of not having a care in the world. Valerie was never fazed by the server's dazed expression when we left the table in the middle of dinner to step outside for a cigarette.

"We will be back, okay?" she'd say.

We did that all night, sipped and puffed and immersed ourselves in nonsense. Once in a while, we'd revert back to work talk, make fun of those who didn't understand the purpose of the project, and avoid the subject neither of us wanted to broach.

What was happening in my personal life? I'd hardly spoken about my family. Who in their right mind would be vaguely interested in a neat little life, filled with clichéd accomplishments like work, career, marriage? Such normalcy embarrassed me.

Instead, we focused on Valerie. She was married too, with parents who owned a Thai restaurant by the Bastille in Paris. She had a brother in school and a younger sister who helped run her parents' business.

But Valerie was different. She wanted so much out of life, and she

9

was living it. She didn't want to stay put in Paris, taking care of her parents. She didn't even want children. She was against everything that tied her down. Every time we were together, she'd share stories and secrets borne out of her ability to keep moving, keep evolving.

I'd done just the opposite. Tied myself down at twenty-five and never looked back.

Valerie wanted to travel the world, move from one place to the other.

When did I start wishing I was like her?

I thought it was my cross to bear. I thought that life was just like this.

You live, you love, you lose.

We were seated with strangers between two adjacent booths, allowing active talk amidst tables to be shared, and secrets to be overheard. Everyone could tune in to what everyone else was saying. Val and I smiled at each other and purposely stayed silent.

The couple to our left was obviously on a Tinder date. The young lady was telling the young man about her job. At the end of her monologue, all he said was, "You don't look like you did in those pictures."

I squeaked under my breath when Val kicked me on the shin.

Four people sat to our right, three women and a man. I only knew it was a man because of his voice. Val kicked me once again as the women across from me strained to speak to the man at the table. They flipped their hair and leaned closer, asking the man where he'd gone the night before when he'd ditched them for a woman at the bar. They spoke in Spanish, but I understood. In heavy accented English, the man said, "A gentleman never tells," in the most melodious intonation I'd ever heard.

Up until then, I'd thought the French language trumped all other.

But not since that day.

Not since you.

10

Chapter Three

Your Voice

That voice was yours.

Did you know it was me sitting so close?

Someone said something, and you stood to give way to your friend, who tapped your hand as she slid off the booth.

"It's that man," Val leaned in with a whisper. Overachiever. She was always the first to recognize people. Point out the obvious.

You hovered over our table. From your wide-eyed reaction, I suspect you were a bit surprised to find us there. When your friend returned, you motioned for her to switch places with you. And there we were, side by side. You unfolded the napkin and placed it on your lap. Val was quick to acknowledge you.

"Hey, we know you!" she announced. "The Wharf guy."

I saw summer. Your upturned lips touched the corners of your eyes. You exuded self- confidence. You smelled good.

Women like summer. I get why those women were falling all over themselves over you.

"Yes, hello," you answered.

But we were too preoccupied with Dylan's arrival. Our trio was complete.

Val and Dylan worked at the same place. He was the project lead, often showing up to check how things were progressing. Dylan had the same puzzled look on his face when he saw you. At first, I thought he wondered why you'd sat so close to me, but then I realized he knew you.

"Matias?" he asked. "Matias Torres?"

"Dylan Forest?"

Dylan reached over to shake your hand while Val and I squinted at him.

"Oh, sorry! This is Matias Torres, the CIO of Majorcorp."

I wasn't sure whether I'd heard him correctly.

He continued, "This is my colleague, Valerie Petier."

You shook her hand and turned to me. "And this is?"

"Carin Frost, CCO of Sardonyx," Dylan replied.

"*The* Carin Frost," you said, offering me your hand. I took it, of course. In the most unsettling way, I knew what was coming next. "What an honor. And here I was, working on a trip to meet you in person. Jim Singer said I needed to get on a plane to Chicago to learn from you."

Majorcorp was a subsidiary of the company I managed. I had heard that they'd hired a new guy out of Spain, but who would've thought it would be the man who witnessed me on my knees, knocked down by a giant bird?

"Join us, Matias," Dylan said. "It would be nice to catch up." And then he addressed both Valerie and me. "Matias and I go back a long way. We started out at the same company, managing the technology integration there."

"Well, it must have been before my time because I'd surely remember if we worked together," Val said, winking at me as you looked away. This time it was my turn to kick her under the table. You waited until Val and Dylan got caught in their exchange before leaning toward me.

"Are you okay?" you whispered. "You were quite upset earlier today."

"Embarrassed is more like it," I said. "I'm sorry you had to witness that."

"Witness what?" You smiled.

Our orders arrived and the other ladies laughed when they saw what the server placed in front of you. Two sushi rolls—that was it. The rest of us had large dishes, mine with steak and vegetables and white rice.

You turned to me with a smirk. "Oops, I don't think I ordered enough."

As the dinner host, I thought I'd make the offer. "Would you like to place another order?"

You smiled. "For some reason, I don't think you're a big eater. If you don't mind sharing with me, I think we have enough."

Your English was perfect. Before another word, you reached across with your chopsticks and brought a piece of meat from my plate to your mouth.

"Sure, help yourself," I said, surprised, not incensed. You were a comfortable stranger. Maybe it was because Dylan was a friend of yours.

"Ca-reen." By this time, both sushi rolls were long gone, and you were picking at my broccoli. The other women seemed consumed by a different topic. "Do you live in California?"

"No. I'm from Chicago."

"Ah. Chicago. The winters keep me away." You winked. "But maybe now, something will make me come back."

I nodded, lost for words.

"And you have a family?"

"Yes, I do."

You pointed your gaze to the hand under my chin. "Married?"

"Very."

This time, it was your turn to nod. I'm not even sure why I called that out, but I noticed a shift in your body language. You sat up taller, straighter, moved slightly away from me. I think it took a while to register because you put forth a delayed reaction. "Wow. No one would think ... you look so young." It was a breathy whisper. *The first of many secrets?*

I smiled. "Thank you."

Valerie leaned in and gently shoved me toward you, slapping my arm. "It's her birthday!"

"Oh!" You smiled. "Happy Birthday."

"Not 'til next week," I muttered, rolling my eyes. I don't know why but I wanted to know how old you were. I guessed you were in your thirties. "And you?"

"No. Never married. Much pressure from my family since I am already thirty."

But when you said that, your eyes drilled into mine. The way you spoke was deliberate. You had a focused look and a slight smirk. I found it arrogant. How was it that a man with such kind eyes could also be so smug?

"Pfft. You're still young. So much time ahead of you."

Five-year difference. It felt safer. For both of us, I guess. I relaxed, relieved that I was the most senior one at the table. It always made me feel in control, drew the barriers between me and the rest of you without even trying.

Don't ask me why I even had the need to do that. Lately, it felt like I'd slapped a sign on my forehead that announced I was available. It wasn't my outside appearance, that's for sure. I was a conservative dresser—fashionable but classic. More Chanel than Alexander McQueen. I never showed skin at the office. And yet Valerie constantly pointed out the attention I supposedly garnered during our late nights out on the town. There she was, constantly reporting things I didn't really care about.

"Carin, I don't think you know how beautiful you are."

Mind you, I always refuted her suggestions. If anything, it scared me to think I was even remotely encouraging attention. I worked, raised a family, kept to myself, and lived life in a straight line. What more was there to look for?

Rest, I think. That was what was missing. I was exhausted. I was searching for something. A breather, perhaps. From what, I didn't know at that time. All I knew was that this trip was a perfect getaway. For a few days, for a few hours. Spending time with the two people who really knew me.

Chapter Four

Home Life

"**W**hy hello there, sexy. How was your trip?"

Jack opened the front door and pulled me in for a kiss. He was still so handsome though the lines on his face were noticeable and his hair was salted evenly throughout. He still did triathlons, so everything about him was healthy. I guess you could call him semi-retired; he made enough money from stocks to trade from home every so often and had taken on the role of stay at home dad. While he trained for his races, while he did his woodworking, when he bought his motorcycle or his boat or his five sets of golf clubs, I worked.

I had three jobs at the same time. A full-time executive position, a tax practice on the side, and the management of my family's business. The tax practice was a choice I'd made when I hadn't wanted to give up three key clients I'd retained while Jack was just starting out. The relationships I built were of importance to me. I couldn't just abandon them despite the fact that I no longer needed a side job. These jobs, these ventures—they just had to be a part of our life. A part of our marriage.

It wasn't Jack's fault. I let him take the backseat for ten years and it had become the norm.

"Great," I said, kissing him back before kneeling on the floor to embrace our English bulldog, Brutus. "Got so much done."

16

Jack was a physical kind of guy. Hugs almost always led to kisses which always led to sex. So of course, I pulled away sooner than he would have liked. Whenever we fought, he would say that the only one who got all my love was Charlie. I'd argue but in more ways than one, it was the truth.

Selda, our maid, was in the kitchen. She shuffled over and stood close enough for me to reach out and place my hand on her shoulders.

"Arriba, por favor." She nodded before rolling the suitcase up the ramp toward the stairs.

"Charlie?" I asked my husband.

Jack slid a large white envelope toward me. I looked up at him, eyes wide with trepidation. He nodded. "He's in. The Gifted Program at Brenard wants him to start right after Spring Break."

There it was. The news I'd been dreading. Charlie deserved to be in a school that would value his advanced intellectual level, but he'd have to go to boarding school. Three hours away by plane, a million miles away from my sanity. "Where is he?"

"Downstairs, playing Switch with his cousin."

Those were the best words I'd heard all week. I loved coming home to the sound of chatter and video games and ruffle-haired boys who smelled like sweaty socks. I scared the sadness away with a big smile.

"Mama!" Charlie yelled while keeping his eyes fixed on the screen and his hands on the controller. Our fifteen-year-old nephew, Paul, sprang up to greet me.

"Hi, guys!" I greeted. Four theater seats directly faced a wall-to-wall movie screen. To the right of the viewing area were two pool tables, a curved eight-foot television, and three bowling lanes. Both boys were seated on the floor, legs crossed, pillows strewn all over the carpet in front of them.

I followed suit and sat between them. "What you playin'?"

I stole a glance at the blank canvas that rested on the large easel pushed to the far corner. I made a mental note to get that out of the way. I hadn't painted since … Well, since my mother left me.

"Paul is beating me at Mario Kart. He won't let me win!" Charlie whined.

"Why would I let you win?" Paul retorted. "I gave you all week to get your game up!"

"Mom! Tell him! Tell him, Mom!"

I placed my arm around both boys just as Jack walked in the room. He sat right behind me in one of the armchairs. "He is busy, Paul," I said in defense.

"Yeah, Paul," Charlie mocked. "Being in all honors classes is very demanding."

Paul flung a pillow far to the side, missing him on purpose. "Then how come you were on Snapchat until one this morning?"

Before Charlie could react, a herd of footsteps came rumbling down the stairs. Four more boys showed up, all in soccer gear, each more colorful than the last. I remembered Jack going all out when we shopped in Madrid for Charlie's goalie uniform. He said the more colors, the better they stood out.

Selda followed them. "Boys! Remove your shoes, please!"

"Hi, Mrs. Frost, Mr. Frost!" they cackled in unison, kicking off their sneakers. I waved Selda off, signaling for her to ignore the mess.

"Hi boys," Jack answered. "What time do you have to leave?"

"Baker wants us there by seven-thirty," one of the boys piped in.

Charlie pouted. He wasn't allowed to go to this party. He was only ten, and this was a big point of contention between us. He hung around older kids—his cousin's friends—but when it came time for parties and girls, he was obviously left out.

"That's still two hours from now, let's keep playing," Charlie ordered. "I'm bored with this—let's bowl."

Jack poured me a glass of Moscato and pulled out a bottle of craft beer from the built-in wine cellar. The kitchen had been newly remodeled to add modern, useless conveniences. To me, wine stuck in the fridge for a few hours tasted the same as wine kept in a ten-thousand-dollar contraption. Granted, Jack loved to cook, but I couldn't taste the difference between the food he cooked on the old KitchenAid versus what he concocted on the Viking. I'm sure he would have listened to me if I had given my opinion, but those were discussions I didn't care to have. Every time I arrived from a work trip, there was always a new hobby, a new fixation, more money to be spent. It made him happy, kept him busy—and out of my way.

"Carin?"

Jack reached out to touch my arm. I sat facing him on one of the leather stools, my glass resting on the marble counter. He leaned forward, eager to hear about my trip.

"Sorry. Yes?" I took a sip of my wine.

"I asked how your trip went. Did you guys finish that contract so you could disengage for the weekend?" He quietly brushed his thumb across my wrist.

"Met the new guy I told you about." I stood and pulled some carrots out of the fridge, washed them and sat back down. "By coincidence, actually. Matias something."

"Coincidence?"

"He was sitting next to Dylan, Val, and me at Butterfly the other night," I said. "Apparently, he's due to fly here soon."

"Val and Dylan. When one's there so is the other. I swear—"

"They are not sleeping together," I interrupted. "Val's married."

Jack rolled his eyes. "Anyway, Torres is his last name. It came out in the Wall Street Journal the other day." He took a carrot and started munching. "Press release."

"Oh, I missed that." I smiled.

"So, how is he?" Jack probed, gently reaching out to touch my shoulder.

"Seems okay, one of those arrogant young hot shots."

19

"He was featured in *Thirty Under Thirty* last year. Young kid." *Chomp, chomp.* He chewed on the carrots. I swigged the wine. "Apparently, he's being credited for turning his old company around— profit was at thirty-five percent right before he left to join your company."

"Huh." I shrugged. "We'll see what he can do for us."

"He has an Instagram account. Have you seen it? It has forty-five thousand followers." Jack circled the kitchen island to stand directly behind me. He pulled me into his arms to show me his phone.

I used to love being held by him. In a way, I still did. I leaned up against his chest.

As if I didn't already know, he pointed out, "He's Spanish."

"I see that."

"Looks like he's into surfing or something." Jack clicked on a picture of him surfing a wave.

"Great. Now I've seen my colleague shirtless and in swim trunks," I joked.

"Aha! Funny that's the one you noticed!" he teased. "That's just one in a thousand others. Photography is his hobby, apparently."

He slid his finger on the screen to make his point. The pictures were all in black and white, most were abstract objects against natural backgrounds.

To me, you looked like a homeless nomad. No roots.

"Yeah, they're okay," I said. "I hope he's gotten all that dillydallying out of his system. He's got a huge job ahead of him."

"He'd be a good hire for a start-up. We should have him over for dinner when he gets into town."

I stepped forward and turned to face him. "Why? Are you planning to start something up?"

He retreated. We were known for this. Turning the mood from good to sour at the drop of a dime.

"Not again, Carin." Jack turned around and headed back to the wine cellar.

"You're wasting really great potential by staying home. We're still young; we should be killing it. You're not much older than him—"

He pulled a bottle of wine out, laid it on the counter and grabbed another glass. "I've done my gig. I've made a lot of money. I'm burnt out."

I couldn't stand to discuss this again. Over and over. He didn't get it.

"You're also spending it all," I spat, but immediately regretted it. I moved toward the dinner table and began to lay out the placemats. Same old thing. Three places for the three of us. There was no way to get out of this cycle. "It's not the money," I followed up under my breath.

"What is it then?" He made no effort to move. I heard the wine swish as he poured more into his glass.

Thank goodness, Selda shuffled over to start making dinner.

"Not now," I said, finding the perfect avoidance and tipping my head toward Selda.

That's when Jack darted over, took my hand and led me toward the gigantic leather couch in the living room—custom made by Marioni, no less. For the record, these couches had the exact same marble colored style at Room and Board. We had yet to sit on it for more than a few minutes. That night was no exception.

Once we were out of Selda's view, he took me in his arms.

"Please, Car. I need to know what you want from me. You've been so distant lately."

I don't want you in my face every day, every night, every hour.

I wrapped my arms around his waist. It wasn't fair, I guess. To bring him down this rabbit hole without a game-plan. "Nothing. I'm sorry. Let's just forget it, okay? I don't know what I'm saying. I think I'm just exhausted."

"Look at us, arguing about a man we don't even know."

"Seriously!" I forced a laugh.

"Are you sure we're okay?"

I stood on my toes, pulled on his neck and kissed his forehead. "Yes. I'm sure."

Chapter Five

Namaste

*D*aily Horoscope: October 1
Friendship could easily turn into romance if you're not careful. Overnight, a platonic relationship could turn passionate, and no one is more surprised than you. It is time to think carefully about where you would like this relationship to go. While you can never go back to what was, you can stop the relationship from progressing if you are uncomfortable with the new dynamic. Think hard—only you can make this decision once.

I was uncomfortable with the new dynamic. One week later and I was still bothered by that conversation with Jack. It had been my chance to tell him something was wrong. But once again, I'd chickened out. Our relationship certainly wasn't platonic.

Unless…unless this is referring to someone else.

You're kidding. We're not even friends! He's smug and condescending and not even that cute. Well, okay, hot is the word, but—

I can't believe his face keeps coming up while I'm trying to concentrate.

I didn't know why I'd agreed to do Saturday morning yoga sessions with my sister, Trish. First of all, she had a class to teach at 9am, which meant we had to do this bright and early at 7:30. Second, I'd rather be chitchatting with her than trying to stay quiet for an entire hour. She promised it would do me good, she said I needed these times to meditate and clear my head.

"Carin."

There I was, flat on my back, staring at the sky. Right arm crossed over my body, left leg stretched out from underneath me. My cheeks burned. White balls of light danced around my eyes, forcing me to shut them. I tried to coax my mind to empty itself, but it didn't work.

What time is it? How much longer until Savasana? I need to send that email out before ten. Should I cancel my morning ride? Did I remember to throw out the old Tupperware? Where did Trish get those yoga pants?

"Where'd you get those yoga pants?" I blurted. "Are those Lulus?"

"Carin! Focus!"

"I can't! I feel like this is such a waste of time!" I sat up and crossed my right leg over my left.

"Bring your hands together," Trish ordered, her gentle voice complementing the soft sound of bells and violins that played in the background. "Circle your thoughts back to your intention."

More music. More silence. It felt like forever to hear the words I wanted to. "Light to all, peace to all, love to all. *Namaste.*"

"*Namaste,*" I answered, dipping my head all the way to the ground and immediately raising it back up.

"Trish," I said, interrupting her head-dipping process.

"What is it?" she asked. We sat facing each other, still cross-legged on our mats, surrounded by the big, beautiful outdoors.

"I just feel weird."

"Weird how?" She stretched her legs out until her toes touched mine.

"Like I'm not in my own head."

A ladybug settled right on top of my mat. I leaned down to blow it away. Trish laughed because she knew I could never touch it. Birds, bugs, the unknown—my list of fears could be quite long. I smiled back.

"Charlie, I know. But both you and Jack agreed this is what's best for him. He's a special boy and needs to be in an environment that will

23

help him develop."

"I'm glad he'll be in Ireland with you next summer. This project is just taking all my time and it's going to ramp up next spring. I want him to have fun with the fam," I said. She saw the betrayal in my movements. The way I nervously balled my fists and set them on the ground, the smile I tried to paste on my face.

"Liam will put them to work on the farm." She laughed.

"Yeah."

"It's work. I know it is. You haven't taken any time off to process what's happened in the last year."

"It's not even that," I argued. "I want to express the way I feel but it doesn't feel authentic. I feel robotic, wooden." I folded my legs and leaned back.

Daisies, hydrangeas, roses in full bloom lined the flower beds directly below the deck. The first level was all outfitted with a built in-brick grill and an outdoor entertainment center. Save for a fire pit, the second level was quite bare. We'd designed this purposely for our summer exercise sessions—the first level for Jack, the second one for me.

She sat quietly, watched me fidget. "Never mind. I know I'm not making sense."

"Car, we do need to talk. Selda told me the other day that there's a stack of bills on the floor in your study."

"I should fire her. She has no right to tell you that."

"I'm your sister!" She raised her voice, but then quickly toned it down. "Who else is she going to tell? She's worried about you. Said she caught you crying in bed a couple of times. Are you okay? Are you short on funds?"

I shook my head. Once, twice. "No, no. Not short."

"Then what is happening?"

I had nothing to say to that.

She tilted her head and kept her eyes on me, waiting for an answer.

"I—"

Jack walked out on the deck, holding my cellphone. "Your phone's been ringing off the hook."

"Who is it?" I was grateful for the excuse.

Just as I walked past Trish, she reached out and gripped my hand. "Please. That can wait."

I turned to Jack, told him I'd return the call and sat back down. This time, I leaned into my sister as she wrapped an arm around my shoulder.

"I don't know what's wrong with me. I can't stand this home. I can't stand Jack. Charlie is the only one who keeps me coming home. If I had a choice, I'd travel all week and never come back."

"What does Jack say? Have you told him?"

"No."

"Why? You used to be so close," she said. "Everyone envied your marriage. You used to be happy."

"Was I?" I'd been thinking about this to no end for the past few months. "Did I even have time to be happy?"

"That's not fair," she countered while frowning at me. "I've been telling you to hire someone for the family business, especially now that Mom's gone."

"Hiring someone takes time, Trish. There's a huge learning curve I don't have time for."

"Well, if you cut down on working so much, the time will magically appear."

"Ha," I said with a scowl. And then an afterthought. "Do you think I ever loved Jack?"

She swatted my shoulder. "What? Of course, you did! I'm your sister. I saw you. You were so happy at your wedding. And when Charlie was born, you had this sense of peace about you. You told me that Jack was your dream come true."

"I did say that, didn't I? Oh god. It seems so long ago."

She looked at me with sad eyes, her lips quivering.

"What's happening to me?" I asked. "I don't feel anything for him, for our home, for the life we built together."

Trish pulled me close. "You miss Mom. I miss her too. But what happened was beyond our control."

I wasn't quite as accepting. I was angry at the person who had so carelessly run a red light and hit her as she'd crossed the street. She had been at Nordstrom, for heaven's sake. One minute she was getting fitted for a brand-new Burberry dress and the next, she was gone. I'd run ahead of her to get the bags in the car, and had been walking back to the store when I noticed she wasn't right behind me. I found her laying in the middle of the street, a small crowd gathered around her while someone banged on her chest, trying to beat the life back into her. She never regained consciousness. And I suppose, in more ways than one, I never regained mine.

Because I'd spent my life taking care of my mother, her death was the end of all purpose. No one needed me as much as she had. My mother's death made everything meaningless.

"I think you need some help processing all that's happened. And you need to go on, pay your bills, get your life on track."

"I have this indescribable sadness." I sniffed. "There's nothing good about my life. I'm constantly wishing for something else."

"Like what?"

"Love. I want to fall in love. I want to be loved."

"But you are!" She emphasized this by throwing her hands in the air.

"I've lost it, haven't I?" I forced a smile despite my anguish.

"You've been running at full speed all these years. It's really time to slow down." She stroked my head while I leaned on her shoulder. And then she lifted my head with her hands and looked at me, eyes narrowed and stern. "Take your time, you deserve a break. But eventually, you're going to have to figure it out. You have a husband who's crazy about you and a kid who's starting middle school. Charlie misses his grandma too.

You need to get it together for him."

Didn't she know? Didn't she know that if it weren't for Charlie, I'd be gone by now?

"I know."

Right at that moment, a gentle gust of wind passed through us. I saw Trish's bangs blow to the side and felt a cold breath on my cheeks. A tiny feather, no bigger than my little finger, landed on Trish's knee.

"Did you feel that?" she asked, breathless and excited.

"Yeah, I did."

"It's Mom," she said, pinching the feather. "Telling us that things will be okay."

Chapter Six

The Plan

rish stuck the feather on my corkboard.

All weekend long, she watched me like a hawk. It was terribly uneasy, the way she fussed over me and made sure I got some rest. Remnants of the Indian summer allowed us to spend the last of the days outdoors. And since Trish lived only two blocks away, she stayed close the whole time, offering to cook, clean, and tidy up during Selda's days off.

"I'll take care of the dishes. Go to your study and catch up on your bills," she whispered to me after dinner that one night. I took her up on the offer by sneaking out the back door to look at the stars.

My relief at being back in the office on Monday was short-lived. I arrived early that morning, only to remember that my assistant, Jane, was out all week on vacation. My calendar was a mess. Immediately, I regretted becoming so dependent on her. When she'd first started, I'd wondered what on earth she would do all day. I liked to manage my own calendar, schedule my own meetings. Once she'd taken over, all memory of ever creating a meeting, let alone a Skype one, had been completely erased. It dawned on me that I couldn't check on all those missed calls.

"Carin." Madden, the CEO's assistant, popped his head into my office. "What happened to your hand?"

I laughed before bunching my fingers into a fist. I'd forgotten about it. "Oh, this! Classic. Grabbed a knife wrong tip up from the dishwasher."

"Well, you'd better be careful not to injure yourself while sifting through all those papers," he said, pointing at the door to my office. "And look." He held up his blue-lined steno pad.

"What is it?"

"Jane gave me a list of your favorite lunches. She wants to make sure you eat. I'm going to bring you lunch every day at noon. It's Prime and Provisions today. Sound okay?"

"That's an old list," I said, waving him off and turning away.

"That's because you haven't been eating for the past year!" he said, his booming voice echoing across the floor. I heaved a deep breath as I walked into my office.

A pile of papers and post-it notes littered my desk. Stacked neatly on the side were four pink slips with messages.

They were all from you.

I matched your call-back number to the missed calls on my phone.

They were from you too.

I was miffed. Not only were you arrogant—that day, I also learned that you were persistent.

I scrolled down to the bottom of my unread emails and began to work myself up.

Someone knocked on my door, and the interruption was upsetting. I needed those ten minutes before the nine o'clock meeting to catch up.

I opened my door to find you standing in front of me. You were in black jeans and a leather jacket, and your eyes were lighter than I'd remembered. I'd thought they were dark brown but that morning, they were hazel. You had the biggest smile on your face; you looked rested and content. And extremely unprofessional.

I was exhausted and unhappy. And compared to you, I felt overdressed in my black and white suit.

29

"Mr. Torres," I stated impatiently. I just wanted to get back to my email.

"Ca—" You glanced to the side to find Madden giving you the evil eye. He was protective like that. Madden was enamored with Jack. He gravitated to all the handsome husbands at every company party.

Madden kept his head turned in your direction as he walked away.

"Mrs. Frost." You moved away, rotating toward Madden to make sure he heard you. "Tienes—eh. I'm sorry. I mean do you have time for a quick chat?"

"No, actually I don't," I replied curtly, returning to my desk. You followed me in. I continued. "My admin, Jane, is out all week so my calendar is a bit messed up. But when she gets back next week, she can pencil you in."

"I called you all weekend."

I feigned ignorance. "What is it I can do for you? I have five minutes but maybe I can help."

"I couldn't stop thinking about you," you said, before catching yourself. "I mean, I was excited to meet with you and present to you my growth plan for 2016."

"New guy trying to prove himself. I get it. Set some time up through Jane and we'll review it."

"I was thinking you'd want to hear it first but if you're too busy, I can present it to the board without you. It's ready to go. I prepared the deck over the weekend."

"Wait, what?" I sneered, displeased by the arrogance. "How can you possibly have one? Who has explained our business strategy to you?"

"I don't care what it currently is. I know what it should be."

At that time, I wasn't sure whether you recognized it. The power move. In retrospect, I should have known that you'd seen it all.

Arms crossed, I moved from the doorway back to the conference table in the middle of the room and sat. "Tell me."

You followed my lead, pulled the chair next to me and slid forward so that our knees touched.

I slid back and reached for my phone. "Hold on." You watched as I typed in a number and pressed the speaker button. "Hi Mad, would you mind pushing my nine o'clock back thirty minutes and have the rest of the day follow? I'm okay to stay until seven tonight."

I placed the phone face-down next to me. "You have thirty minutes. Pitch it."

You moved toward me again. I placed my good hand up, palm almost in your face. "I can see from here, thank you."

Your presence unsettled me. The way you addressed me with your eyes was something we didn't do in the business world. I could glance anywhere in the room and still come home to those eyes. They found mine every single time. I kept thinking it was a cultural thing. You know, like when Val said I needed to make eye contact when clicking glasses and saying "cheers".

You cleared your throat. "Okay. Everyone in the industry thinks you're slow to expand. That you've been too squeamish about taking chances."

"Hmm." I'd heard this assessment from my Board of Directors. But like them, you had no idea how difficult it had been to build this much capital. I didn't want to let it go when the market was still in flux.

You continued, "There are different ways to raise capital without tapping into your own resources. I'm here to build a strategy and then find you the means of financing it."

"So your strategy is what? Expansion?"

"Pretty much."

I wondered whether you knew just how attractive you were. I bet you did. I bet you'd used it many times to your advantage. Your deep-set eyes and your super thick eyebrows, all in perfect symmetry with your cheeks, your lips. I willed myself to concentrate on your words, but for a moment, that was all I saw.

"That's not rocket science. I just didn't have the bandwidth to explore, given the resignations I've had."

And then I softened. I needed to trust my advisers. And I did. Even if one of them was you. "I'm interested in hearing more about it."

You spent fifteen minutes showing me some charts and studies and graphs on your computer. All the while, I leaned over to look at your screen without pushing my chair closer to you. Weird, I know. My thoughts began to vacillate between confidence and doubt. As you moved close to me, I felt like a schoolgirl—conscious all of a sudden about the way I looked, the way I smelled, the way I sat. By the time it was over, my right hip hurt and my left leg was cramping from leaning in the opposite direction.

But the charts were good, meticulously prepared, complete with animation. The metrics you presented were well-researched and supported by a bibliography that looked longer than my grocery list.

"I have to prepare for my next meeting, but Jane should put some time on our calendars. A working session to get everything together to present to the others." I stood and walked back toward the door, intent on escorting you out.

"Carin," you countered, placing your hand on my arm. "If you're really interested, why wait? Let's continue this over dinner. Tonight."

"But—" I started. "I don't have time today."

"It's in the interest of the business. We can't wait. I will let Madden know where dinner will be."

Chapter Seven

Voicemails

Three weeks later, we'd had three dinner sessions and made a lot of progress. Your plans were surprisingly clear, your strategy unquestionable. Of course, once presented to the board, it flew. You talked too much. Bossed me around even more. I didn't have to do one thing—you prepared, discussed, and connected with everyone who mattered.

I would never admit it, but it was nice not having to do a single thing to convince the team.

Our first expansion plan: Asia. The market was booming, consumers were clamoring for real estate investments. This demand inflated property values.

Since that first discussion in my office, I'd been traveling to and from Europe. Jack even managed to get Charlie on a plane to Heathrow, where we spent five days together, just the two of us. Like the old days— the boy who loved to sit in his stroller and go wherever his mother took him. The boy who would tell people how much he loved shopping with his mom. There was so much of that boy left, but you had to dig to find it, buried under the cool ten-year-old facade of wanting to stay in and play video games all day.

I spoiled him. I really did. Bought him everything he wanted, everything he saw. He didn't want much, but when he asked for something—like those little armored truck models and civil war soldiers we saw by Buckingham Palace—he got them.

You were on that trip too, except we only met at the London office and stayed in separate, distant hotels. So you can imagine my surprise when we ran into you while shopping in Piccadilly that Sunday.

Charlie was sitting on the sidewalk enjoying an ice cream cone and I was buried under a pile of shopping bags. Fall came earlier in that place, so we were bundled in coats and scarves under the ever-graying sky. There was some sort of demonstration going on at the square—young people carrying placards and waving flags. I held on to my bags while I watched Charlie's head turn from left to right, following people's footsteps as they walked in front of him.

"You were right, Mom," he declared before taking a bite of his cone. "I should have brought a hat."

"You cold? We can get up now and start walking," I answered, placing an arm around his shoulders. "Ice cream was a terrible idea."

"No, it wasn't. It was delicious."

A pair of men's sneakers appeared in front of me. I looked up to find you in a black overcoat and a gray cap, looking down on us with a smile. The crowd swarmed around us as police sirens wailed in the distance. You knelt in front of us and laid your bags on the ground. "Fancy finding you here," you greeted. "Hi."

"Hey."

"And this young man must be Charlie?" You offered him your hand. I noticed that you had no rings, but you did wear a black leather bracelet. I compared you to Jack. He liked wearing men's jewelry. I myself didn't care much for it. "I'm your mom's friend, Matt."

Charlie shook your hand. "Did you just come out of that store?"

"Which one? That one? No, but I did come out of another store," you answered.

"Oh." He turned back to the crowd.

You remained fixated on the shopping bags. "Buy much?"

Before I could answer, Charlie did. "My mom likes to shop."

"Because she can," you answered. "Are you having fun, Charlie?"

"Yup! My mom and I go on these trips a lot. When I don't see her for a while because of work, she'll take me out of school so we can spend time together."

"You have a great mom, young man."

Charlie nodded, eyes still on the people around us. We all stood at the same time.

"Where are you guys headed next?" you asked.

The crowd thinned out considerably after a few uniformed policemen formed a line by the fountain. We started toward the sidewalk. Just as we were to turn the corner, Charlie turned to you. "My mom and I have been eating all the fish and chips we can. I'm trying to see which ones are the best." Then he turned to me. "Where to now, Mom? We need to find our next restaurant."

"Fish and chips, huh?" you responded with that same smile. The spontaneous one that's full-blown eyes, lips, teeth. "How's it been so far?"

I couldn't look away. I was hypnotized. Even then, your delight was contagious.

"Nah." Charlie shrugged. "Eights."

I knew you'd win him over.

"I think I know this place in Covent Garden with the best fish and chips in the whole world."

"Like, how good? Like a ten?"

"Like a ten," you said with a laugh.

"Can you take us there?" asked Charlie, tugging on my sleeve. "Mom, can Matt take us there?"

"Oh, I don't know, honey. Matt is here for work. I'm sure he has things to do."

"It's Sunday," you reminded me. "I'd be happy to take you there."

I looked at you and then at Charlie, his head bobbing like a puppet.

35

You never liked waiting for an answer. There you were, taking my bags from me and steering us through the clumps of people who stood in our way.

Those awesome fish and chips? The ones Charlie rated number ten, we had those with you.

And when we got back, I tried my best to maintain some semblance of normalcy at home. Trish and her mindfulness mumbo jumbo. Being in the moment, pushing past thoughts from my head, all that stuff—I cut off all meetings at six o'clock every evening and made sure I was home for dinner. Which didn't really make a difference because Charlie had so much homework, he gobbled everything down in three minutes. And Jack's attention was on football. He played and replayed every Bears game, stayed up all night watching post-game analytics, went to bars with his friends during weekend games, tailgated when he could.

I used to love seeing him so happy, so ecstatic about sports. Was that a sign? When you love someone, you just want them to be happy. Wasn't that how it should be?

On a Thursday night in October, Jack cooked a wonderful meal of Vietnamese beef stew. Charlie finished his work early and was down in the game room. We sat outside in the cool air, the fire pit providing just enough heat for the evening. I wrapped a blue blanket around myself and watched a squirrel hop from branch to branch. Jack had ESPN on, but he was focused on playing word games on his phone. Brutus had lain on my right foot, the weight of his body warm and secure. Lately, he'd been clinging to me, looking up at me with those soulful eyes. As if he was searching for something in mine.

The landline announced itself rather loudly. I made no effort to move from my seat. I'd been that way for months now—our voicemail box had over a thousand messages that needed to be retrieved. Was it a crime to wish they would just erase themselves?

"Who is it? Do you need to get it?" Jack asked, giving me a puzzled look.

"Nope, let it go to voicemail."

Jack pressed the Caller ID button. "It says American Express Plat. Shouldn't we be getting it?"

"You get it if you want to," I said. By this time, voicemail had picked up.

"Car, they've been calling all day and all night for weeks. What's happening? Are we in trouble or something?"

I sighed before rolling my eyes. "I've just been so busy, Jack! Why don't you call them back if it's bothering you that much?"

"I wouldn't know what to say," he said quietly. "You've been handling this for so long. If you tell me to leave it be, then I will. I just want to make sure our credit is okay."

"Everything is fine. I'll take the next week off to catch up on stuff here at home," I assured him.

He nodded and reached out for my hand. "Come move next to me," he said. "I've missed you."

"I missed you too." I did miss him. Or maybe I missed missing him. It had been like an out-of-body experience for me. I was there, but I was flying ten feet above the ground as an observer. Everything around me was a story playing out with me as the star.

Another ringing phone; this time it was you. I stepped away to take it. All you wanted to know was if I'd gotten home safely because there had been an accident on I90. I thanked you for checking on me, laughed when you told me you texted Jane instead of me.

"Who was it?" Jack asked.

"Torres. Some data he needed." I avoided his eyes. I don't know why because peers and colleagues have called me at all hours of the day before.

"You didn't tell me Charlie got to meet him in London."

"I didn't? I thought I did."

I was relieved when he smiled at me. "Charlie thought he was one of the male models from All Saints since he came out of that store."

"I didn't even know our son was that observant." I smiled back.

Jack squeezed my hand. "They hit it off rather well at dinner, apparently. Charlie knew all about the history of Catalonia and the soccer team that won the finals."

"Did you ask them what they talked about?"

"Not really. Charlie just kept talking about him."

"Ah."

"What about you, Carin? Is he as wonderful as his Instagram pictures make him out to be?"

"I don't really know him. We've been so focused on working on our plan."

"So I shouldn't worry, then." He squeezed my hand and smiled. It was a sad smile, his eyes frozen despite the slight curve of his mouth.

"About him? No." *I'm a different story.*

"Sometimes I feel like I'm losing ground with you. I don't know what to do about it. If I push, the more you'll resist."

"Jack. I work in a man's world. This isn't new. I've been working with men like that for fifteen years," I said. At that time, I found it ludicrous that he would worry at all. I moved closer to him. We were still holding hands.

"I know, I know," he said, looking up at me. "But Car—"

I waved my hand in front of my face. Not the rabbit hole. And certainly not with him. "No, no. Not now. Let's enjoy the peace and the lovely weather. There's time for all that. It will come."

Chapter Eight
Triple Date

$\mathcal{I}$ craned my neck to scan the place while tapping my fingers impatiently on the table. The weeknight crowd at one of the hottest restaurants in Chicago was as expected. Young women in black halter tops, their hair cascading over their shoulders, their skirts tight, their arms looped around the handsome young men leading them through the thick mass of people. The more mature patrons were dressed to the nines.

Lemmings. That's what came to mind. Too many designer bags, red-soled shoes, shiny sequined dresses, large diamonds.

Jack and I were shown to a booth in a semi-private corner of the restaurant. It was C-shaped and bulky, set for three but could really fit five, which means we were able to spread out.

"So, we're missing Charlie's parent barbecue for this?" I asked, exhaling loudly to show my annoyance. "How'd you get us this table anyway? It takes months to reserve at this place."

He took my hand. "You look nice. So sexy with those pants. I can't wait to—"

"Thanks," I answered, pulling my hand away. "Seriously, how'd you get this table?"

"Jody."

"You called the owner directly?"

"Yup," he said, looking up at the waiter who began pouring tap water into our glasses. He waved his hand before placing it on top of his glass. "Sparkling, please."

I rolled my eyes again. "Tap water is fine with me." I smiled sweetly at the waiter and turned serious when I faced Jack. "It's a Thursday night and I have an eight A.M. meeting tomorrow. Why are we here?"

"Because it's important."

"What is?" I shook my head.

"I want to meet the man you're working very closely with. Is that wrong?"

"It's stupid," I said, arms crossed at the table's edge.

"Everything's been stupid to you lately."

I pretended not to see you swagger toward our table, surprising Jack when I grabbed his hand. He smiled at me and stood as you approached us. I remained seated, right hand in Jack's.

"You must be Jack," you greeted with a grin.

Jack shook your hand firmly. I saw his muscles tense at the forearm and his elbow lock in place. "Matias, it's nice to meet you. Glad you could join us. Please, sit."

"Hey," I said, just as your eyes caught mine. How many leather jackets did you have? That night it was gray, faded and worn at the elbows.

And there we were. To my right, Jack wearing khaki pants and a blue Burberry blazer. To my left, you in your trademark Armani jeans and a leather jacket. I couldn't help it. I started to map out the differences between the two of you. Clearly one was seasoned in the finer things in life, the other without a care in the world about it.

The waiter came to take our drink orders—Moscato for me, Old Fashioned for Jack and a beer for you. Such diverse tastes. I don't know why, but I inscribed those differences in my head. Then there was me, feeling like a harlot in leather pants and a tube top. I did have a blazer over it. A sparkly, shiny one. Gucci was into metallics that season.

the year i *left*

As Jack perused the menu, you leaned over to whisper in my ear, "You look stunning."

I moved closer to him. Farther away from you. We'd had dinner with friends before, colleagues of mine or Jack's. Never had there been this air of … I wouldn't have called it tension. It was more of excitement. The thrill that seeps through every part of your body, insides vibrating. Fast pulse, lightheadedness. I crossed my legs and then uncrossed them. This was going to be an ongoing thing all throughout dinner.

"You've never been here before, have you, Matias?" Jack asked.

"No, I haven't," you answered, your eyes moving left to right as you propped up the menu so it stood on the table. "What's good here?"

"They have this spicy broccoli that's to die for. And this thing." I skimmed my finger across the page in front of you. "They have your favorite."

"Here? Better than the one we had from Star?" you asked.

"I think so!" I clasped my hands, taking the right one away from Jack. I could see where Jack's mind was heading and I threw a roadblock in front of it. "Jane always gets us lunch from there almost every day." I skimmed through my words to show nonchalance.

"Of course, that makes sense. You know each other's favorites."

You egged him on. "She's a creature of habit. She never changes her order. Everything plain. No sauce. And with white rice. I don't know how your wife stays so slim with everything she eats."

"Ha!" Jack crossed his arms. "My wife," he enunciated, "is always on the go. She's on a perpetual treadmill."

I laughed. A forced one that sounded more like a cough. Dinners like this were so predictable. In three, two, one, he was going to order his favorite seven-hundred-dollar bottle of champagne. And then he was going to talk business and then insist we get some dessert.

"Carin tells me the deal with the sellers in Asia is almost in the bag. Let's celebrate." Jack waved the server to our table. "How's Cristal for you?"

41

The server waited patiently while you hesitated, lips pursed as if you were holding your words back.

"It looks like we may close in early spring, but we shouldn't celebrate prematurely," you answered. "If you don't mind, I'm going to stick to my beer."

"Ah. Here we have a superstitious guy," Jack said. "Fine with me."

"Speaking of ..." I turned to you while Jack studied the menu again. I caught him looking at us from behind it. "Did you send your crew to the site just to look at potential issues that may come up in terms of infrastructure?"

"Yes. There are none." You paused for a second before you quipped, "Other than the fact that it's in a typhoon belt as well as on a fault line."

"And still, we decided to sink a significant amount of money into this. It had better be worth the investment."

"Car, are we ready to order?" asked Jack from behind the menu.

The server whipped a pad out of his pocket, pulled the pencil clipped on his ear and assumed the writing position.

You deferred to Jack, who ordered one dish from every category. You'd think we were feeding a platoon or something. So far, I still hadn't said much, my head whipping left to listen to you and right to listen to Jack. It felt like a ping pong match. One of you whacking the ball as if it would crack in half, the other volleying right back.

First, it was about work. You spoke about your experience, how you had graduated at the top of your class at Wharton and then gone to work for the top consulting firm in the world. Jack hit back, not with his credentials from Northwestern, but with the fact that the equity of his company had tripled in value only three years after he started it. You changed the topic to hobbies—yours was surfing, his was buying and selling cars. Your favorite place in the world was Belize. Jack's was Russia.

"In the dead of winter," I added. "Jack loves going there when there's nothing to see but wooly hats, marshmallow-man coats, and frozen churches."

Jack smirked at me, his lips stretched in a straight line. "As you can see, my wife hates the cold."

You laughed. "Well, my fiancée loves it. I'm more of a beach guy myself."

I felt my neck twist in a knot as it boomeranged from Jack to you. I caught myself in the middle of the jumbled mess in my head, opened my mouth to say something and then quickly shut it. Jack watched as I nervously took a drink of my water and placed the glass down before bringing it back to my lips.

I'd been wrong all along. In my warped head, I'd thought you were making a play for me. Turns out, you were just a really friendly guy.

"Apparently, you don't know everything about each other," Jack said in a hushed tone.

I left both of you to your own conversation and focused on the sounds around me. Someone dropped a glass.

No, someone had *flung* a glass to the floor. It was a woman, now wagging a finger at a morose man who stared at his feet. All that drama in public, I never understood.

I traced my fingers along the grooves of the table and imagined it was a winding road that led me to a buried treasure. Neither of you noticed how I was in my own little world, making up a story about a girl who followed the squirly rainbow and fell in love with a leprechaun.

Love.

Here we go again with love. Why does it always have to be about love?

"Carin?" You brushed your fingers across my arm.

"Where's Jack?" I asked, snapping my head sideways.

"He went to the washroom. Are you okay?"

You had noticed.

"Yeah, why?"

"I just don't think you're here."

Chapter Nine
Pretty Woman

S elda was off on weekends. It used to be the best day of the week to reacquaint myself with my home. During the week, I'd hand over the reins to Selda who constantly rearranged the Tupperware, the dishes, and the pots and pans. I tried a few times, but the repetitive instructions just got too exhausting, took too much energy from me. Saturdays were my days to put everything back in its usual place. I prided myself on that.

Or at least I used to. Now, Saturdays were my days to hide. For the past few months, I'd sit at the top step of our long winding staircase and stare at the branches of the big willow tree just outside our front door. My mind was blank on most days, but on the days I got myself together, I'd curl up in front of the TV and watch movies.

I had just managed to crawl out of bed with the intent of brewing myself a cup of tea. The doorbell rang once. I thought it was a package. I ignored it until it rang again, thrice, and then incessantly.

You stopped pressing the button as soon as I opened the door.

"Matias?"

"Did you get home okay? I left before the valet—" There you stood holding a basket wrapped in blue cellophane.

"I drove," I said, interrupting you. "Jack had quite a bit to drink."

"I'll say." You smiled. "He's very …" You paused as if in deep thought. "I don't know the word, *carinoso* in Spanish. All over you."

"Well, he's my husband."

"And he gets what he wants, I suppose," you said under your breath. I pretended not to hear you.

"May I come in?"

I nodded before retreating against the door.

You stepped inside, smiling as you kicked off your shoes and offered me your gift. I stood speechless for a second, hands on the basket, eyes on your psychedelic colored socks. You walked toward the living room, ignoring the fact that I was still in my favorite Target red and black striped pajamas and a long-sleeved camouflage shirt. Mismatched to the hilt.

"Nice," you said as you moved your head from side to side, observing the all-white décor and gray and black accents. "A little too cold for me, but I'm sure you weren't the one who designed this room." You bent down to touch the lambskin pillows. "Spanish, no?"

"What are you doing here?" I repeated.

"Movie day," you said, your eyes pinched tight and your grin kind of cringy. You rocked back and forth on the balls of your feet, like a child with a secret he couldn't wait to share.

"Movie what?"

"Look in the basket," you instructed, taking it from me and splitting the wrapper right down the middle. "We have popcorn, M&Ms, a bottle of your favorite, Mesh and Bone. And your three all-time favorite movies."

"How did—?" I sat on the couch and gestured for you to sit across from me.

"Jane. She gave me some intel on your favorite snacks. Madden, on the other hand, told me all your favorite movies."

"And you're in my house because …?"

"Because I'm a loser in the US with no life and I need the company."

"You're not a loser," I offered.

45

"Well, neither are you," you offered back. "Even if you stay in your pajamas all day."

I dipped my hand in the basket and pulled out three DVDs. "*Pretty Woman. Breakfast Club. Less than Zero.*" I laughed. "I can't believe Madden even remembered. It was that mad crush I had on Andrew McCarthy and Richard Gere!"

"Who are both very old by now," you reminded me.

I shook my head, suddenly realizing how unkempt I looked with my hair in a bun and not a trace of makeup. My mother's golden rule was never to leave the house without your eyebrows. Technically, I hadn't left my house. You had just invited yourself to it.

"Look, I really appreciate this. It's so sweet of you. But I've got things going on today."

"Like what?" you asked, leaning back into the couch and stretching out your right arm. "I also know from Jane that Jack is away in Arizona on a golf trip and that Charlie is at a sleepover."

"I'm going to kill her."

"I thought she knew your calendar a little bit too much." And when I didn't lighten up my glare, you said, "Come on, Carin. I am trying here."

I sighed, my shoulders arching forward. It wouldn't hurt to have some company that day. If you weren't at my door, I wouldn't have gotten out of bed. If I hadn't gotten out of bed, I would have sunken deeper in my thoughts and taken out my anxiety on something more harmful than snacks and a movie.

Besides, I began to notice this thing about you. You were funny in your biting sarcasm, and you actually saw through the façade I worked so hard to place in front of me.

And then all of a sudden, I felt guilty. There was a man in my house. I was alone with a man in my house. Not just any man. Someone I actually enjoyed spending time with.

"Fine. But the snowcaps are mine and the M&Ms are yours."

Instead of leading you downstairs to the game room, I walked straight through the living room and out of the glass French doors. At least no one could say we were alone inside my house. We would be alone outside my house. Well, not really alone. We had Brutus and the wooden owl sitting right on top of our deck to ward off the birds.

"Holy shit." You followed me through the doors and into the all-brick deck complete with an outdoor stainless steel kitchen and a brick-enclosed TV.

"Outdoor TV? Do you have to take it in during the winter?" You survived on touch, I think. Using your hands to establish contact. You ran your fingers along its edges.

"Nope. I think it's a special one. We leave it out here in the winter, uncovered. And it survives the snow, the cold, the rain."

"Now, this is cool. Are those Martin Logan electrostatics?" You pointed to two tall cylindrical speakers on either side of the bar. "Built in?"

"Matias! You are being very technical right now. I have no idea! These are all Jack's little toys." I waved my hands and directed you to the couch directly in front of us. "The DVD player is underneath the wine cabinet." I handed you all three discs before walking to the steps to summon Brutus. "Buddy! Where are you?"

Brutus emerged from under the built-in seats at the bottom of the deck. He crawled slowly toward me, his ID tags making the all-familiar clinking sound. His footsteps were heavy and slow, no matter how excited he was to see me. I ran down to pick him up, letting out a silent grunt in the process. "Come here, you heavy baby," I whispered in his ear. "Don't tell Daddy."

I recognized the movie you chose to watch first. We sat down at the same time, Brutus between us. He laid his head on my thigh as I scratched his ear. "Now, we're complete." I smiled at you. "And *Pretty Woman*. Great choice."

The sounds of summer were all around us despite it being early fall.

The birds still chirped; the warm breeze and the oscillating leaves of the willow trees made it a perfect day to be outdoors.

There we were in the early afternoon sun, drinking wine and eating peanuts. We laughed when Brutus began to snore. Vivian slowly fell in love with Edward and I … well, I forgot that just hours ago, I'd been sad.

"Matias," I began, maybe as a way of cutting through the stickiness of the on-screen kissing scene. "I'm sorry about the other night. I guess I was really just so tired."

"Don't apologize. We all have our things."

"Our things, yeah." I laughed. "I'm sorry about my thing."

You took a sip of your wine before refilling your glass. "You'll learn that I also have my thing."

We smiled at each other before slipping back into a comfortable silence.

When she allowed Edward to kiss her, you turned to me.

"So tell me, how many frogs did you have to kiss to get this one?"

"Jack's a frog now?"

I sat up. Before then, I had been fully relaxed and reclined, my head on the armrest and my legs tucked under my knees. Brutus no longer separated us. For some reason, he'd ended up on your right. I think he moved when I went to get us more snacks. I hadn't noticed. I was too happy to have company. Happy that the day was going to pass without a smidge of regret or deep thought.

"You know what I mean," you answered, still looking at me.

"Guess."

"A hundred."

"Zero," I squeaked, raising my chin, triumphant. "He was my first."

"Huh. You didn't date in college? Were you weird?"

"I was too busy studying and working and trying to take care of my mother. Jack just appeared and swept me off my feet," I said. "And maybe a little weird. You?"

"Finally settling down," you said, then downed what was left of your wine. You didn't look me in the eye as you would normally. Instead, you stared straight at the screen just as Edward climbed the rickety fire escape to rescue Vivian.

We sat in silence until the credits rolled.

"How sweet. She got the fairytale." I let it slip out and then regretted it.

I stood and crossed over your knees to take Brutus back into my arms. When I leaned down to reach for him, you ran your fingers along my cheek and tucked in a piece of my hair behind my ear.

"Did you get yours, Carin?" You spread your arms in the air. "All this. Is this your fairytale?"

"Yes. Of course. Of course, it is."

Chapter Ten

Trouble

Ⓘ did a pretty good job at subsisting for a few weeks by living in the moment and casting aside the changes I felt. It was like fending off an impending storm, with just enough divine intervention on my side to get me through each day. Working insane hours helped a lot. By the time I'd arrive home, dishes were done, homework was ready to be checked, the laptop was open and ready for more emails until it was time to go to sleep.

Jack seemed happy. We had always been such great friends, making sure to talk about our days and do some immediate planning regarding Charlie's frenetic sports schedule. That third week in October, when I pulled in the driveway after a school pick-up, Trisha stood waiting by the door. She wore running shorts and a silly-looking fanny pack with her hair up in a bun and earphones hanging from her neck and past her waist.

Even in her most casual moments, she was stunning. We were like night and day. Trish with the exotic dark hair and dark eyes, covert and often furtive, and me with the lighter complexion, light hair, and transparent eyes. My mom used to say that secrets couldn't survive in these eyes. I guess her passing took that light away too.

I waved at her and motioned for her to wait.

"Charlie, get the mail, please. I'll be outside with Auntie Trish if

Dad looks for me."

"Yup," he said, springing out of the car, kissing his aunt, and running off in two seconds flat.

The closer I got, the more I could see how unhappy she looked. I pointed at the brick steps and motioned for us to sit.

She remained standing, both hands on her hips, her face expressionless but her tone admonishing. "Did you check your messages?"

I pulled my phone out of my purse. "No."

"Check them now."

I looked up at her. Something was unraveling. "What is this, Trish? Just tell me." Ashen face, sweaty palms. Just like in high school when my mom caught me skipping class.

"Jack has been calling you all day. Where were you?"

"At an offsite! We had to surrender our phones at the door. You know I can't—"

She stared straight ahead, showing me that she was done listening to all the reasons I'd repeated over and over again. "Your husband called panicking. He tried to buy a car today, called me when he couldn't reach you. His credit was denied, and he was so sure your credentials got hacked."

"Shit." I buried my face in my hands. "Shit! Where is he now?"

Brutus came to me, nuzzled his nose into my chest, ecstatic as always that I was home. I held on to him as though doing so would make everything go away.

"At the bank, straightening everything out."

I stood up and hastened back toward the car. "I need to get to him. It's not the bank's fault."

"What?" Trish chased after me. "Carin, text him back but don't leave. We need to finish this conversation."

I turned to her and slumped against the car door, then slowly slid down until my backside hit the ground. "I haven't paid the bills." I held my head between my knees. "It's my fault."

Trish took her place on the ground next to me. "Being late once doesn't do that to your credit, I don't think."

"Sometime earlier in the year, I just couldn't get myself to sit down and pay the bills. I was just so tired of doing everything myself. Then the next month came, and the next, and I'd get so overwhelmed every time I tried to get caught up. I haven't answered our phone since February."

"That's eight months ago," Trish said. "Oh god." And then a realization. "Charlie's tuition?"

"Jack paid it last week when they called him directly." My eyes began to cloud with tears. "I missed Brutus' latest checkup. I can't get myself to do anything related to our home, let alone take him to the doctor! All I want to do is work and get as far away as possible from here."

"Why?"

"I feel like a fake. I don't love Jack anymore. Everything's changed."

She gave away no reaction. Sat still, staring at a big, tall tree. "You do. That doesn't just change. I think it's your work. You're burnt out."

"You keep saying that. Exhaustion doesn't change feelings." I lifted my arm to rub the back of my neck.

"What's that?" she asked.

"What?" I quickly balled my hand into a fist, afraid she'd noticed the scars.

"This." She tugged at my red bracelet. "Is that new?"

"No," I said, pulling my arm back.

"A new bracelet. Cartier, no less." She gasped, still staring at the red silky string knotted around two white gold rings clasped around each other. "Why?"

"I was so stressed last week I needed to occupy myself. Buy something."

"You're spending like crazy and not paying bills. You're sleeping all day on weekends. Carin! Do you see that something is seriously wrong? You used to yell at me about money management all the time! You were the organized one, the one who never took risks."

"I feel trapped. Like I'm in a coffin with no room to breathe. I can't stand to be near Jack. I resent everything about him."

She drew her shoulders back, eyes wide and her hand to cheek as if I'd slapped her face. "What? Where is this coming from?"

"I don't know. After Mom! Did I ever really love him? Was it just because I got pregnant with Charlie?"

"If that's the truth, if that's how you feel," she said, "then you have to tell him."

"Tell him what?" I asked, exhaling loudly. "It's not like he did anything wrong. It's all me. It's the way I feel about him. About my life. About everything."

"He can help you sort things out. If not, you can go get help. The two of you can get some counseling."

I shook my head. There were dead leaves all around us, blowing in the wind. The pretty summer flowers were gone, and instead of the majesty of fall, I saw winter. I saw the loss of life, the bland, white blanket of snow and the frigid ground.

I shuddered to think about what my heart would be like then— slowly decaying. There was nothing beautiful around me anymore.

We both stayed silent, and she took my hand. "There's someone else, isn't there? That guy. Jack told me about him."

"What guy?"

"The new guy at your office. Charlie told Paul he met him in London. Jack says he calls you a few times a day."

"For work, Trish," I said calmly. "I need to build him into my succession plan. That's all."

She looked away. "We still don't have any plans for the first anniversary of Mom's death."

Tears filled my eyes. Every day, I'd imagine her busting through my front door, picking up Charlie's scattered shoes and hanging up jackets flung across the stair rails. "I can't do it."

Her eyes held pity. Not contempt, but real concern and love. She pulled me into an embrace. "Oh, Car. I'm here. You can talk to me, okay? I know it's been really tough for you, trying to keep it together after losing Mom. Listen," she said softly, grazing her fingers over my shoulder. "I'll take care of the planning for the service. It's in two weeks. I'll pull something together. You have nothing to worry about. It could be just us—just immediate family at mass and then we'll just spend the day together to remember her. Okay?"

"Okay."

"You haven't paid the bills yet." She looked straight at me.

I shook my head and gazed at my feet.

"While I'm at it, give me the password to your accounts. I'll catch up on your bills for you tomorrow."

"Trish." I tried to bring her back to the issue. It wasn't just the loss of my mother or having bad credit.

"What is it?" she asked, twisting to face me directly. There she was, trying her best to understand me. How could she when I didn't know myself?

"It's—it's not just about Mom. Or the bills."

Just when I thought she was about to stand, she cradled my face in her hands. Her thumbs gently skimmed the skin underneath my eyes. "Oh, honey. You look exhausted," she said, her fingers now finding their way to my cheeks. "You've lost a bit of weight and I haven't heard that wonderful, gregarious laugh in ages."

"I don't want to be this way," I answered.

"Promise me, Carin. Promise me you won't give up. Whatever is happening to you, fight it. I love you. I need you here, in this world, present—you're all I have. I need you. Your family needs you."

Chapter Eleven

The Godfrey

Hiding was impossible when you worked in an environment like mine. You were surrounded by people everywhere—in the halls, in the elevator, in the lobby, in the restroom. They knew who I was, the voice behind those weekly emails, the woman on the executive floor with the corner office. It was pretty much the same story with the restaurants in our area, as you quickly learned. And oh, forget about Thursday nights. Somehow, our brains were synchronized into needing a drink at exactly six in the evening, and the nearest bar was filled with working people like … us.

I had a spot, though. It was tucked in an alleyway between my building and the next, a shaded brick enclosure only three people wide. Certain times during the day, it would be completely empty; other times, especially in the summer, it would be insanely full. Smokers had claimed it as their space, but I liked it because no one would ever think to find me there. And although the area was a straight line, its dead-end branched out, providing space that was obscured from view by pillars on both sides.

Did you follow me to my secret place that first day in November? Because there you were, standing in front of me, watching me squeeze myself into the corner, leaning against the cold brick wall with my eyes closed and my arms around my knees.

I opened my eyes and saw you, and I was so surprised that I fell sideways. It was a moment of great transformation. I saw you in a different light. It was like the weeks we'd spent working together had never happened. I was meeting you for the first time, at a time and a place that felt right.

Maybe it was because you'd stepped into my private universe, the place where it was just me. Not the wife nor the mother or the determined superwoman. It was me at my most vulnerable, in the place where I lived in my head. I was getting good at pretending everything was fine. That I had just as many chances as everyone else to find happiness. Here, in this place, I was just like everyone else.

The pressures, the pretenses, all dissipated that afternoon. It was outside of work, outside of home—in a neutral place, I supposed. I saw you as you were, all man, all face and hair and lips. I hadn't looked at a man that way since Jack swept me off my feet three weeks before graduation.

There were feelings I couldn't define. Good ones. The ones that made one feel beautiful and invincible at the same time.

"Hi," you said, squishing yourself in the tiny space between me and the wall.

"Did you follow me here? How did you know—" I could feel your thigh against me, your right arm wedged behind mine. I didn't know whether to get up or to stay. It seemed like every time we were together, we pushed a little more. A touch here, a brushing of the hand there.

"You come here every afternoon between three and four," you stated, matter-of-fact. "Sometimes, you smoke. Most times, you sit and stare straight into space. I followed you once, three weeks ago."

"Geez, Torres! First my house and now my secret hangout." I smiled, embarrassed.

"That one time the clients paid us a surprise visit, and you were nowhere to be found."

"Swear to me that you won't tell anyone!"

"I swear!" You laughed and held up your right hand. "It's Jane you have to control. She's the one who told me!"

"You're kidding! I guess I'm going to have to hang out in the stairwell," I answered.

"Jane says worse things happen in there," you teased. I observed the way your eyes crinkled at the corners when you raised your eyebrows. "But hold on a minute. I came down here to find you to tell you something more important."

"Oh, no! What happened?" I asked, afraid that the deal we'd been working on had fallen through.

You glanced around before leaning in, your lips inches from my ear. "I found out where everyone goes to use the bathroom in this building if you know what I mean."

"What?" I broke out in laughter. "What are you talking about?"

"Just saw Holt and the mailroom dude come out of the second floor. The one where construction is currently taking place!"

I laughed hysterically, throwing my head back.

"I love the way you laugh," you said. And when I didn't answer, you asked, "Are you done with your work? I know a place where we can continue this conversation and have drinks at the same time."

"I wish! I still have a few hours of work to do." I finally decided to stand. You followed me instantly. "I want to finish this work so I don't have to worry about it over the weekend."

"Come on." You tilted your body sideways, touching your shoulder to mine. "Please?"

"I'm just so crazed right now, I need the time to work on the proposal."

"It's my birthday," you whispered. "Please celebrate with me."

I turned to look at you. "Really?"

"Yes, really. So please, one drink."

"Okay, but I—"

"I'll wait," you said. "I'll come for you at seven." And then you turned around and left me.

"Is the weather normal for this time of year?"

There we were, on the rooftop of the Godfrey, watching intently as the DJ was about to spin some tunes. It diffused some of the awkwardness between us. We'd stop and start, ramble on about work and then lapse into silence. You struggled to engage me in conversation while I really just wanted to think to myself for a bit. The place was already packed. Extra seating had been eliminated to give way to a tiny dance floor, and you and I sat side-by-side at the edge of a stiff, white couch supported by black metal legs. They reminded me of high heels, wobbly and unsteady. Maybe we would have been more grounded if they had been wedges instead. I scooted forward to give you room to lean back.

I smiled. "No, we've been really lucky. Fall is turning out to be quite mild this year." I took a sip of my drink. You had ordered it for me. I don't remember what it was, but it was sweet and very strong and made me lightheaded. Just as I was about to say something, the sultry little server appeared right next to you.

"Miss, we'd like to order now, please."

We would?

She batted her eyes and took out her little pad. "I'm all yours." She knelt beside you, gave you a good view of her boobs.

You didn't miss a beat. "The green bean tempura and some hummus and flatbread. Also, the roasted broccoli and a few of those steak sliders."

"Anything else I can get for you?" she asked, still leaning forward.

"Yes, water for my friend over here." You had the cold, steely look—the same one you had when clients tried to pull a switcheroo on you over contract terms.

I couldn't help myself. I giggled.

"What?" you asked.

"You can be brutal," I said. "Thank god, I haven't had the privilege of getting on your bad side. Although we've had our differences in opinion. Remember that one—"

The server came back with two glasses of water and some plates. You unfolded one napkin and placed it on your lap, then unfolded the other one and laid it flat on mine.

I pushed your hand away. "I can do it, thanks."

You twisted to face me. "I'm done talking about work. I want to talk about you, Carin Frost."

"What about me?" I asked, a bit self-conscious about the way your eyes danced across my face. I took a swig of my drink and finished the glass off.

"Your story. What's your story?"

"I don't have one!" I laughed. "What's yours?"

I tried to draw my hand back but you were too quick. You held it up, moved your face closer and frowned. "What do you do to your hand?" You traced your finger along the tiny, pink scabs on my right palm.

"Just a nervous tick," I answered, pulling it back. It was only a partial lie. I forcibly lightened my tone, put forth a little girl voice. "I'm waiting for your story."

"Okay, I'm only going to start because it seems that you're the get and give type of girl. With *get* coming first," you grunted. "Next week, I'll be going back to Barcelona for a few days. She wants me to see some venues for the wedding."

"Exciting!"

"Is it? I'm not feeling that way yet." Your tone turned serious. "I guess I'd just been too busy with work. Next week will be telling."

"Telling how?"

"I don't know. I'm still waiting for things to sink in. It's a big deal, I think. Getting engaged. But I had to leave for this new job so I haven't been able to see or speak to my family yet," you said. "There's so much pressure to be this perfect son, perfect husband, perfect heir."

I didn't want to get into it. Didn't want to tell you that if this wasn't the happiest phase of your life, it would never be. I wanted to tell you to run away as fast as you can. Find the woman you couldn't wait to marry.

But instead, I said, "Show me a picture! It doesn't seem like she's in your Instagram."

"Do you know why?" you asked while moving your finger across your phone. "Because she has her own account and it's bigger than mine!" You held the phone up to my face.

I'd seen her before. There she was—a thin reed of a model and looking so familiar.

"Is that—"

"Yes." You bowed your head as if in apology. "Isabella Rossi. She's been in a few movies."

I bounced on the couch. "A few! She's famous! And gorgeous!" Long flowing dark hair, round eyes, sultry lips, five-ten, thin and lanky. Everything I wasn't.

"Thank you." You scratched your chin. "Now, your turn."

"Seriously, Matias. I have nothing. Everyone knows about my life."

You tilted your head and blinked before continuing your death stare. I guess I had to keep going or things would get uncomfortable.

"Well, Charlie got into boarding school."

"And that's not a good thing?"

"I'm going to miss him. Selfishly, I guess. He's the only one that—" I took a sip of my drink. One more. And then another.

He waited. I looked away.

"Ask me something else," I said with a laugh. "I'm just being an overprotective mom."

"Okay," you began in a low, gruff tone. "How do you do it?"

"Do what?" By this time, my head was spinning. I leaned back and found that you'd had your arm around me the whole time. I settled in, dizzy, exhausted, happy.

"How do you walk into a room and command everyone's attention like you do? Like you're the only one in the room. How do you cross those long, sexy legs of yours at board meetings without a clue that all eyes are on them?"

"What are you talking about?" I giggled. "Are you talking to the right person? Are you drunk?"

"I'm as sober as I could ever be." You leaned into me and brushed your lips against my ear. "How do you drive me crazy without even knowing it?"

"Where is she?" I said, swaying unsteadily as I stood. I needed to get some air. "Where's our food? I need to eat, I think."

You hopped up and took my hand, but not before waving at another server who approached us. You asked him to follow-up on our food and pulled me away from our table. "Let's get on our feet for a while," you ordered. "I love this song. Let's dance."

"Can't," I said. "People from work just walked in."

You stepped forward and I trailed behind, my fingers clasped in yours. I had no idea where we were headed but I didn't object. I loved this new passivity, the ability for me to follow instead of lead. It was nice, just going with the flow.

You pulled me through an exit, past the kitchen where cooks and servers hustled about, and onto a narrow path that led to a tiny landing on the roof. We were all alone under a dark and cloudless sky, but the music was loud enough to hear. Not far from us, the observation deck of the Hancock illuminated the city and everything around it.

You pulled me into your arms. "One dance and I'll take you back, I promise."

"No." I stepped back despite the fact that your arms stayed in place.

"Hmm. Birthday? Are you forgetting?"

"Okay, one." I stepped into you, placed one hand on your shoulder while you held the other. "Matias, this is so wrong. We really shouldn't—"

"Shh," you whispered. "Feels so right, doesn't it?" There you were, interrupting me again. And when your eyes met mine, you whispered, "If you don't hold her in your gaze, she might get lost."

"Happy birthday, Torres," I said quietly.

A song we both knew played. I closed my eyes and leaned my forehead on your shoulder. You buried your lips in my hair as you took the lead, slowly swaying me back and forth and singing the words in my ear.

Can I be him?

Chapter Twelve

My Brutus

We didn't talk about that night when I saw you the next day. It was business as usual—you in your element and me in mine. Negotiations for the purchase of that resort in Southeast Asia were going swimmingly well. I asked Jane to let you know that the sellers were ready to talk about integrating the latest technology from the vendors you'd lined up. You stuck your head in my office. There was a different dynamic between us now. Although I couldn't define it, I knew we'd moved past the formalities. We had become friends.

"Hey."

"Oh, hi there," I answered, looking up from the contract on my desk. "Closing day is coming, I can feel it." I stood and walked around the desk before settling on its edge, stretching out my legs and crossing them at the ankles.

"Tsk, tsk." You smiled, stepping in and closing the door behind you. "Those legs, Mrs. Frost ... What did I tell you about those legs?"

"Matias, I'm in pants."

"Still ..." You chuckled, taking a seat at the conference table and keeping a healthy distance. "Anyway, you know I leave tomorrow."

"I'm excited for you!" I clasped my hands together. "Don't worry about work. It will still be here when you get back."

"I kind of don't want to go. I don't want to leave in the middle of the discussions." You held a pack of yellow post-it notes and flipped its pages back and forth. I think we both welcomed the ruffling sound, which made up for the absence of words.

"But I'm here. I'll handle whatever comes while you're gone and debrief when you're back."

"It's not the work I'll miss," you said, leaning forward and resting your elbows on the table. "I mean, this is far more exciting than—"

"Oh, stop!" I countered. "You will see your family, your friends, have a week to relax and plan the most important event of your life!" I pushed myself off the desk and approached you, offering you my hand. "See you in ten days?"

"See you in ten days," you responded, shaking my hand. "Hold the fort and be good."

"I will," I answered as you released me and walked away.

I didn't hear from you while you were gone. Not that I expected it. I pictured you having the time of your life back in Barcelona, home with those you loved. That's what I tried to do too, stayed at home as much as I could, immersed in the domesticities I'd sworn off for the past few months.

I baked zucchini bread for Charlie to take to his teachers.

I paid our bills, went to school to prepay Charlie's tuition.

I wanted to get better.

But instead, things took a turn for the worse.

They say it takes just one thing to push you over, to rouse you from your sleep. For me, it was a long time coming, shedding parts of myself and what little resilience I had left. But that day broke me. That day, I lost my spirit.

I knew it as soon as Jack pulled into the driveway with Brutus in the front seat. That same uncanny feeling of loss hung over me. I ran out to meet them and pulled the car door open as soon as it came to a stop. Brutus stood, his stub of a tail still wagging, the clinking sound of his tag a sound I can still hear.

"He has cancer," Jack said as he slid out of the driver's seat.

"He has what?"

"It's bad, Car," he said. "Doctor Toni says the cancer has spread to his lungs—that's why he can hardly breathe. He's had a tumor all along."

Brutus jumped down and stood at my feet. I knelt to hold him. "When can he have surgery? Did you try to schedule it for today?"

"We can't."

"Tomorrow, then. I'll take the day off." I walked toward the front door. "Come on, Buts."

"Carin!" he called to me.

"What?"

Jack caught up with me and led me to the stoop by the entrance. "He's not going to get better."

"We can afford to find someone who can fix him. He's part of our family. Money's no object, Jack."

He took my hands and tugged at them. "There's nothing they can do. Listen to me! Dr. Toni said that the most humane thing we can do is to put him down. Today. He's in a lot of pain."

"Put him down," I repeated. "Put him down. Just like that." I covered my face with my hands. "Just like fucking that."

Jack kept his gaze on the ground, his shoulders stooped in defeat.

"Say something," I challenged him. "Take charge. For once, tell me it's going to be okay. That you'll fix this. Fix this, Jack. I'm tired of being the one who has to pull shit together!"

"This isn't the time for confrontation. We have to agree on the next steps before Charlie gets home."

"How can that be? He's been with us for eleven years and we give

65

up on him in one day? Dr. Toni doesn't know what the hell she's talking about!" I squealed.

"Your defiance isn't going to get rid of the tumor."

I turned to Brutus who stood right in front of me. His right hind foot hung in the air. His belly was distended. It dragged on the ground. That was why I'd asked Jack to take him in that day. That morning, as I waited for him to come up from the deck, I noticed that his stomach had reached the ground. It was my fault. I was too selfish to see him disintegrate before my eyes. I thought it was just a part of getting old. But cancer takes a while to ravage a body. Where had I been all this time?

"No!" I cried. "Jack, listen—I'll take a leave to take care of him. He's been with us since before Charlie was born. He was our first child. He's my only friend."

"The way we can show him how much we love him is to let him rest," Jack said calmly.

"No," I sobbed, knowing these words were futile. We were going to lose him that day. We had no choice in the matter. Which one was better? No goodbye or a planned goodbye? "When?"

"I told the hospital I'd speak to you and then call them if we decide to follow through with it. I figured we'd wait until Charlie came home from school and allow them to spend time together. They close at six, so we should be there by five."

They say that an animal's intuition is stronger than a human's. I supposed it was because their pattern of behavior, their way of communicating with each other was based solely on instinct. Brutus was not only my best friend. He was the keeper of my secrets, the silent observer of my tears.

I knew he knew. I knew he knew it was his last day with us.

In the hours we spent together, he had a renewed burst of energy. Keeping close to us, but running through the yard just like when he'd been a puppy. We took many videos and pictures of him; he chased Charlie around, followed his every command. I could see him watching all of us. And as the time came closer for us to leave, he took tours of the house, walking through his favorite parts of the family room, his bed, his crate. Charlie was beside himself, crying and then laughing, giggling and then going back to crying again.

By the time we arrived at the hospital, I thought we were all at peace with our decision. The doctor explained the process—they would take him away and insert an IV in one of his legs so that they could administer the medicine.

Charlie kept his gaze on Brutus, tears streaming down his cheeks.

"I just want you to know," she said, hand on his shoulder, "that the medicine may take about a minute to work. And when their heart stops, sometimes, they don't have time to close their eyes. Okay, Charlie?"

Charlie turned to me in despair. "Mom!"

And then they led Brutus away.

The next time we saw him, we were seated on a colorful printed rug in the middle of a private room. We wanted to form a circle around him, the three of us, his family. Brutus calmly walked in a few minutes later and stopped to circle around each one of us. First, he went to Jack, and brushed his head against Jack's chest. Then he went to Charlie and licked his face. When it came to my turn, he walked straight into my lap and laid his head on my thighs.

But first, he looked up at me. "I'm so tired," he said, tears in his eyes.

"I know," I whispered.

He rubbed his nose against my hand. "But will you be okay?"

I kissed his face and placed my lips by his ear. "I will be fine, I promise. Rest, my love. Go now and rest."

He stretched his legs out to the side and closed his eyes.

We set our hands on him, six pairs all over his back and his chest, as the doctor injected the IV tube in his leg.

"I'm sorry," I lamented. "I'm sorry, I'm sorry."

And that was it.

In fifteen seconds, he was gone.

Jack wailed, a loud keening sound I would never forget.

Charlie shouted, "Brutus! Come back, please!"

I sobbed as I'd never sobbed in my life. Our screams and howls could be heard from the outside. We held him for thirty minutes before we were told we had to leave.

We knew that the loss of Brutus was more than just the loss of our pet, our friend, a member of our family. It signaled the beginning of a new time in our lives. Brutus symbolized the early years. The simple years when money had been hard, and it hadn't mattered where we lived or what we had. When Charlie had played with boxes and worn hand-me-downs and our vacations had been car rides to the dunes instead of trips around the world. It had been a time of simple joys, of gratitude and hard work, of raising a family and a partnership rooted in adversity.

Those days were long gone, and on that day, Brutus took with him the last thread that held our family together.

Chapter Thirteen

Imagine No Dragons

We picked up his ashes a week later. None of us could bring ourselves to bury him. We kept him on the bookshelf right next to all his things.

Jack was dealing in his own way. He immersed himself in Charlie's activities, helping out at school as the king among the lunch moms. As for me, I worked. I worked until I was too tired to think. I worked until I passed out on the couch in my office. I took showers at the gym next door and shopped at Nordstrom for clothes and underwear to wear the following day.

It had been three weeks since Brutus left us, and I continued to nurse my wounds in London.

"How are the boys?" Valerie asked, handing me a bag of freshly roasted chestnuts. "Dylan's over there getting us some spiced cider."

We continued to walk arm-in-arm toward the many stalls in the Christmas market. Earlier, we'd walked across the London Bridge in search of more shopping prospects and had stumbled across this instead. The air was crisp and cool, tiny Christmas lights connected each light pole from the bridge to the square. There were funnel cakes and spiced wine and many pieces of jewelry laid out on wooden, velvet-lined tables. I could have stayed there all evening if we didn't have reservations at

Nobu that night.

"It's been tough. We still think he's home waiting for us at the end of the day. It's like our whole family is in denial."

"Ah, that is so hard," she said, pausing to look at me. She was different that night—calmer, more subdued. There were no plans to dance at bars or smoke cigarettes, no stilettos or skirts. Jeans and flat black boots instead, her hair in a ponytail. Her eyes looked tired—dark circles had inserted themselves onto that flawless skin. "But are they okay not having you there for Thanksgiving?"

"Charlie is having so much fun with his cousins. They're all camped out in the basement watching a horror movie."

I tried to make light of it, but she wouldn't let me. "Carin, don't you think you should be with them after what happened a few weeks ago?"

"Believe me I thought about it a lot. But somehow, I figured I had to save myself. I'm not well. I feel like the more I'm around Jack and Charlie, the more I'll pull them down with me."

"Pull them where?"

"Into whatever it is I'm going through," I answered.

We found Dylan carefully making his way through a crowd of people with his hands full, concentrating on keeping the cups from tipping over. "Here you go," he said once we reached him. We each took a cup and found a bench.

I noticed Valerie reaching out to him but pulling back once she caught my gaze. Dylan pulled out a napkin and wiped the edge of her mouth with it. It felt strange. Something was going on, but I was afraid to confront it.

They watched as the phone on my lap rang incessantly. Twice I pushed the DECLINE button, and twice it rang all over again.

"Isn't that the new guy who started? Why aren't you picking it up?" Valerie asked, seeming happy to deflect the attention back to me.

"I'm on vacation," I snapped, upset by my suspicion, not the phone call. "It can wait." I took a swig of my mulled wine, forgetting how hot it was and how it could scald my throat. It did just that.

"What's going on?" Valerie asked. "Why does he keep calling?"

"You tell me, Val," I said. Dylan sat straight up and took her hand. "Is something going on between the two of you?"

"Yes," Dylan said. He had no fear in his voice. It was resolute, straightforward. "We're in love."

Valerie stayed silent.

"But she's married," I argued, turning to Dylan since it looked like Valerie wasn't going to participate in this. "Is she getting a divorce?"

"Don't talk about me like I'm not here," Valerie finally spoke up. "Yes, I'm going to speak to my husband as soon as I get back to Paris."

"When did this happen?" I asked, baffled. First Brutus, now this. Where had I been? Too engrossed in myself to keep up with those I love? At that moment, I wanted to rush home to Charlie, check to make sure he was okay. I shuddered to think I might have missed something with him too. My heart ached all the more. I thought about Brutus and how much I missed him.

"Six months," Dylan answered.

"Oh, my god. That's why Val didn't want to stay in the same room with me in San Francisco. I thought she was pissed about something!" I said, thinking back at how shady she'd been. "I'm so sorry I didn't see this. You're my best friend and I didn't know."

"It's fine. I know you're going through a lot too," she said. "I'm really happy. I love him so much."

"But how?" I asked, still wanting to know more. "Why only now are you deciding to tell your husband?"

"It was just a work fling. Or at least we thought it was. Love wasn't supposed to happen."

"But it did." Dylan leaned over to kiss Val's cheek.

I nodded and sat still, listening to the sounds around me. "Little Drummer Boy" was playing softly through the market, kids were running around us, lovers were huddled in the stalls in their boots and coats. I missed Brutus and his joy with every year's turkey and mashed potato meal. I missed Charlie and I missed my mom. I could still hear her laughter reverberating through the house late at night.

I missed you. I missed you, Matias. I realized then that it was you who made things bearable, it was you who made me want to go on. While I was invisible to the world, when no one saw or understood the change, the pain, the yearning. You did. All the more, I had to fight it. Because admitting this would mean I knew you were more than a friend to me.

The truth is, I was jealous of their happiness. Val and Dylan were going to hurt people for each other. There was something so utterly brave about that. Most of us live our lives accepting what we have because we're afraid to hurt those we love. When in reality, we're being unfair to them. They deserve to be with someone who can love them as much as we wanted to but couldn't. They deserve to find their happiness because we make them sad. We had fooled them into a life of lies and they deserved to live in truth; that we can't love them the way they should be loved.

I couldn't help but die inside.

After a few wordless minutes, Valerie piped up. "Can we talk about you now, Carin? We are worried about you. We just want you to be happy."

"I think you're depressed," Dylan piped in. "You're eternally unhappy. You look sad all the time. And now we're concerned that what happened to Brutus will push you over the edge. There's too much loss in one year."

"I'm trying to cope," I said, tossing the cup into the blue bin across from us. I was content to mask the silence with the cracking of chestnuts. I peeled them hurriedly and threw them in my mouth. My fingers turned black from the soot.

"Here," Valerie offered. "Give me your hands. I've got a wet wipe. Let me clean them." She twisted my hand to turn my palms up.

"No! No. It's okay," I said, flicking my arm upward.

"Oh-kay," Valerie quipped, her eyes squinted. "Talk to us then. That guy—why does he keep calling?"

"We're in the middle of this huge Asian deal. That's my life right now. Work." I smiled in a weak attempt to lighten things up.

"That's how it starts," Dylan said. "Is he interested in you?"

"No! Definitely not! Look, guys, I can't even find myself right now. Why would I cause more problems?"

The phone rang again. You just wouldn't let up. I'm sure you knew I'd cave eventually. Not that night, buddy. I was too involved in choking back the tears, controlling my emotions after all the things I had realized that night.

"It's him again? What the—" Dylan snorted. "Do you want me to tell him to fuck off?"

"Yeah," I said, laughing. "You go tell him, Prince Charming."

And wouldn't you know, you called again.

"Give it to me," Dylan said, taking the phone from my hand. He pressed the speaker button. I wondered what you would think—the bits and pieces of our evening condensed through the sounds you heard on the phone.

"Torres, it's Dylan Forrest."

"Forrest, what are you doing with Carin's phone?"

"She's here with me and she doesn't want to talk to you. Take this up at the office next week, dude. She's on vacation."

He pressed the end button. In two seconds, Valerie's phone buzzed. She brought the screen to my face. "Oh my god, it's him!"

I exhaled loudly, took the phone from Val, blew out a breath, and answered, "Hi."

"Carin, hi. I arrived back and was hoping to speak to you," you said.

I tried my best to suppress a smile. Something about your voice made me want to be there and not here. "Is it about work? What happened?"

"No, I—" you stammered.

73

"Then it can wait. I'll be back in a few days. Can we talk then?"

"I wanted to apologize about the day I left for Spain. I wanted to tell you that things changed for me after the night at the Godfrey, but—"

"Changed how?" I turned to look at the newly outed couple across from me. They strained to listen to every word I was saying, eyes wide.

"There's something here, Carin," you whispered.

In a moment of panic, I pressed END on the phone and handed it back to Val.

Dylan signaled for us to get going. Valerie took his hand, and I followed them.

"Geez," Dylan said, as he led us back up the stairway to cross the bridge to our waiting Uber. "He's pretty aggressive, isn't he?"

"When he wants something, he wants it." Valerie laughed. "I guess that's what makes him successful!"

Chapter Fourteen

Crazy Phase

$\mathcal{I}$ walked into the house on Thanksgiving Day, taking all of London's soccer souvenirs with me. I was intent on offering them at Charlie's feet out of remorse. A mother should never leave her family in the middle of the holiday just to watch a concert with friends.

The house was filled with people, relatives, friends—all forty of them gathered around the large white island in our kitchen. Jack was the center of attention, regaling his audience with the story of the marlin he'd caught off the Gulf of Mexico during his October golf trip. I'd apparently missed dinner. Trish had her back turned to me while rinsing off the dishes. Something was baking in the oven. It smelled like apple pie. The ones Jack used to bake from scratch when we were newly married.

"Carin! You're back!" Trish exclaimed, waving her hands wildly and running over to take me in her arms. "How was the concert?"

I hugged her back. "Hey, look at you. Love that velvet dress."

Jack quickly laid a tray on the counter and shuffled over.

"Hey." I looked around the room. Everyone was staring at me. There were his parents, his three brothers- and sisters-in-law and some people I didn't recognize.

"Carin, these are our new neighbors, Cheryl and Kevin. I also invited the guys from down the street. They're all in the living room.

And Mom and Dad, Eric and Jake and their families are staying until Sunday. They're all set up in the guest bedrooms."

"Okay," I said, smiling. "Happy Thanksgiving, everyone."

They all nodded at me and went right back to their own conversations. I could hear the rumbling of pins from the game room below us. This was typical. I was never around long enough to form any relationships with any of them.

I rolled my suitcase out of the kitchen and toward the staircase. Trish followed suit, taking my coat from my arm and slinging my purse on her shoulder.

"Mom!" Charlie's footsteps were loud and heavy. Something he got from his dad, for sure. We used to talk about how he was Jack's son in looks—strapping and bulky—but my son in heart.

"Baby! Hi!" I shrieked, dropping my suitcase and wrapping myself around my son.

"You're early! You came home for Thanksgiving!"

"London's not the same without you."

"Did you check out the fish and chips at Saint John's?"

"Sure did. Val thought they weren't that fresh. I thought they were delicious."

Charlie scrunched his face, his lips almost touching his nose. "The French don't know their fish and chips."

"You may be right," I said, kissing his ear and allowing him to lead me to the living room.

I gasped when I saw the twinkling lights of a ten-foot Christmas tree. It was all decked out in red and blue, golden garlands and silver ribbons twisted around each other. Charlie's annual ornaments hung on every branch, his large fourth grade picture surrounded by dried pasta noodles in the middle of it all.

"Auntie Trish and I and Paul and Daddy put this all up for you."

Trish and Jack snuck up behind us. I felt his arms around my shoulders as he pulled me against his chest. "You like our surprise?"

"I love it," I answered quietly, careful not to alarm them, make them feel that this was inadequate, not enough to bring me back. "Thank you all for doing this."

"Is this your best Thanksgiving, Mom?" Charlie asked, beaming at his dad.

I forced a smile and leaned into their loving arms. "Yes. Yes, it is."

I couldn't get away fast enough. Everywhere I looked, I only saw strangers. No matter how long we'd known them, Jack and I—the laughter, the voices, even the home itself, were all so foreign to me. It was like being in someone else's environment, certainly not mine. I noticed things I was sure I'd purchased but couldn't for the life of me remember when. Even the tree skirt, the tree stand, the angel perched atop its highest branch looked different. The throw pillows—they used to be checkered, not striped? And I don't think I would have spent all that money on embroidered leather covers. Did I? When?

As people wandered into the living room and listened to Jack and Charlie recount their tree-cutting experience, I quietly made my way up the stairs and into the dressing room. Jack rarely ventured there, just because there was no need to. I had set it up as my sitting room as well—a chaise and a lounge chair adjacent to a bookshelf in the far left corner. Drawers and closets with mirrored doors surrounded me, their content meaningless, inconsequential. My heart was racing, my mind running just as fast in different directions. I thought maybe, if I got myself ready for bed and read for a while, I would be fast asleep by the time Jack came upstairs.

"I like the new color in here. The gray in the sage-green really makes it pop."

I looked up to find Trish brooding over me. She tapped my feet, signaling for me to fold my legs in so she could sit at the edge of the chaise. She shook her head, her eyes in a hard, fixed stare. "Reading. Now? Are you kidding me?"

"I started this book on the flight and want to finish it."

"Carin. There are fifty people in your house right now, celebrating Thanksgiving."

"And?" I asked, my gaze still fixed on my Kindle. "Jack has it covered. You're there."

"Carin."

"What?" I snarled, slamming the Kindle cover shut. "Can I please have some time for myself? I was just on an eight-hour flight, for god's sake."

"You just had alone time with your friends. Your family deserves your presence."

"I've already changed into my pajamas," I argued. I didn't recognize my words—they spewed out faster than I could even gather my thoughts. "Please don't make me go down there. I can't stand to see them, all of them." I began to cry.

My mother's voice assailed my thoughts. *"Stop running,"* she said *over and over again.*

How do I do that? How can I make Trish understand what I'm going through when I can't even figure it out, myself?

Trish's hand flew to her mouth in surprise. "Oh, honey," she said, stroking my shoulder. "I didn't mean to make you cry. But I don't want people to think you're being rude. Everyone is asking about you."

"I know." I sniffed. "I guess I should get dressed and go downstairs."

"Listen," she said, standing up to approach one of the cabinets. She pulled out a wool blanket and draped it across my lap. "Go ahead and rest for the evening. I'll let Jack know you're not well. I'll come by tomorrow so we can talk about the plans for Mom's." She blew out a breath before massaging her forehead, shoulders slumped, defeated.

"Okay," I answered, swiping my hand across my face. "I'm sorry, Trish. I'm a disappointment to you, to everyone. I'll rest tonight and try to get better."

"Let's talk tomorrow," she said, looking back over her shoulder before shutting the door behind her.

the year i *left*

You continued to call. I continued to avoid you. Even while at the office, I kept my door closed and canceled all my meetings. The ones with you in them, that is. I'd tell Jane that I wasn't prepared or that I had a conflict, and she'd email you with some flimsy excuse. I guess in the back of my mind I expected you to barge into my office demanding an explanation, but you didn't.

What an irony, the fact that we chose an outdoor columbarium for my mother's remains—out in the middle of a big wide field, supposedly filled with blooms and trees and never-ending sunshine. Except that she died in the late fall when the light was nowhere to be found and stubs and dried branches were all that was left of the blooms and trees.

On the first anniversary of her death, there we gathered, bundled up and cold, sitting on the frozen ground and pretending to have a picnic. Trish had it all planned out—a congregation of those close to my mother, her best friend Lourdes, her priest, the nail lady, the Nordstrom lady, three people from her bible group. And then there we were—Trish, Liam, Paul, Jack, me, and Charlie.

What were we doing there?

This wasn't how the holidays were supposed to be. My mother would have had all our presents wrapped, our menus planned, the Christmas cards sent out. She'd lived with us for all of my married life. When my dad had decided he no longer loved her, I swore I'd make it up to her, take care of her once I could afford to live on my own. She didn't need any money—her parents were real estate tycoons who'd given her a fair share of her inheritance. But her heart. That's what I tried to fill up, making sure she had a home with us just like the home she'd built for Trish and me. I tried to make up for her loss. And the funny thing was that she wasn't here to make up for mine.

We came in the late morning and stayed until early evening. The wind was biting cold by then, and although the fire pit had helped to warm us up, our hearts were cold, our tears were frozen. We laughed and cried and talked about her for hours. Until there was nothing more to say and no more memories to be relived.

I didn't want to think about her. I wanted to touch her, feel her skin, hear her voice. Things I knew were impossible. When everyone left to go home, I told my family I had things to do at the office. They nodded in unison as if they'd expected it. I wanted to get as far away as possible from that day, but the clock just stopped spinning and I moved in slow motion. It wasn't any different from the days that had passed since we'd lost Brutus.

The underground parking garage was empty on a Sunday evening. I should have known it wasn't like any other day because Henry wasn't there. Henry was always there. He'd made a home out of this parking garage when his family kicked him out of their house. Like a ghost or guardian angel, never hurting anyone, just hanging out to greet us as we drove in. Henry had jumpstarted my car when it died two winters ago. He'd also cleaned my car in the summer with an overused rag and a water bottle. He'd wait for me on Fridays when the rest of my lunch money for the week was his for the taking. Henry called me "young lady" and always told me how beautiful my smile was. On late nights, he would walk me to my car and stand guard while I packed up my trunk.

"There you are," I muttered, turning around as soon as I emerged from my car and locked the door.

You weren't Henry.

"Ca-reen."

I hadn't seen you in three weeks. Something was different about the way you looked. It seemed like your eyes had gotten darker and you'd been hibernating in a cave for a while. You hadn't shaved. I wasn't sure if that was your new look.

I did a quick about-face and walked away, focusing on the sound of my shoes against the shiny concrete floor. I heard you following me.

"Carin, wait!"

"Matias, please. Not now."

Of course, you'd catch up with me. Long, steady strides versus stumbling high heels. You grabbed me by the elbow. "Stop, please, Carin! Why have you been avoiding me?"

I turned to face you, hyperaware of the fact that you still held my arm. I yanked it away and stepped back. "Will you stop following me?" I yelled at the top of my lungs.

You flinched, eyes darting back and forth, expecting someone to materialize in front of us. "Carin, please." Your voice was gentle, quiet. Nothing like mine. Your hand slid upward—up, up, up, the tips of your fingers like barbed wire, pricking my skin—until it reached my face and stayed, your thumb lightly skimming my cheek.

That gesture was so heartfelt it took my breath away. If you want to know about the moment that defined us, you and me, that was it. I couldn't help but cry. The events of the day just came rushing back, and for some reason, my mother's voice was in my head, telling me to stop running.

"It hasn't been a good day, please," I sobbed. "Please, Matias!" My knees gave way and once again, you held me up. This time, your arms were wrapped around me, one hand rubbing my back, pressing me closer. I lost my words, snuffed them out against your chest. "She wasn't supposed to leave me! No one knows what I'm going through. It hurts so much!"

"Shh, *Carina*," you whispered. "It's okay. Everything will be okay. I am here."

"I'm so tired," I said, looking up at you. "I'm tired of pretending everything's fine. Jack and Charlie, they put up the Christmas tree for me. And yet—" I cried. "It doesn't feel right. I don't feel anything." I took a deep breath and went on. "I should be grateful, my life is so good. I have nothing to complain about. They've been trying to get me back, but I'm so far gone. I'm so far gone!"

You tightened your hold on me, tilting your head so that your nose touched mine. "Don't pretend," you whispered, right before cradling my face and touching your lips to mine.

I kissed you back, allowing you to devour me with your lips, teeth, tongue. Your hands were on my face, on my neck, all over my hair. And then you touched my skin, slowly slipping your hands underneath my blouse.

"Leave him," you whispered, licking a trail down my ear, your hand hot on my flesh. "Tell me you're leaving him."

"No," I whimpered. "No, no."

You silenced me with your mouth, kissed me some more before pushing me away and stepping aside, leaving me in a daze.

My knees betrayed me. I lost my balance and leaned against the cold, hard wall. I stared, dumbfounded as you came closer, gently straightening my blouse and smoothing down my hair. Ever the gentleman, even in moments of chaos.

"Matias."

"I'm sorry," you said before walking away. "This was a mistake."

Chapter Fifteen

Not This Time

What were we supposed to do with what happened that night? Were we supposed to walk away from it, the mistake you made, the feelings you stirred in me?

That kiss destroyed me, gave me life, made me hopeful and sad at the same time. I spent days wondering whether I loved you. How could that be when I hardly knew you? Could love come that quickly? Could it die in haste too?

I stayed home that entire week, immersed myself in my life—went to Parent-Teacher conferences and volunteered as a lunch mom. Jack wondered aloud whether I was in trouble at work. It just wasn't like me, going offline for a whole week. No phone, no computer. Just lots of naps and sleeping and television. I used the cold weather as an excuse to stay in and lay dormant, knowing I'd have to face the music one day.

That day came just before Christmas, in New York, where Jack, Charlie, and I were spending the holiday. I'd flown there two days early to spend time with Trish. We thought we'd do some last-minute shopping and catch *Mean Girls* before its final run on Broadway.

I finally turned on my phone ten days after you touched me. It was full of messages from you.

The last one said that you too were in New York, at the company apartment on Park Avenue.

"Please, see me. For an hour, a minute, ten seconds. I have to see you before I leave for the holiday. My mother is not well and I need to see her. We need to talk, *Carina*."

And so, on a cold, gloomy winter's day, I took the subway over to 59th and Park, after making some sort of excuse about running to Bloomingdales for some gifts.

My heart was pounding, head swimming in a bowl full of water, noise popping in and out of my ears. I rehearsed my words in the cab. I was going to curse you, hurt you, make you regret everything you'd made me feel and do.

As I stood outside the door to the apartment, I pulled my jeans up to my waist, tightened my belt to hold them up from all the weight I'd lost in the past two weeks.

When you met me at the door, you looked somber, your gaze on the floor, your shoulders slack. You hid your eyes from me and kept your hands in your pockets. Hardly the reaction I expected from someone who had literally begged to see me.

"Well, I'm here," I said, my tone flat and icy.

Still no words as you motioned for me to follow. We ended up in the middle of the living room. To my right were wall-to-wall glass doors showcasing an expansive view of the city. The moon was full but its light was shrouded in a smoky haze.

"What game is this? What game are we playing?" I asked, waving my hands in the air.

You didn't move. Stood your ground and spoke calmly. "Games? Who's playing games?"

"The other night—" I stopped myself and exhaled loudly. "You asked me to come here!"

"You never told me what you were doing in London with Dylan Forest."

You were being ludicrous. It fueled my anger. "What? After all this time?"

"You've been avoiding me for weeks! I need to know! Answer me. What were you doing in London with him?"

"Oh my god. Are you serious? Dylan is with Val! They're in love! She's getting a divorce."

You looked surprised, eyes wide with disbelief. "Valerie was there too?"

"Of course she was! What would I be doing there alone with him? We planned that concert a year ago."

"I'm sorry, Carin," you said. We were still standing feet apart from each other. "It was driving me crazy. I don't know what to think. I don't know how to feel. I don't understand why I'm jealous of any man who—"

"I've never been unfaithful to Jack," I finished your sentence for you. Saying those words hurt me more than I could describe to you. They minimized how I felt about you. How could you think I'd been there before?

"Of course, I know that!" you said loudly, taking two steps forward. I took two steps back.

I turned and took a seat on the black leather couch that wrapped around the west side of the wall. Our corporate housing team did a great job with the place's décor. I remembered wondering how much we'd spent on this. Everything was modern, well appointed. Black leather couches and chrome accessories. Red and yellow accents filled every open space. You took a seat on the ottoman facing me.

There we were, a few feet apart.

"I needed to see you. To apologize for what I did in the garage. I'm sorry, Carin. It's just that you looked so lost that night. I was overwhelmed with my feelings for you."

"Feelings?"

"Yes, feelings."

When you lifted your head up to look at me, I finally saw your eyes. They no longer held the luster that always captivated me. What could I do to wake them up, take away their misery?

You were illuminated by the moon. I could clearly see the lines of your jaw, the perfect symmetry of your face.

"You shaved," I said quietly.

"I'm trying to get out of my crazy phase," you laughed.

"Crazy?"

"For months, you've been driving me insane. I get that I can't have you."

"You're engaged," I reminded you.

"I don't have to be," you answered back. "And you're married."

"Yup." I tried to lighten the conversation, nervously bouncing up and down and placing both hands alongside my legs. "It's easier to undo an engagement than a marriage."

You shrugged, lifting your eyebrows in acknowledgment. We stayed silent for a few seconds, lost in the sounds of the city. I caught your gaze when I raised my head after staring at my shoes.

"Matias, why are we here?"

"You're the one who's here."

"I mean in New York. In Chicago," I clarified. "You should just go home."

"I had it in my head that I could swoop in and save you. Take you far away from here."

I had to laugh, from consternation, mostly. Did I really seem that way to you?

"I'm not a charity case," I said, my tone curt. "I don't need your pity."

"I never said that," you muttered, reaching out to wrap your fingers around my wrist. "It's me, not you. I want to take care of you. Take you out of your sadness. This feeling I have, I just can't walk away from it. I can still see you on the day we met. You had the most profound void in your eyes. It drew me to you, your beauty despite that darkness. You have captivated me since then, and I don't know why my feelings for you won't leave."

I shook my head. "It's impossible to change things right now. I'm unsalvageable, unsaveable."

"Are you happy, Carin?"

"No! But that's the thing. I've been this way even before you came into my life. It's not you. It's not Jack. It definitely isn't Charlie. Once I figure it out, I will get better. I can fix myself."

"I want to fix you. I can fix you." Your tone changed drastically. I'd never seen you so meek, never heard you ask for anything this way. You were Matias, the negotiator. The peacock that showed off his feathers with much pomp and circumstance.

You leaned forward and reached out to me. I held out my arms and you clasped both my hands in yours. We leaned forward, our foreheads almost touching, but not quite.

"Listen. You have a gorgeous fiancée and a great life ahead of you. Don't ruin it for an old washed up hag with a son and a husband. This will never bode well. Impulse is always for naught."

"For what?" you laughed.

I laughed right back. "Doing something out of impulse isn't worth it."

You kept a strong grip on my hands, tugging to make a point. "But that's the thing. This isn't being impulsive. I've been thinking about you, being with you, having you, since I met you three months ago. You've invaded my thoughts every minute of the day."

I was at a loss for words. How could I tell you that I felt the same way? How could I tell you that you were the only light I'd seen in months? That the feelings I had for you kept me alive, made me want to get better?

"How could we be so cavalier about this? I have ten years with Jack."

You stood and took a seat next to me. You hooked your arm around my shoulder and I leaned on your chest. You buried your nose in my hair and kissed the top of my head. "Time is nothing. People can be married for fifty years and be dead inside for just as long. What you feel, *Carina*. What I feel, here and now. I could die tomorrow and it would have been a lifetime for me, to have held you like this for ten minutes."

I looked up at you and smiled. "A bit dramatic, don't you think?"

You kissed my forehead and brushed the tiny wisps of hair that covered my eye. "We invented telenovelas."

"Oh, Matias. Please, don't. Please don't make this harder for me. I'm so confused. I'm not myself. And these feelings, they distract me. "

"So I am a distraction?" you asked.

"You're more than that. I wish I'd met you earlier in my life."

"It's never the wrong time. Things happen and you make it work. You fit it in your timeline. You don't get to choose where or when."

I scooted away from you so that nothing about us was touching. I had to break this connection. I wanted this so badly; I knew that if I stayed much longer, I would give you everything you wanted from me.

"I do," I said, alighting from the couch while you watched me in stunned silence. "I get to choose the time and place. And this can't be it." I bent down and brushed my lips upon your cheek. "Please let this go, Matias. For both our sakes."

Chapter Sixteen

It is Him

I left the apartment in time to find Trish combing the makeup aisles, searching for me. I adamantly insisted I'd been there all along before we left; *Mean Girls* was starting in thirty minutes.

After the show, Trish thought it would be a good idea to have drinks at the Robert. Unlike the opaque mist that blanketed the afternoon, the evening skies were clear. We could see skyline so clearly, the bustling of the commuters, the buses, and the tourists twenty-eight floors below us. We sat at a table by the window; to my right was Columbus Circle and in front of me was Central Park.

"Can I tell you again how nice you look tonight?" It was my second Cidre Pomme of the evening. I loved the taste of anything apple. Trish knew that well enough to take me to a place that served it.

"Surprise! No leggings." She laughed.

I couldn't stop thinking about you. I knew I'd done the right thing by walking away, but I also knew that I'd done it against my will. I hardly heard what Trish was saying, lost in deep thought about the things you and I had talked about.

"Carin, did you just hear what the gentleman said?" Trish leaned over and tugged on the hem of my sleeve.

"Oh no, sorry?" I looked up to find a young male server holding two glasses of white wine.

Trish rolled her eyes.

"The two gentlemen over there." He pointed toward two handsome, much younger men with the glasses in his hand. One had dark hair and a perfect nose. The other was the complete opposite, light-haired and fair skinned, just like me and my sister. "Would like to buy your drinks for you."

Trish waved at them with a smile. "Please let them know we said thanks."

The server set both glasses down and scurried away.

"You see," Trish teased. "Now you're even working your magic all over New York City."

"Please." I set the wineglass to the side.

"What's wrong? You've been quiet all evening. Did anyone call? Anything happen?"

"It's just ... I'm so tired of this. It's all based on the outside. The outside isn't always the best side."

"You're not making sense. Outside, best side, what?" Trish was losing patience with me. She spoke with a tight jaw, her mouth hardly moving.

"It's just that everything is based on looks. No one knows what's truly going on inside someone's heart. Nothing is ever as it seems."

"Are you referring to yourself, Carin?"

"It's a general statement, really."

She got this look whenever she didn't believe me. The same eyebrow raised in unison with the corner of her mouth. "Sure." She leaned back and crossed her arms. "I saw the text pop up on your phone last night. From your coworker."

"Why can't you say his first name? His name is Matias."

"He's the reason for all this ... this change in you. You're not yourself."

"I don't even know what being myself means," I answered.

Before she could respond, we watched as the two men who bought our drinks approached our table.

"Let me handle—" Trish started. I grabbed her hand to stop her from standing.

"Let them," I smiled. "This might be fun."

We spent half an hour with these two guys, Nate and Jake. They were clearly on the prowl, despite having been informed we were married. The classic New York transients—men on business trips with no ties, no commitments. I remembered Val and Dylan and the way they had been before they had fallen in love. In a foreign city brimming with life, surrounded by beautiful people. Who wouldn't want to partake in that? Nate suggested we go somewhere else—a salsa club by Times Square for some dancing. Jake wanted to take me home. To his place. Trish watched as Jake openly expressed his attraction to me. And as she stood to leave, she whispered in my ear. "Get this out of your system. I'll see you at the hotel."

Nate stood to walk her to a taxi.

Jake stayed seated, his eyes glued on me.

"You are so beautiful. You sure don't look like the mom of a ten-year-old."

"Actually, I feel more like the mom of a twenty-year-old." I laughed.

He was quite the looker, with those baby blue eyes and full red lips. So young and so successful. He was a real estate broker in commercial property. I'd heard once that those brokers made millions in commission. He looked very branded—Rolex watch, Yves Saint Laurent shoes. Very much like Jack.

"Listen, what do you say we boot it out of here? I've got a suite at the Dream—we can have drinks and hang out at the rooftop."

"Sounds great," I answered. He looked shocked. I think he'd fully expected a rejection. His face broke out in a smile as he jumped off his chair.

"Let me go and freshen up first. I'll meet you outside," I said.

I never did meet Jake outside. Instead, I exited through the back door, out toward an alley and into a waiting Uber.

I was met with the dim light in the kitchen when I walked into the suite. CNN played at a very low volume, something Trish did whenever she traveled alone. The door to her bedroom was slightly ajar. It was dark in there—I didn't bother to see whether she was sleeping.

I took a bottle of water from the fridge, slid the door open to the balcony and sat on the dusty, weathered wicker chair facing the sky. Thirty-five floors below me, cars moved back and forth, sirens wailed and the laughter of partygoers echoed, their voices traveling through the levels between us.

I rested my chin on the glass barrier and hung my head loosely off the edge. Such a peaceful sight. Everything seemed suspended in time. The cars moved in slow motion. The voices began to blur. Even the sirens played a melody. These sounds beckoned me closer, made me want to float in them.

If only … what if … If I ended it all now, threw myself off this balcony … Would they be better off? Who would receive the life insurance proceeds? Would it take care of Charlie? Would it be enough to send him to college?

For a while I got lost in these thoughts, until a jarring voice whispered to me, reminded me that love didn't mean leaving. Love was about staying. Seeing things through. Most of all, the voice in my head told me that courage and bravery were a product of unconditional love.

I stepped back and lifted my head. Instead of looking at the ground, I switched my gaze to the sky.

I had to tell her. If there was anyone I needed to be honest with, it was my sister.

I ran back inside the suite and knocked on Trish's door.

"Trish?" I whispered, my voice low. "Are you still awake?"

No answer. I pushed the door open. She faced away from me, fast asleep.

"Trish." I sat at the edge of her bed and gently rubbed her arm.

"Carin?" She shot up and leaned against the headboard. "What is it? What's wrong?"

"I'm so sorry to wake you." I took her hand in mine.

"What happened? Is it over? Did you …?"

"No, no." I shook my head, still hanging on to her hand. "I left him at the restaurant."

"Oh." Trish held out her hands and touched both sides of my face. "Are you okay?"

"Yes, yes. I just needed to tell you something."

She nodded, her palms resting on my cheeks. She wiped the tears that began to form at the edge of my eyes.

"Trish, I love him. I don't want to be with anyone else but him."

She dipped her head to the side, gesturing for me to climb into bed with her. "Tell me."

I slid under the covers and laid my head on her shoulder. "He makes me feel alive. Is it possible, Trish? Could it be that he's my first love, not Jack?"

"Alive, how?"

"He sees me. He sees me for what I am. I can't explain it, but he's not into ostentation. There's nothing flamboyant about him. I'm tired of living on the outside. I want to feel alive. But inside. My inside wants to live."

She pulled me closer, wrapped her arms around my shoulders and kissed my head. "Oh, Carin!" she exclaimed. "Only you can see that. If all is lost with Jack, there's no sense in keeping this up. I want you to be happy. I just want you to find your peace."

"What do I do? Where do I go from here?" I cried. I let it all out of me, sobbing, wailing, shaking uncontrollably. "There is no reason for this! There is no reason to be so sad! To be in love with another man. No, reason. No reason."

She held me tight, tried to keep my body from wracking, wrapped the comforter around my shoulders and said nothing.

"When he's around, I live for a few brief moments. And then I die all over again."

"You're right." She placed her lips on my forehead and kept it there for a few seconds. "You can't live like this. No matter what, you're my sister and I love you. I'll support whatever you decide to do, okay? But take your time to think about it. It may be that you're looking for a change. It doesn't have to be love. It could be that you've outgrown this life and those you love just have to keep up with you."

"No matter what happens, I have to tell Jack. I will. I'll tell Jack. And then maybe I'll stop being afraid of my feelings."

Chapter Seventeen

Gone

e left New York three days after that. It was difficult to spend time with the boys knowing what I'd just confessed to my sister.

But it all worked out. I didn't forget about you, but Charlie's excitement over the holidays worked its magic. It helped me to focus on him, on our family. Whether it was going to stay that way or not, it didn't matter. Jack was his father; he was my son. We were going to play a part in each other's lives whether together or apart.

In Chicago one week later, I was back at the office. The weather had turned on me. It was the middle of winter, after all, but one never gets used to the frigid air that swirls around the city. The drabness feels new, even the sting that creeps through your clothing—you're never really prepared for it, you never really get used to it. Everyone was back from the holidays. Not a single trace of Christmas was left. All that remained of the fifty-foot tree in the lobby was the makeshift stage where violinists and guitar players and young singers had, just a few weeks ago, charmed us with their Christmas carols. Every wreath, every Christmas ornament was gone. New Year. New blank space. That's symbolic, isn't it? A clear template to carve out the next three hundred and sixty-five days.

Jane was the first one I saw when I entered our floor. She was busy sifting through her signature post-it notes, sticking one on top of the other as she checked them off her list. "Happy New Year!" She jumped up. "How was your holiday?"

"Great! And yours? Did the kids just love the stuff you ordered from FAO?"

"Our family room looks like a battlefield," she answered with a smile.

"Enjoy it. It won't be long before you'll be wishing your family room wasn't so empty."

I continued walking toward my office. She followed right behind me. "I've organized your meetings for the week. The good news is there's no travel until the end of the month. Your calendar is updated as of this morning." She paused before reaching out to touch my arm. "You look different. Rested. Peaceful."

There was something to be said about admitting what was in my heart. I placed my hand on hers. "Thank you."

"Let me see." I took a seat at my desk and logged on to my computer. She stood across from my desk and waited. "Can you get Mr. Torres on my calendar this week? I think we still have open items from the Asia deal."

I scrolled through my calendar, typing a note here and there.

"I canceled all your meetings with him."

I looked up.

She continued. "He left. Said he'd be leaving you a folder of papers, but I haven't seen it yet. Madden said he was going on an indefinite leave to address some family matters."

"When was this?"

"While you were away in New York. Sorry, Carin. I thought he would tell you directly."

My heart plummeted so fast, I felt it fall to the ground. I could feel the color drain from my face, first a burn that turned ice cold in seconds. There was a stinging in my eyes and a loud thumping in my chest. I felt faint, my arms falling to my sides. It took a great effort to lift them up and start sifting through the stuff on my desk. Before I realized it, Jane was staring at me, eyes wide at my reaction.

"Are you okay?"

"I was so busy with the boys. Maybe he didn't want to bother me," I answered. "That's okay. I'll send him a note. Maybe we can do a conference call."

I switched the tone of my voice. Made sure she couldn't hear my devastation. Still, I couldn't get enough air inside me. I was out in the open and yet everything had closed in. I was in the dark. In a box.

You'd taken away my only hope. Hadn't I just told Trish you were my only light?

I wanted to tell you. Right after I let Jack know.

"Do you want me to contact him? See if we can put some time on the calendar?" Jane asked.

"No, no. I planned to tell you I'll be working from home next week. So I'll connect with him myself."

"Okay," Jane said, her face unchanged. "Let me know what he says and I'll move your schedule around."

"Great."

Chapter Eighteen
You're My Buddy

At exactly 12:01 A.M. on a Sunday, we were in a line of teenagers, Charlie shifting back and forth, waiting to purchase a game he'd wanted for weeks. These were precious moments for me—in the middle of the night with my son who had simple joys and few expectations. This was normally something Jack would do with him, but I jumped at the chance of taking him while Jack was on a golf trip with friends. It was a ritual father and son had adopted for the past few years, midnight releases and a midnight snack at our favorite neighborhood ice cream parlor. I was one in a slew of bleary-eyed parents, all with the same objective.

When it was his turn to pay for his game, he proudly showed his points card and grabbed the disc from the cashier's hand. Once his coveted prize was in tow, we walked to the Shakers next door and took a seat at a booth facing the parking lot. He happily ordered a steak burger and a milkshake; I ordered the same.

"I'm so excited to play this game!" he exclaimed. "Thanks, Mom, for coming with me."

I smiled. "We should have these dates more often. Remember the time we came here with Dad and you guys ordered the kitchen sink?"

That thing had been huge, filled with ice cream and fruits and condiments I hadn't even known existed.

"Dad finished it all," he said.

"You helped a lot."

Our orders arrived shortly after, and Charlie spoke animatedly about the new game—the graphics, and the fact that he was going to beat his friends at all the levels. He told me he would show me the new microphone he wanted for his birthday so that he could record his voice while gaming on YouTube. Half of the things he mentioned were foreign to me, but the light in his eyes and the lilt in his childlike voice filled me with so much joy.

"Gosh, Char, you are so smart."

"They tease me at school all the time. My friends say they don't understand what I'm talking about half the time. They talk about baby-ish things and sometimes I get bored, Mom."

"Well, you won't feel that way anymore in your new school."

A swift nod of his head. "I guess."

We'd been called to the school office before. Some kid complained about Charlie's analogy of the asbestos in toys made in China.

"Well, what did we tell you about trying not to alarm the other kids about things they don't know about?"

"I know," he said, looking at his plate. "It's just that they should know those things. I was trying to help them."

I reached for his hand. "You are. But those kids don't have older cousins like you do. They also don't hang out with adults like you do, so you are a little bit too advanced."

"Like the time I told Mrs. Meyers about Brexit? She actually liked it, Mom. She said I taught her so much about it."

"You taught all of us about Brexit." I laughed. "And the DACA, and immigration. You're just way ahead of your time, monkey."

He smiled and sipped the rest of his shake. I pushed a napkin toward him before standing and making my way around to sit next to him. He scooted close, placing the weight of his body against mine. He relaxed his head against my shoulder. I could tell he was getting tired.

99

"Char, you know you don't need to get into trouble at school just so I can leave work to come and get you, right?"

He didn't answer. Instead, he began to peel the nail off his little finger. It was his nervous tick—a habit he'd always had ever since he was three years old.

"Are you scared about transferring schools?"

"Nope."

"About living in a dorm? Away from home?"

He buried his nose on my shoulder, sniffed me once or twice. "Not really. I know you and Dad will be there every other week."

"We will."

"And I'll have all my games." He smiled. "And you have Life 360, Mom. You can track me anytime."

The truth behind a child's wisdom. He was assuring me instead. "Do you know how much I love you?" I asked.

"More than anything."

"Do you feel that way, baby? Do you feel loved by Dad and me and Auntie Trish?"

"And Grandma," he interjected.

"And Grandma." I laid my head on top of his thick, coarse hair.

"Mom, you're not okay, right?" His voice was markedly low, almost a whisper.

"I haven't been well lately, honey. And I'm so sorry. I'm trying so hard. I'll try harder."

"Like you've been sleeping a lot lately. And you don't like talking to Daddy. Once, I saw tears on your pillow. You're still sad about Grandma?"

"It has nothing to do with you, baby. I need you to know that."

"I do, Mom." A slight pause, and then, "Mom?"

"Yes, Bubba."

He laughed. "Am I the boy with ten thousand names?"

"You know it!"

"Mom?"

"Uh-huh?"

"Do you still love Daddy?" he croaked.

My heart broke for him because I knew the answer.

"He's my best friend." This was true. This was the truth of the matter. I loved him like a friend, a part of my life I would never give up. It would kill me to lose Jack's love. It would eviscerate me, blow me up into pieces. For many years, my marriage had defined who I was. It spelled out my future, characterized exactly how things would turn out in years to come. If I lost Jack, I would lose my old self. Even if I didn't know what my new self was all about, I knew I had to hold on to the good parts of the old me.

He continued, "When I have a wife, I want to be the one working. I don't want to stay home all day like Dad. It looks boring."

"Hmm. Char, you don't know what Dad does while you're at school. He's working too, trading stocks and doing things around our house. Remember the shelves he made for us? And how he finished the entire basement and built your computer? Mommy couldn't do that. And your games! He's been to every game and every school activity! He takes care of you and us, so well. Don't you think?"

"Yes, he does," Charlie agreed. "But you try really hard too. We have all these nice things because of you."

"Things aren't as important as love and a home and the happy times we have when we're all together." And then I realized. The important things were gone. At least in my head, all the things that mattered to me were no longer of any value. This instance further solidified my resolve to let Jack know. Let him know that everything that had mattered to me no longer did. And that this wasn't the life I wanted to live.

How ironic. I'd worked so hard to gain his love. And now that I had it, I didn't know what to do with it.

Charlie stayed quiet, processing everything in that spent little head of his. "I'm getting tired."

I gestured to the server to bring us our check. Charlie stifled a yawn and looked up at me. "Love you, Mom."

"I love you, Mookie. You have to know that my life is nothing without you. You are the light of my life. Okay?"

"Okay."

"Remember the song we used to sing when you were two or three?"

"Nope," he said, nervously picking at the one fry left on his plate. "I don't."

I laughed. "Okay, it was a long time ago." I left cash on the table and we both slid off the booth to head back to the car.

Just as I unlocked the doors, I sang at the top of my lungs a song I'd made up when he was younger—a toneless, tuneless profession of my love for him. It was our goodnight song, sung as I tucked him in each night.

"You are my sunshine, my only sunshine. You're my buddy too."

And just as loud and raucous, he answered.

"And I love you."

Chapter Nineteen

Love

When the universe aligns, it does so with a vengeance.

The day I decided to speak to Jack was the day I received your note.

I clutched it in my hand, its sharp edges digging into my skin and the world falling apart around me. I had no doubt who it was from. I just didn't know what to do with it. I barely had ten minutes to react when Jack unexpectedly arrived home.

"Hey babe," he called excitedly from the kitchen.

I slipped the note in the back pocket of my jeans, wishing I'd had more time to collect myself. "Hey."

I lived that way in the months after I met you, functioning when called for and retreating inside myself when I wasn't needed. My shoulders hunched and my head jolted when the back door slammed shut. I wondered why he was home early. He was supposed to be gone for a few more hours, meeting with a contractor for the prospective vacation house he wanted to build in Michigan.

"Why do this in the middle of winter?" I'd asked him.

Jack felt it would be good to get a head-start so we could break ground in the spring.

He knew. He felt it too. He knew we were pulling away from each other. How could he not?

He tried to distract us from the inevitable, moving around constantly, afraid that if he stood still, the obvious would tear past the walls he'd built and force him to confront the truth. I knew this, because for the past ten years, winter had been his retreat. This particular season came with a vengeance—freezing the roads, train tracks, and each body of water around us. School had been called off a few times due to the extreme cold.

And yet, there was Jack. Working in the garage to build me a shelf I hadn't asked for, taking cooking lessons, going crazy on his exercise bike. Instead of slowing down, he fought like hell to keep changing things up, allowing a constant flurry of activity to invade our home every single day.

I'd hardly spoken to him for weeks, especially after our trip to New York. When I said goodbye to you, I came to resent him even more.

Even before you sent me that note, it was over.

That night, I had started on dinner when Jane stopped over to drop off my mail. I was taking more days off in that time than I ever had before. The walls of the office felt toxic, suffocating. Everywhere I looked, all I could see was you.

"How was your day, Car?" Jack asked in between dipping and munching on a piece of celery.

"Uneventful," I answered. "Jane just left. I just woke up when she stopped by."

"Yeah. That," he muttered, looking away. "You've been doing a lot of that lately. Sleeping."

"And?" I asked, irritated with his passive-aggressive way of bringing it up.

"And nothing. Just making a comment. It's been ongoing for months."

"You're still blaming me for what happened to Charlie," I said, stepping in front of him, trying to confront this, make it real and concrete.

"Being in the principal's office three times in a row is a call for help, Carin. You still haven't cut down on your traveling. We need you here with us, not in New York or Paris. Not sleeping but awake."

"I know that."

"Then, if you do, let's move on. I don't really want to get into a discussion with you right now," he said.

"I just haven't been feeling too hot." *Ask me why I'm sleeping so much,* I screamed in my head.

I could always predict what his response would be. I didn't know why, but I could. His demeanor changed. I could tell he was trying to save the night, find a way to detour the conversation back into joviality.

"What do you mean?" he asked, his lips upturned into a sly smile— a total change from the strain of a few minutes before. "You're always hot."

"Ha," I said with a smirk.

It was his standard peace offering. It used to work every single time. It didn't anymore, and it made me so sad.

I was in no mood for any of this, but I laughed anyway. "Go change into your comfy clothes and I'll have dinner in about fifteen minutes."

He turned around to do so, but not before grabbing the remote and turning all three televisions on. They had to be on—all of them—the one above the fireplace, the one in the family room and the built-in mirror one right in front of the kitchen table.

All this excess. It bloats you up like a balloon flying aimlessly for a few short-lived hours.

You can't choose who to love.

That's what your note said, in barely legible handwriting, ink smeared flat across the yellow paper. You were trying to be funny, I supposed, slipping it in between the pages of your report—the one you'd asked Jane to give me right before you left for the airport. I never saw you after that night in New York, although you surfaced in emails, in conference calls, in conversations with peers. It was a game we played, you and I. The push, the pull, and the excruciating silence. When I didn't hear from you, I felt insignificant and unsure. It was like I only existed to be chased by you. And so your note to me was in many ways, a victory. A vindication that what happened between us hadn't been imagined. You see, I spent half that time going through the motions of my ten-year-life; I was never really sure what was real and what was perceived. And right there, in an unmarked envelope addressed to me was the note that threw my world off kilter.

Because if I could, I would choose you.

Chapter Twenty

Divorce

By the time I received your note, I had already planned to end this vicious cycle. I had to find a way to get better. I didn't have a plan, nor did I know what saying those words would mean. But I knew that if I didn't take a step forward, remove myself from the place that triggered my distress, I would take my family on this downward spiral right along with me.

Jack's mood had shifted back into his safety zone. Sometimes I thought he tried too hard, but I never faulted him for that. That night, he was overly solicitous, and it broke my heart. He talked nonstop about his day, asked me about mine, tried to get me to tell him about the latest deals, asked about each of the people he knew at my office.

I tried to act as normal as possible, filled him in with what he wanted to hear.

After putting away the dishes and clearing the sink, I knocked on the door of his study and asked if we could talk.

"Of course." He smiled. "What's up?"

I sat on the chair directly facing his desk. "I need help, Jack."

"What's wrong?"

"I haven't been well for months."

"I know, Car. First your mom and then Brutus. It's been a tough year. Maybe we need to go away. Take a break or something."

"No, no." I shook my head furiously, choking back a sob. "I haven't been well for a while. I think I need to leave."

"Leave?" He winced and jerked his head back. His eyes were so narrow, the lines on his forehead were so pronounced, they looked like ridges on a piece of potato chip. "For where?"

"I don't know."

"Leave for where?" he asked again.

"Anywhere, actually. Anywhere but here."

"Aren't you being a bit too rash? I know things have been difficult for you but we have to go on. We have a son, we have a life. How are you just going to get up and leave?"

"I don't know," I whispered. "All I know is that I'm suffocating. I can hardly make it through the day."

"We can go to counseling or something. Is that what you mean? How do we make this work?"

"Jack, please listen to me," I stressed again.

"I'm trying, Carin. You're not making any sense."

"All these months, did you even notice this?" I opened my right hand and placed it in front of him, palm up. Scabs and mottled pink patches streaked the skin.

"Oh, my god! Carin! What—" He staggered back and leaned on his desk.

I'd been suffering from so much anxiety I'd scratched the skin on my hands until they bled. Late one night the previous week, I'd played a game with myself, tried to etch new lines on my palms, disconnect the old ones—hoping my fate would change. *If it did, would you be in it? Would you be my new future, Matias?*

Tears began to form. I raised my voice, strained to make myself heard. This newfound strength that came with accepting the truth. "Last week, when we were in New York, I actually thought of throwing myself over the balcony. I was thinking that you and Charlie would be better off without me. I haven't been present. I've stopped wanting to function as a mother and a wife."

"You're depressed, maybe?" he said, still in denial. "Or is it the Porsche? Is it the new house? Is it stressing you out? Because I can—"

"Jack! Please, please, listen to me!" I cried. "That's all you ever want to talk about. Things! Material things! I don't care about those fucking things!" My tears were flowing, my words squeaked out between deep breaths and sobs. "I want a divorce."

"You don't know what you're saying. Let's call Trish." He stood and leaned over to pick up his phone. "She can help us figure this out."

I grabbed the phone and threw it on the ground. "No!"

"Goddamn it, Carin! You are being so unreasonable. You have a son. You have a family. What the hell are you telling me?"

"This has nothing to do with Charlie."

"Of course it does. He knows that his life means two parents living in the same house," Jack defended.

"And he will always have two parents. A divorce doesn't change that."

"A divorce." His eyes grew dark. Anger manifested itself in many ways with Jack. Normally he would clam up, turn silent and then walk away. I remember the early years when I would chase after him, challenge him to fight back. He would turn his back on me and leave.

"You didn't really pursue me."

"And we are revisiting this why?" Jack clenched his fists and began to pound on his lap.

There was no turning back. I threw the first dagger and buried it in his heart.

"I got pregnant two months after we met and you married me out of responsibility. You didn't even return my calls, never tried to contact me. My mother had to chase you down, hold you to your obligation."

"Bullshit. I loved you."

"No. We didn't love each other. Raising a child doesn't constitute love."

"Okay. So, let's say we got married too quickly. I've learned to love you since then. And for the past years, I've been faithful. I've been a good husband and a father. I don't know what else you want from me!" He slammed his fist on the table. "Let's forget this conversation ever happened!"

"You also said I was average-looking, made me feel as if I was beneath you when we were newly married."

Truth be told, for years I had lacked confidence. Thought I was plain looking until I'd made enough money to adorn myself with exceptional things. Turned out I didn't have to do that because eventually, this average duckling had turned into an average swan.

"Oh, my god! How many times during our marriage have I told you how beautiful you'd grown over the years?"

"And that makes it better?" I asked. "And my mom!"

"What about your mom?" he asked through clenched teeth and bright red cheeks.

"When she died. You never really talked to me about it!"

"I was giving you space!"

"YOU GOLFED THAT WEEK!" I yelled.

"Carin! It's not like you've ever asked me for help!" he roared back.

"I didn't need space!" I sobbed, trying hard to form my words. "I needed you, your love, your assurances."

And then something happened. I sensed a shift. I saw it in the way his jaw tightened, his shoulders pulled back. There it was—the imaginary slap on the face. His pride. His ego. The competition.

He moved closer to me and stared me down. "It's him, isn't it? You're in love with that bastard. Did you sleep with him?"

"No!" I squealed. "This has been a long time coming. Jack, please listen to me. I can't breathe. I'm suffocating. Every day, I lose a part of myself. I don't even recognize myself in the mirror. Do you see me?"

He turned around and faced the window, hands at his sides, his fingers twitching.

"Listen to me. Can you see me?" I asked again.

"Yes," he mumbled.

"I haven't been here!" My voice reflected the frustration I'd felt all this time. "Please, Jack. Please turn around and talk to me." I stepped toward him and pulled on one of his hands. "Please."

He sighed deeply before facing me with tears in his eyes. At that moment, I wanted to erase everything I had just said. I wanted to hold him and tell him that I changed my mind. Maybe if it lingered a few minutes more, I would have acquiesced, agreed to fix my head while he held my hand. I would have done so if he hadn't given up.

But he did. "You're right. You haven't been here for a while."

"I'm so lonely."

"I am too," he admitted, slowly backing into one of the five Oculus armchairs he'd purchased and sagging into it. Jack had insisted they provided great balance for his back.

"But five?" I'd asked.

I remained standing.

"I love you, Carin. Maybe it wasn't love at first sight, or a head over heels kind of meeting. But over the years, you have shown me how blessed I've been to have you as my wife. This change in you, this just happened months ago, after you lost your mother. I'm afraid to throw the towel in too soon. Maybe it's a mid-life thing. I know it's because Charlie's growing up too."

I stepped forward and knelt in front of him, cupping his knees, keeping them from unfolding. He didn't move but kept his eyes on me. I choked on my words; hearing myself say them sealed my decision. "I got lost somehow. I don't know when. I don't know where."

"I didn't comprehend the magnitude of all this until you stopped paying our bills and our credit was ruined. It was just so out of character for you. That event confirmed to me that you'd lost your sense of self. Your family used to be your world. Now I think you've outgrown us."

111

"I'm so sorry," I cried. For him, for me, for our family.

"What could I have done different?" Jack asked, his tone somber, his voice soft. His face went slack, his mouth hung open and his breathing was labored.

"I think we both focused on the wrong things. We changed as people. Your priorities were different. We worked so hard to accomplish what we have, but those things weren't important to me. When my mom died, I think I realized that I never had the chance to be my own person."

"What does being your own person even mean, Carin?"

I spun around with my arms in the air. "All this. It doesn't matter to me. I'm still sad. I'm still despondent every single day."

"Is it him? Are you in love with him?"

"No." I paused. "And yes."

Jack closed his eyes. "I know I haven't been involved in our life. But you haven't been here. I haven't been able to find you. It's like you're in deep with something that's not here, not in our home."

"Maybe the idea of him," I continued. "There's something missing. I need to mourn my mother. Mourn the loss of our old life. I need to think about what I want, what I need. I need to figure out why I'm feeling this way about another man. He's engaged to be married. Nothing will come out of it."

"You've lost respect for me because I don't work."

"Yes, I think so," I answered truthfully. "It never used to bother me, but now it does."

"I can't change that. Even if I looked for another job, what good would that do for us? We have enough. Why does it mean so much to you? Is it because you feel it's unfair? You're working yourself to the bone because that's who you are. Not because you have to."

"You are absolutely right, Jack. Maybe that's why I need some space. Nothing but Charlie brings me happiness these days."

He stayed silent for a moment, staring at his hands, and then looked straight at me. "When did I stop being part of your life?"

"I don't know."

"What will we tell Charlie?" he asked, his voice meek.

"The truth. He knows, Jack. He's the most intuitive, mature ten-year-old I know. I'm going to tell him that I'll be living downtown for a few months while this expansion project is going on. He'll be away at his new school, and then come summer, he'll be traveling with Trish and Paul for a bit. It will give us the time we need to sort things out. And when he's in town, he can stay with me. We will have many times together. I think the space during the week will help me clear my head."

"Car. How do I make you find your way back to me?"

"I need to find myself," I repeated. "And then I'll look for you."

Chapter Twenty-One
New Normal

One week later, I moved out of our home. With Jack solemnly standing by the door, Trish holding my hand, and Charlie packed up in the car, it was as uneventful as I'd imagined it could be. Two people with nothing in common, both fearful and unsure, each letting go for a different reason.

"Come back, okay?" were his last words to me. Even then, I wasn't sure I wouldn't.

No matter how intuitive a child is, still he remains a child. It couldn't have gone more sideways with Charlie. He was mad, angrier than I'd ever seen him before. He'd called me selfish, told me his dad had taken care of us more than I did. He'd asked me to give up my job, made me promise that a break was all it was. He'd cursed—and I'd reprimanded him for it—and cried and held on to me, his disposition shifting from hatred to vulnerability and back again.

Does this mean divorce?
What if it did?
WTF mom!
Don't dodge the question. Why?
I hate both of you. You're selfish.
You made a promise, and you can't work it out?

We won't be a family anymore
If you stopped loving each other, how do I know you will love me?
You said the same thing to Dad!

It lasted for a few days. He sulked in my apartment, focused on his video games and Face-Timed his dad at every free moment. I deserved everything he did and said—the implications of my actions a penance for disrupting this perfect, happy family.

Timing is everything. A friend of a colleague was looking to rent out her condo at the Marina Towers. The place was a steal. A one-bedroom, open-floor concept overlooking the Chicago River. Although the sole bedroom was mine, I converted part of the living room into a loft for my son, complete with a makeshift wall that gave him some privacy.

I filled the walls with Beatles memorabilia. Val sent them to me from London as a favor. Charlie, a huge Beatles fanatic, gasped at the life-size mural of himself walking down Abbey Road—a housewarming present from his dad. It was important for me to give him a home that would feel just like the other one. In a matter of days, I truly believe he got that message loud and clear.

Winter was slowly easing into spring. Snow turned into rain, cold air turned into dampness that seeped into your bones. Charlie and I sat on the leather couch facing the clouds, watching a rerun of *Stranger Things*, but not watching anything at all. The floor was littered with empty shopping bags that surrounded a large blue suitcase. Both sides lay open next to three pairs of size 8 boys' sneakers.

"Mom?" he said, turning to look at me before leaning his head on my shoulder. We'd spent many quiet moments like this while getting him ready to leave for school.

"Hmm?"

"Did you know you were moving out that night you and I went to Shakers?"

"No, not really," I answered, reaching for his hand and holding it. "I knew I had to make myself better, I didn't want to think it meant

115

leaving your dad."

"Are you still sad now?"

"A little. I mean, this is so new to all of us, you know," I answered. He lifted his head and stretched out on the couch, placing his feet on my lap. I caressed them lightly while he folded his arms under his head. "And while you're away at school, I'm going to be making sure I get better."

"Sometimes, you can't help it. Sometimes, it's clinical, you know," he stated nonchalantly. I felt like I was speaking to someone my age. "Like you need medicine or something."

"How did you know that?"

"Google," he said with a thumbs up.

"Ah."

"Besides, you're not as bad as before."

"Was it that bad?" I asked.

He nodded furiously. "Oh, yeah. You didn't laugh at all or smile. Sometimes, I wouldn't even know you were home."

I didn't argue, didn't even try to respond.

He went on. "But not anymore. I've been counting the times you've laughed since we moved here. I'm at eighty-eight."

"That's a lot of laughing!" I said with a chuckle.

"Yeah, because I'm a funny guy." He kicked his legs into the air and sat up, his head turning from side to side. "And Lola." He pointed to a wall-sized portrait of my mother.

Did I ever tell you she had been Miss Illinois back in the day? In that picture, she had her trademark pixie cut hair and large gold hoop earrings. It had been taken in the seventies when she was just thirty-three.

"You talk about her all the time now. You never wanted to say her name before."

I held his head between both hands and kissed it. "Yes, being alone in this apartment has given me time to think about her and celebrate the times we had together."

Charlie fished out his phone from underneath him as it rang. "It's

116

Dad," he said, pressing the green button on Face-Time. "Hey, Dad."

"Hey, buddy." Jack's face appeared on the screen. Charlie sat back up and rotated his phone.

"Say hi to Mom," he commanded.

"Hi, Mom," Jack complied. "Char, I'm just calling to check in and make sure you're okay and ready for our flight to Florida tomorrow."

"I am. Mom and I were packing. I mean, we were packing and then decided to watch *Stranger Things*."

"Huh," Jack responded. "Carin, so you're taking a car service to the airport? I'll meet you at the Priority Check-in Line?"

"That's the plan," I responded. "He doesn't check into the school until Thursday, so we have a day to visit the area. We have two rooms at the Hilton."

Jack avoided my eyes while nodding. "Okay, I'll see you guys then."

"Bye, Dad," Charlie said as Jack's face disappeared from the screen. He turned to me before sliding completely off the couch. "Hey Mom, I forgot to tell you. Do you remember Stella, the lady who worked with Dad when I was five?"

"Oh, you mean Dad's colleague at the old company?"

"Yeah, that one. The one with the red hair and super high heels?" he said.

"Yeah. She was so nice."

"Dad had dinner with her last week. I think it was a date. Aunt Trish stayed with me until he came home."

I inhaled deeply before pasting a smile on my face. I'd started this—I wanted this. Jack deserved to be happy. Come to think of it, they had been kind of alike even back then. They were a good-looking power couple, complementary and supportive of each other.

Charlie stood and pointed at the shoes on the floor. "Okay, so we have three pairs. Which one should I take to the school with me? I can't decide."

"Take all three," I said, joining him in the middle of the living room and gathering the bags that were strewn on the floor.

Chapter Twenty-Two

Away We Go

We stayed in adjoining bedrooms at the Hilton across the street from campus. Jack was in 1803 and I was in 1805.

"Hey," I greeted as I closed the hotel room door. We'd agreed to meet by the elevator for Charlie's official first day of school. Brenard Preparatory was an all-boys school in Florida, specializing in the development of gifted students. "Is he ready?"

Jack shut the door quietly behind him, ruffling his hair before giving me a kiss on the cheek. "He's putting his shoes on."

"How is he?" I asked.

"Excited, I think," he replied, rubbing his hands together before exhaling loudly. "I think we're both more nervous than he is."

"So true."

Just then, Charlie dashed out, his Fortnite backpack swinging from side to side. "This is happening!" he squealed, causing us to laugh out loud.

Ten minutes later, we stood outside his classroom after meeting his guidance counselor at the admissions office.

"I'm going in now, Mom, Dad," he said, first turning to me and then to his father.

"Are you sure?" I reached out to smooth his hair down over his ears.

"She did say you can take your time."

"I'm going," he said in warning, as if giving me and Jack some time to digest his next move.

"We'll be here to pick you up at two," I said. "And then we'll take you to your dorm."

"Mom! Dad! Do you have to do that? I'm okay, really. You can all go back to Chicago and I'll see you next weekend."

"No, no. We planned to stay until tomorrow. Make sure you're settled in," Jack repeated.

Charlie rolled his eyes and began to walk away. "Okay. But I told you I'll be fine."

And there we stood, side by side, watching as the classroom door closed in slow motion. Our thoughts and emotions screamed on the inside, but on the outside, we remained silent, absorbing the gravity of the moment.

Jack's voice broke through at the perfect time. "He's only going into sixth grade."

I laughed. "I know."

"So we save our tears for college." He looked at me with a smile. His eyes looked sad. I'm sure they mirrored mine. This is what we do as parents. We make sure that life goes on for our children, even if it comes to a screeching halt for us.

"Deal." I took a few steps away from him, signaling for us to leave.

"Car," he said, catching up to me. "Want to have coffee or something?"

"Sorry, no, I have a conference call in ten minutes. Was going back to the hotel to work."

"Okay, let me walk you then," he said, pushing open the exit door and leading me down the steps to the sidewalk.

I wanted to notice him, what he was wearing, what he looked like one month after our separation. I was afraid I'd miss him, regret everything once I saw him.

There was a kind, handsome gentleman in front of me.

But that was all I saw. I had been married to him once, but he felt more like an old friend to me. I refused to over-think this. We were there for Charlie and nothing mattered more than that.

We crossed the main street and headed toward the hotel. A strong, warm breeze drifted through, causing the branches of the trees to sway and the leaves to fly around us.

"Charlie says you're better," Jack began as we approached another crosswalk. He guided me down the street, lightly touching my elbow.

"He did?" I smiled. "I'm so glad he thinks so."

"Are you taking the time you need to figure everything out?"

"I am."

"I was really angry about your leaving," he said as we stopped in front of the hotel's sliding door.

"I know," I answered, glancing at my feet. There were times I wondered whether it had been worth it. What was the alternative? Float through life as if it were a dream? Life was too short to pretend. There was someone else out there who could love him like I should. "I'm so sorry."

"Listen," he said, as we stepped in. "I just wanted to tell you that I realized the part I played in changing how you feel about this marriage. If something wasn't amiss, if your heart was full, you wouldn't have allowed him—" He paused and switched gears. "I would change things if I could."

"No, no," I said, taking both his hands in mine. "Jack, I didn't mean to hurt you. I just couldn't live with the sadness."

"There's a chance, isn't there? There's a chance you'll come back?"

Slowly, I stepped back, releasing his hands. He kept his eyes on me, waited for an answer.

"Let's focus on Charlie, okay?" I muttered before taking deliberate steps away from him. "I'll see you this afternoon."

Two months later, I arrived in Asia, anxious to seal the deal on my independence. Financially, this was going to set me on track, help me to take care of Charlie, empower me to live on my own.

The look of disdain on the stewardess's face was classic. There I stood, in line to disembark with a phone to my ear and three carry-ons instead of two. TSA pre-check, global entry, first class seats—all that doesn't matter when you're in another country, far away from what you've grown accustomed to. There was no Jane to help me with my schedule, no Henry to walk me to and from the office. No Matias to confuse me, no Jack to make me want to leave.

"Char, are you there?" I checked in with Charlie as soon as we touched down. "Landed safely. I'm dropping my stuff off at the hotel and going to my meeting. I'll text you pictures if I find the Pokemon you're looking for."

"Okay," he answered.

"And I ordered more uniforms before I left. They will deliver them to the school office so you can get them from there."

"Okay," he said again.

"I love you," I declared, hoping my words would one day erase the pain I'd caused him. "Don't forget you're staying with me during spring break. We'll take trips to the Science Museum—maybe go to New York for a few days."

By this time, I was close to the door, waving at the pilot and copilot who stood enmeshed between the food cart and the microwave.

"I love you too," he answered.

"Okay, bye for now."

"Mom! Wait, Mom!"

I slowly made my way down the stairs, holding up the line while trying to maintain my balance. It became hard to breathe, the air so thick and torrid, it arrested my movements.

"What's wrong, Charlie?" I asked, panicked. "Do you want me to fly back sooner? You know I'll be back in time for your break." It was the middle of March, after all.

"Nothing's wrong, Mom. I'll miss you, that's all. I think I see you more now than when you lived at home."

"Do you like that, Charlie?"

"Yes, I do. And I'm sorry for everything I said. Paul said that you also have a right to be happy."

"Don't be sorry, baby. We'll talk when I get back. I love you, too."

The ride from the airport was uneventful. The Plaza Hotel was a bed-full of contradictions. In all the majesty and opulence of its marble floors and luxuriously decorated lobby, it was less than a mile away from an entirely different scene, where shanties and makeshift wooden homes lined the pothole-laden streets and soot-filled ground. I checked into a room overlooking the bay and grabbed an hour of sleep, mindful of the fact that I was about to embark on the biggest deal of my career.

There I was, about to meet the man whose island in the middle of the South Pacific was up for sale, with my company on the way to making the most generous investment to develop the first all-inclusive resort in the area. There were security concerns—this was a third world country beset with political unrest that simultaneously welcomed this type of intrusion. It was a quandary, really. Opening a world untouched by modern conveniences to the riches of the western world, where a price was always paid for change. I thought about this to no end, felt sorry for those poor souls who didn't realize what was about to happen. With change there is pain.

Progress always came with a trade-off.

Two hours later, there we sat in silence, me and a legal team of three on one side of a long boardroom table made from handmade seashells bordered with coral and jade. Directly above us was a line of antique Spanish chandeliers, their stems filled with precious stones that shone like diamonds. Opposite us was a kindly gentleman named Dr. Fernandez, his legal team and his son Vincent, who had brokered this sale.

I spoke up, finally, after exchanging many pleasantries. "I think we're ready to sign the papers," I started out. "The team has reviewed the contract and we are thankful for this opportunity."

A woman named Josefina piped in. "No, I think we are waiting for one more person from your team. He called to say he was on the way."

The heavy wooden doors swung open and in you walked, wearing a navy blue suit and loafers. I turned to glare at the person beside me, handing out my surprise to anyone who would accept it.

"He insisted on coming," she said helplessly, glancing over to the man next to her, her eyes beseeching him for help.

"Hello, everyone, apologies for the delay." You took a seat next to me without acknowledging my presence. The room grew warm. The women at the table sat up taller—one flipped her hair, the other adjusted her neckline. I wondered whether you noticed them—these tiny petite, dark-haired Asian women with olive skin and fine features.

As you leaned back into your seat, I turned to face you. "I thought you—"

The room grew eerily quiet. I shuffled my papers, hoping to draw everyone's attention away from us.

"Management wanted me to complete this deal, see it through." You looked at me, your eyes unblinking. There was harshness in your tone. "I shouldn't have left my unfinished business."

"You forgot to wear socks," I muttered under my breath.

The doctor cleared his throat and nodded, prodding us to get on with it. "Ms. Frost, Mr. Torres."

"Yes, yes. Ladies and gentlemen, what a privilege to be here. Want to ensure you have no further questions before Ms. Frost over here"— you turned to me with a smirk—"finalizes the sale."

I wasn't going to fall for your antics, at least not in front of these people. I opened the folder and leafed through the three-hundred-page agreement. I'd read each and every page about ten times to ensure there was nothing of concern.

"Well, there is one point of clarification," Dr. Fernandez said. "Page two-hundred forty-four, the elimination of an underground gas pipe requiring additional funds to be placed in escrow. Ms. Frost, are you amenable to this?"

Gas pipe? What gas pipe? What the hell was he talking about? I had no knowledge of this. Had I missed this page? How was this possible?

"Did this come up in the due diligence, because I—" I stammered, frantically thumbing through the pile of papers in front of me so they spilled onto the floor.

The doctor leaned back on his chair and pushed backward, preparing to disengage.

You cleared your throat. "What Ms. Frost meant was whether this was the only item found through the due diligence. If you turn to Exhibit H, you will see proof of escrow which was transacted two days ago."

Dr. Fernandez relaxed and leaned over to his son, who quickly showed him the page. "Very well. Let's get this deal signed and sealed." He smiled. "Mr. Torres, you have saved the day."

Chapter Twenty-Three

History

Shaken and flustered about what had happened at the meeting, I retreated to my room, intent on redeeming myself the next day.

How could I have missed that addendum? Unless it had been done at the last minute without my knowledge at all. It wasn't the right time to get to the bottom of it—I was still reeling from your unexpected appearance. I just couldn't handle facing you, facing my embarrassment, facing the buyers at this point.

And so I focused on Josh Lucas.

Josh Lucas had the bluest eyes I'd ever seen. The moment he turned Reese Witherspoon after she ran to him in the rain never failed to make me swoon, no matter how many times I'd seen this movie. Of course, it took me a few minutes to get over the fact that *Sweet Home Alabama* was showing on a local channel all the way in the Philippines.

It was two o'clock in the morning in the US. I had to wait for a few more hours before giving instructions to the bank to ensure Jack had access to the funds just deposited in my commission account.

After the closing, I'd retreated to my hotel suite, intending to take a nap before venturing out into the city. I had scheduled an evening tour of the place they called the Walled City of Intramuros, the site of pre-war churches and post-war ruins.

Despite a separate bedroom and a walk-in closet, I decided to camp out on the living room couch, complete with a blanket and pillows, magazines on the floor next to the coffee-table and four paperbacks I'd taken on this trip with me. I wasn't much of a reader, but this time alone was still part of my new life that required some getting used to.

Staying in bed all day, getting lost in my thoughts, replaying scenes over and over again—I realized how much time I'd wasted in the months that had passed. Those days were slowly disappearing. In their place was a new person who loved to explore and learn new things. It was like living all over again, getting familiar with all the senses I'd lost.

I was besieged with guilt at abandoning my boys, often wondering whether I had done the right thing. In its place, however, were nights of restful sleep and the slow but sure birth of a clearer mind. I didn't want to die anymore. I was excited to live.

The room service menu had a separate leaflet called *merienda*. Google told me this was a light meal or snack, sort of the equivalent of afternoon tea. So that's what I ordered. Jasmin tea and three pieces of rice cake called suman, cooked in coconut milk and wrapped in banana leaves. I think I dozed off, because Reese was back, this time doing the "bend and snap". What a diversion, to discover a Reese Witherspoon marathon in the middle of the afternoon.

I sat up slowly to answer a knock on the door.

It was the room service man, carrying a little round tray with my *merienda*.

And you.

Dressed in jeans and a black T-shirt, you allowed the man to set his tray on the coffee table before walking in with a bottle of Cristal and two champagne glasses.

"Thank you, Simeon," you said, taking the leather billfold and signing for my charges.

"Enjoy, Mr. and Mrs. Frost," said Simeon, smiling.

I sat on the couch with my legs folded under me, trying to think of something smart to say. I had nothing. Instead, I tried to cover up my tank top with the blanket, thankful that my bulky pajamas covered the rest of me.

"Way to go, pulling that off this morning. What were you trying to do, impress me?"

"Hardly," you answered. "Things here move so slowly. The inspection was completed while you were in flight. I didn't want to lose the deal, so I handled it."

"I arrived two hours before the meeting. You could have told me."

"I could have, I guess," you admitted. "But I didn't want to give you time to react when you found out I was here."

"Why?"

"Because all I wanted to do was to see you. I didn't want you to run away."

"I wouldn't have."

"Well, so far, your record has proven otherwise." You moved about the bar and rummaged through the drawers until you found what you were looking for.

"You've been gone for three months. You don't know how things have changed."

"Look!" you said excitedly, placing a piece of paper in front of me. "We can retire!"

"Ha," I snorted, unimpressed. Money wasn't the answer to anything that had happened to me. Money had caused my marriage to disintegrate. It couldn't bring back my mother. Or Brutus. It sure as hell wasn't going to give my son his two parents back.

I didn't think you heard me. You popped open the bottle, poured it, and handed me a glass half-full of champagne.

"Would it hurt you to celebrate for a little bit?" you asked. "You just made two million dollars."

"Well, so did you. And you can be happy enough for both of us."

You didn't say a word—no smart comeback, no anger either. Just a slight nod of your head and a puckering of your lips.

"I'm sorry. That was uncalled for."

"Oh well," you said, taking another swig of your drink before standing. "Just wanted to congratulate you on a job well done. I'll see you at the site visit tomorrow."

I remained seated, staring at the floor, noticing the cork that had rolled right next to my shoe.

"Matias, wait!" I jumped up, forgetting about the flimsy bra-less look and dropping the blanket. You stopped, hands in your pocket, rocking back and forth on your heels, eyes wide, staring at me as I moved closer. I realized what I had done and crossed my arms against my chest. "Give me some time to get dressed. I'm going on a tour of the city—would you care to join me?"

"Yes, yes. I would love that." You smiled as if every stupid thing I'd ever said to you had been forgotten.

"Great. I'll meet you in the lobby at five o'clock."

We sat side by side in the front row of a tiny passenger van, together with two other couples on the same tour with us. One couple was from London, the other from Costa Rica. You spoke to the Spanish couple animatedly in your language while the older English woman took copious notes while listening to our tour guide, Marina. I heard you asking how long they'd been married. They were newlyweds almost—married only three years. When they asked you about us, you said not long enough. I would have said six months because you'd had my heart on the very first day we met.

Did you feel the tension between us? Your thigh against mine, my shoulder touching your chest. I felt your breath on the back of my head, held your face when you buried your nose in my hair. It was a slow dance, a seduction, happening in front of five other people. I wonder if they felt it too.

Intramuros was located in the historic heart of Manila, the meaning of the word, "within walls". Surrounded by a three-mile-long brick barrier, it had been the seat of government, the center of religion, economy, and education during the Spanish colonial period in the late 16th century. Its cobbled streets and old stone structures had been mostly destroyed during World War II. But what remained to this day still emanated richly in history and the heroism of the Filipino people.

The van dropped us off at Fort Santiago, once a defense against invaders from the sea and now a historic park. You held my hand as we walked through old jail cells and dungeons, wrapped your arms around me as we listened to the story of the country's national hero, observing the crowds walk in and out as we watched a short play about his life.

I asked for some time alone to call Charlie, told him how much I missed him and recounted the history of this country and its people. He said he regretted not coming and made me promise to take him back during the summer.

And when our tour was done, we joined the other couples at a place called Barrio Fiesta that served authentic food from the country. We were treated to a folk show where the country's history was told in song and dance. You held me close throughout, ordered my food, took care of my needs and never left my side. I didn't stop you from touching me, placing your hand on my thigh and slowly trailing it underneath my skirt.

I wanted you more than anything in this whole world.

In two days, we would be done.

In two days, we would return home.

And you'd do what made the most perfect sense. You would go on with your life.

Chapter Twenty-Four

Because of You

"*Dahil tayo!*" I sang, swinging my hands back and forth as we rode the elevator to the suite. You pressed yourself against me and I giggled.

"I'm sure you're wrong. It's *Dahil sa you!*" you argued.

"How do you know that? We only heard the song once!"

"Yes, but they said it fifty times in the song. Plus, I'm Spanish. I know their words," you bragged, taking my hand and leading me down the hall of the fiftieth floor.

"*You* is an English word," I laughed.

"And I'm pretty sure it's in their language too. Google it. I'm sure I'm right."

So I did. "It means because of you, I want to live."

"Because of you," you repeated. "Because of you." You started to sing the song again.

"Shhh." We turned a corner and then another corner. "It's one in the morning. People are sleeping."

"Or fucking."

"Shh. Oh my god," I said again as we turned another corner. "Here I am, 5100."

"Here you are," you whispered, heat emanating from your eyes, burning a hole right through me. I pushed you away, unlocked the door, and walked inside, hearing your steps but refusing to turn around.

This was it. The split moment decision that would change my life. For no matter what happened after this, you would be the only other man after ten years of Jack.

I felt shy all of a sudden. The insecurities of the past began to creep in. I wasn't pretty enough, sexy enough. I had a child. You had a model. Or two. Or three.

"Carin," you called out to me.

I stayed rooted in place, looking out the window at the boundless bay that touched the sky. There were boats of all sizes, the smaller ones swaying with the waves in a monotonous beat as they surrounded the towering cruise ships.

"Carin," you said again, your voice louder this time, and every word enunciated. "Don't be afraid. I won't ever leave you. I came back for you."

Did I think about my marriage? Of my son? If you knew me, you'd know. Spontaneity was not my thing, and so I wouldn't say I didn't. But all throughout that tour, I knew I would give myself to you if you wanted me.

Slowly, I made my way toward you.

"I didn't leave him because of you," I stated clearly, making sure you heard every word.

"I know," you answered, head bowed. "It doesn't change anything I just told you."

"I left him for me." Tears began to flow with those words. I raised my hand to stop you from rushing over to me. I needed to shed those tears. They'd weighed me down for so long.

"I know, *Carina*."

You gasped, swallowed audibly, as I undressed in front of you. Unbuttoning my blouse, slipping it off, unhooking my bra and revealing myself to you for the first time. "But," I choked through my tears. "If

131

you want me tonight, I am yours."

Two large strides and I was in your arms, being kissed by you, touched by you, caressed by your fingers, your mouth, your tongue. I pulled away for a second, allowed you to watch as my skirt and panties fell silently to the ground. I backed away, intent on showing you who I was. For months I'd survived by pretending. This time, I wanted you to see me for me. Vulnerable, open, in love.

I stood in front of you, legs slightly apart, completely naked.

"This is who I am."

Your eyes grew dark, your lips in a tight straight line. "I've wanted you since the day you fell on your knees. You looked like an angel, exquisite, helpless. The most beautiful creature I had ever seen."

You were the beautiful one. Handsome and strong. Perfect in every single way. I'd wanted to touch you too, hold you, fill myself up with you.

"Make love to me, Matias." The first bridge I'd burned. The first of many, in following my heart. After this, there would be no turning back. No begging Jack for forgiveness. I knew that once you'd touched me, it would mean that I was yours.

You didn't need to be asked twice, lifting me and carrying me to the bed. Slowly, you laid me down, and I reached up to take you in my hands.

"Look at how much I want you," you growled. "Touch me, Carin."

And I did. I held you in my hands while you leaned over and trailed kisses down my face and neck, settling yourself on me, biting, nipping, driving me wild. I'd discovered love before. I'd swooned over words and promises and believed that if we were lucky enough to have one single moment of true love, we should take it. But this.

This felt impossibly new.

Your touch made me shudder. It broke me and then revived me all at the same time.

"Now," I moaned. "I want you now."

Gently, I placed my hands on both sides of your head and pulled you up, aligning my lips with yours. I spread my legs and arched upward, pleading for your body to invade mine.

"I've wanted this for so long," you whispered as you buried yourself in me, your eyes locked on mine, watching me react. "Tell me what you want."

But you see, I didn't have to say a word. Because you saw how overcome I was, how tears streamed down my face, how my muscles trembled. How perfectly we fit each other when you filled me. How we moved to the cadence of a song I'd never heard, its melody soothing, its words reassuring.

"Take me, take all of me!" I huffed, breathless and reaching the peak of my pleasure.

With those words, you pushed one last time, gasped sharply, and released yourself. Your brows were furrowed, eyes were closed. I savored the seconds I had you in me, wishing we could stay like this forever.

When it was over, you rolled to your side and held me close. You kissed me once more before settling your head on your pillow and falling asleep.

The plight of the jet-lagged. In my dream I arrived so hard, I screamed out loud. I woke myself up with a shudder at two o'clock in the morning, finding you under the covers with your mouth on me. At four o'clock, I was on my knees, asking you to tear into me. To our dismay, we overslept, waking up at nine the next day and missing our seven o'clock flight to the island.

We got dressed quickly after making a few phone calls—you to your hotel, asking them to send your suitcase to the airport and me to let our colleagues know that I was running late. We agreed to arrive at the airport separately, sit separately, and interact separately.

"What are we going to do?" you asked, taking my hand and bringing it to your lips while we sat in the sitting room.

"We go on as we have been. The deal is done. You have your commission—you're also on to a great life in Spain." I tripped all over my words, tried to sound as upbeat as I could. Despite a broken heart, I was thankful to have had you even just for a day.

"That's not good enough for me anymore," you declared. "Carin, I will leave her. I want to be with you."

"Don't do this," I said. "Don't change your world for this. You have everything ahead of you. You'll forget this ever happened and move on. You have to."

"You have no right to tell me what to do, how to feel," you argued. "Did last night not mean anything to you?"

I cowered, allowed you to envelop me in your arms. "Of course it did. But all this is temporary—things like this don't last. We steal the moments that belong to others. You and I don't have a right to them."

I looked up at you and for a while, I thought that maybe I was wrong. Maybe we had a chance. Until the phone rang—our ride to the airport was waiting in the lobby.

"We have to go," I said, resolution and concession fighting to the surface. Last night was the first time I had let go of myself, relinquished all pretense. Today, it would come back with a vengeance—the fight to survive regardless of the circumstance. You'd come into my life way too late.

It was too late.

Chapter Twenty-Five

Into the Sea

Neither of us had much to say on the way to the airport. Entry into the island was currently limited to the doctor and his family and so a private plane was the only available means of getting there. There were six of us again—two lawyers, two architects and us. One of the architects was a personal friend of Jack's. It was only respectful for us not to interact too much during the entire scouting trip.

I smiled when your eyes grew wide at the sight of the Gulfstream G150. You were like a kid in a candy store, appraising the lushly appointed leather seating, the extended bar, and the three large television screens.

You didn't know how much flying terrified me. As we sat across from each other, I tried my best to mask my fingers under my sleeves so you didn't see them digging into the armrest. It was a forty-five-minute flight, a quick take-off and landing—and as the pilot was giving us last-minute instructions, you motioned to me not to turn off my phone.

You're so beautiful.

We have to talk. I can't leave tonight.

Don't push me away.

Uncross your legs for me.

I want to be inside you.

Want to join the mile high club?
I know what you're wearing underneath that skirt.

I laughed out loud a few times, stole a few glances and fell head over heels for your lopsided smile. My heart sank when we landed. All I could think was that it brought me closer to the time when we would have to say goodbye. What you had given me the night before would keep me alive for the next twenty years. Not everyone got to soar as high as I had that night. Sometimes, life keeps you pretty close to the ground. There are no guarantees that one day you'll take flight.

In our convoy of golf carts, I was way up in front and you were in the back. In my car were the doctor and his son, in yours were the architects.

I missed you. So many times, I wanted to turn around and check on you. Instead, I listened to the woman with a megaphone walking us through a history of the island as well as its geographical location. We passed through the town before ending up by the ocean. Slowly, we made our way through the village where happy, toothless people waved us on. Many children played in the streets, among tooting horns, speeding cars and crackling motorcycles. The sounds of life were different here. There was a vibrancy in the air, an affirmation despite the dilapidation and poverty. How could there be misery when they didn't know what they were missing?

"And this is the largest island in a group of how many?" I asked Dr. Fernandez.

"Yes, Lubang Island is the largest. There are other islands in this group, but the land you purchased is right here. We will be there in two seconds." He paused. "Ah, here we are."

The carts circled around a stone landing and before we knew it, we were in paradise.

I caught my breath at the sight before me. Sand, white as snow, stretched as far as the eye could see, sparkling like sugar crystals, untouched, unspoiled, spotless.

"Can we stop, please?" I gasped, leaning down to remove my shoes. I didn't wait for a response; my feet were on the fine white powder, running toward the shore.

The doctor stayed in the cart while his son tried to catch up with me.

"My god! I never knew a place like this existed! Look at the water! You can see everything underneath. It's amazingly clear!"

Vincent smiled. "This place has been kept a secret for a long time."

"Carin!" you shouted, running toward me, loafers and all. I shielded my eyes from the sun with one hand and held the other one to you. You grabbed it, despite the fact that the whole world was watching.

"Look at this, Matias!"

"It's gorgeous," you answered. "Just stunning."

"You see over there?" Vincent pointed to the right side of the island. "That's the island of Cabra. Do you see the lighthouse at the very tip over there? That is where the Virgin Mary appeared to a young girl, a student, in 1966."

"A place for miracles," you said, your eyes never leaving mine.

In a matter of minutes, the people from the village began to descend upon the beach. They were curious about the foreigners who had entered their world. Three little girls in shorts ran up to me and touched my skin. One of them gently tugged at my hair, giggling and saying something in their language.

You watched this all take place, never letting go of my hand. The crowd filled the beach.

"There must be two hundred people out here. Where did they all come from?" I glanced around. The island began to look small, a country of many compressed into one place.

"I don't know."

There were women dressed in sarongs and men in dark-colored

pants. Strange, I thought, that fishing boats were pulling in so early in the day. Maybe they'd started out in the middle of the night. Maybe they were the day shift. In a matter of minutes, the water line began to rise. People started moving backward—what had been a shoreline at my ankles was now up to my knees.

You looked at me with worry, tightened your grip on my hand, squeezing my fingers firmly, as if signaling a course of action.

"Ms. Frost! Mr. Torres!" Vincent called to us. "Please come here!"

We pushed our way through the crowd until we reached the golf cart. "We should leave now. There is word from Golo Island that there is some volcanic activity on Ambil. They experienced a small earthquake a few minutes ago."

Golo Island was one of the islands, I guessed.

"Okay, okay," you said, pulling me toward the second cart.

A shrill, screaming siren cut through air, leading to an uncanny silence.

People stopped in their tracks, immobilized and shocked.

And then a rumbling. A soft drone right before the ground began to shake.

"Carin!" you yelled above the screams. People were running in every which way. I feared a stampede, but you—you looked so calm and collected. You took my hand and led me away from our colleagues.

I could hardly hear you yelling.

"This is our chance. This is our start! Carin, can you see it?"

"What? What are you saying?" I yelled back.

"We can start over! Leave our lives, be together. Erase our past!"

"How?"

"By getting lost!" you answered. "We can let it all go, right here and now."

"No!" I cried. "My present has Charlie! And Jack! And Trish!"

"You will always have them! But this! Me and you, a life together! Can't you see that?"

I started to cry. More than anything, I wanted you.

"I'll never leave you, Carin. I will always be here. I don't want the life everyone has planned for me. I want this life." You reached for my face, cradled it gently between your fingers. "With you."

From the distance, a glowing red light emerged from the ground.

"Run!" you bellowed at the crowd. "Something is happening!" You grabbed me with both arms, lifted me off the ground, and slung me over your shoulder. You climbed a huge mound of hardened soil, huffing and panting until we reached the top of a small hill enclosed by a break wall. The golf carts were gone—there were strangers all around us.

People ran from the water, tripping on their feet, trying desperately not to be swallowed by the sand.

There was a rumble, a slow one, the waves thrashing in and out. You encircled me with your arms, holding me against your chest, anchoring me to the stony ground.

And then a deafening sound—a thunderous clap followed by a loud boom. The ground shifted and we were met with the ear-splitting sound of an approaching freight train.

You held on to me, kept me from falling. I felt safe with you. The waves rose higher and higher, crashing against the wall and drenching us. I thought of the Godfrey, when getting lost in your voice, in your song was the only thing I could remember from that night. I felt that way again except this time, I didn't want it to end. I wanted to be lost forever. With you.

You looked at me, and I looked right back at you.

"I love you, Carin."

"I love you, Matias."

"Let's throw our old life into the sea," you beseeched, tears in your eyes.

In every life, there is that one time.

When for one miniscule moment, you are selfish, self-serving, even hedonistic.

139

You become a mercenary for yourself, an advocate for your own happiness.

That moment for me was profound and absolute. It was the end of my world but also the beginning.

The apocalypse and the birth. Our origin.

I watched you pull out your wallet and your cellphone. When you turned to me, that same storm was brewing in your eyes. They were conflicted, swirling like the clouds above and yet sparkling.

You were giving me your heart. How could I refuse it? Slowly, I pulled out mine too—my wallet, my cellphone, and slipped the diamond ring off my finger. You nodded and, without a word, we flung ourselves far out into the angry, grumbling sea.

Part II: OUR SPRING AND SUMMER

"People go
But how
they left
Always stays. "

Rupi Kaur

Chapter Twenty-Six
The Place for Miracles

March 2016

"How much farther?" I asked, holding on to the crook of your arm, my footsteps unsure and reluctant. We were on sand, I knew that much. It felt cool and compact, like it had been touched by water. I could hear the rushing sound of the tide and smell the salt in the air. But those were a given, a new normal for the two weeks we'd been living by the sea. I lost all sense of time and place. I was with you, and that was all I cared about.

Our origin. It began in a dingy little room somewhere in the middle of the earth, where the temperature was punishing and the dust seeped in through the windows. We clung together, on a bamboo bed with a sunk-in futon, unsure of where we were or what we were going to do, but filled with anticipation about what was to come.

The night of the earthquake, we disappeared together with the others, evacuated to the opposite side of the shore. Its magnitude was recorded at 5.8. There were no deaths—or at least no dead bodies.

Just the missing.

Buses and tricycles transported us to a more touristy side of the island with small hotels and resorts. You said we couldn't stay. That it was the eventual place where people from home would try to find us. So we took a tiny motorboat across the island and ended up here.

"Just a little bit more," you answered, adjusting the blindfold settled snugly on my nose.

"Where are we exactly?" We'd taken one jeepney and one tricycle and walked a heck of a long time on the beach. You carried this out so well, so secretive, like a stealth mission. "How'd you even find this place?"

"The other day, when you were getting some clothes at the village, the lady at the hostel introduced me to some guy who knew another guy who owned some abandoned properties."

Your voice had a lilt to it. A tinge of excitement. I knew you were doing all you could to convince me that we'd made the right decision.

"Ha, yes. These clothes," I said, before turning to you with a smile. A tiny dive shop by the beach with clothes at tourist prices had sold me three sets for a hundred dollars. Of course, dive shops don't really carry many essentials.

You read my mind. "I told you we don't need underwear."

"It's quite liberating—literally and figuratively." I laughed. "To think I was a slave to my outfits for years and years. Here, we get to wear the same thing every day."

"Don't worry," you assured me, "we'll take a trip to one of the bigger resorts once we're settled and get you all the stuff you'll ever need." Finally, you stopped, pivoting to the left and guiding me to turn away from the water. "Here we are."

A few hundred feet in front of us, behind two coconut trees and a smattering of tall grass, stood a modest raised bungalow with wooden shingles and a low, pitched roof that extended over a porch. I let go of your hand, dropped the knapsack on the ground and made my way closer to the dwelling. The porch was littered with leaves, the front door hung loosely on its hinges. The large bay windows were boarded up to protect them from the elements.

"Blue and white," I muttered to myself, observing the scaly, blistered flecks of paint that now exposed the clapboards. I saw the gentle hues of the sky and the clouds and the deep blue sea dispersed around the good portions of the structure.

You wrapped your arms around me and leaned your chin on my shoulder. "I know there's some work to be done, but I can do it in no time. All it will take is a little bit of—"

"It's beautiful," I countered, tightening your arms around me, craving to touch your face. "How much did it cost?"

"Five thousand," you answered, skimming your nose against my cheek.

"For a house?" I had no perspective at all.

"He wanted more, but I pointed out all the stuff I have to do to fix it," you explained.

"That leaves us with …?" We started with fifteen thousand between us. It seems like a lot to bring on a work trip, but truth be told, I had plans to shop in Hong Kong on the way back to the States. It looked like you had planned to do the same, too.

"Ten thousand more." Gently, you twisted me around so that I was facing you. I saw the worry in your eyes. "But Carin, you don't—"

"I'm not worried," I declared right before I kissed you. I kissed you with the fervor of someone who'd been found. Someone who'd just realized the magic of a kiss. Someone who was in love for the very first time. The kind of life-changing kiss that said "you saved me".

I surprised you, I guess. Because when we pulled away, you had that glaze in your eyes that only happens when tears begin to form.

"That was nice," you whispered. "Do it again."

I planted soft kisses on your forehead, your nose, your cheeks. "Let's see our home," I whispered.

You lifted me with both arms and carried me up the wooden steps, laughing as the porch floor creaked and the wind blew the door open. When you set me on the ground, I was paralyzed, overwhelmed with emotion.

"I know it's small, but—"

The house was completely empty, save for yellowed, stained formica kitchen counters and a tiny white stove. Rectangular and narrow, it stretched from side to side—the kitchen on one corner and a white door on the other. Slowly, I made my way around the house, touching the counter, running my fingers along the window ledge. I pushed the door open to find an empty room illuminated by a green metal lantern with two sleeping bags neatly laid out on the floor.

"You found our bedroom." You ran your hand through your hair before fidgeting with your chin. I supposed it was because I had yet to say a word. You cleared your throat. "As I said, I know it's small—only seven-hundred square feet, but I can build an addition here." You stretched your arms across from one corner of the room to the other and walked around the sleeping bags. "Tear down the wall to use up some of the porch space. We can also extend the kitchen."

I stepped in front of you, took your hands in mine and held them to my lips. "No. It's perfect. I love it, Matias."

"You do?"

"I do." I answered. "It's big enough to hold our dreams."

"I love you, Carin."

"I love you," I whispered, softly pushing you down toward the floor until you were seated on one of the sleeping bags. You pulled me down with you, guiding me while I spread my legs and straddled you. Your kisses were wanton, your touch fierce. You lifted me up, your eyes instructing me, telling me exactly what you wanted without saying a single word. So I settled myself on you, filled myself up with you, surrounded you, swallowed you, and made you a part of me.

When kerosene runs out, there is a flickering of light and a dim haze. We stayed wrapped around each other, whispering softly, as if the whole world was listening in on us. There was no one there, of course. Our world as we knew it had dissolved, down to just you and me in a strange land, in a house filled with everything despite having nothing.

We floated in and out of sleep, intermingling the conscious with the subconscious. Dreams with reality.

"Carin?" You breathed into my ear. "You awake?"

"Hmm." I stretched my arms up over my head before looking up to face you. "What time is it?"

You smiled at me, trailed your finger in a straight line from the tip of my nose down to my neck. "Only four. I should let you sleep."

"I'm not that young anymore. You tired me out." My tone was playful, but I had to admit, I was exhausted.

"You are perfect. This"—you cupped my breast—"is perfect."

"Hmm," I said again, holding your face with my hands. Our noses touched. I felt your breath on me and it gave me life.

"'Did my heart love 'til now? Forswear it, sight! For I ne'er saw true beauty till this night.'"

"Shakespeare." I kissed you. "Is that us, Matias? Are we the star-crossed lovers?"

"On the contrary," you answered. "We are rewriting the story. Right place, wrong time doesn't have to end in heartbreak."

"I like that," I said.

"Rest well, my Juliet."

"And you, my Romeo."

Chapter Twenty-Seven

Woodpecker

ap. Tap. Tap.

The knocking on the window had a tempo of its own. I opened my eyes and strained to listen, its rhythmic beat lulling me back to sleep. The sunlight was blinding. It burned through the sheet that you had hung as a temporary curtain. You were fast asleep, your chest rising and falling deeply, your arm draped over my chest. With eyes half-closed, I felt for my watch on the floor next to me, trying to see what time it was.

The woodpecker disappeared. In its place was another bird, bigger probably, because it kept crashing against the door.

Bump! Bump! Was it a cat, maybe?

Bang!

You sprang up, whipping the blanket to the side, covering me completely. "What's that?"

I shot up too, crawled across the floor to grab my underwear.

"Stay here," you instructed.

You shut the bedroom door behind you, pulling it twice because the wood was warped and disfigured. I heard voices through the wall. Low, mumbling. A woman and a man. Quickly, I pulled on the first pair of shorts I found, grabbed the shirt I'd worn the night before and tied my hair up in a bun. It was the very first time I thought that maybe they'd found us. I wasn't going to let you out there all alone.

You were all startled by the creaking sound of the door, turning toward me in unison.

There was an older man, half your height, wearing khaki pants and a white embroidered long-sleeved shirt. I had seen it before—the men at the sale closing all wore the same thing. The woman next to him was petite with ebony-dark hair. She looked at me and smiled.

"Hi," I said, waving at the woman. She waved back hesitantly. Hand halfway up, fingers folded.

You ran over to me and took my hand.

"We are so sorry to have bothered you," said the man. "My name is Ariel, and this is my wife, Diana. We were sent here by the owner of this house, who is traveling abroad, to collect the payment and sign the papers."

"The papers," you said to me with smiling eyes. I nodded and smiled back. We stood in silence, allowed a few seconds to pass, waiting for Ariel and Diana to make a move. Ariel pulled a white envelope from his briefcase.

"I think I have a pen," you said, dashing in and out of the bedroom quickly.

"Thank you," Diana said, shaking her head. "Sorry, we did not get your names."

Names. Right. I offered her my hand. "My husband's name is Roman. And I'm Julia."

You caught up to me, placed your arm around my shoulder, squeezed, and kissed me on the cheek.

"Ah, here," Ariel said, pointing to the kitchen counter where he laid out the contract. You handed him the cash in a worn brown envelope and proceeded to sign the papers. I wondered what you were doing when you paused to glance at the floor and tugged on the hem of your shorts. You slid the document toward Ariel who folded it up and placed it back into his briefcase.

"Thank you, Mr. and Mrs. O'Neill. I have a truck parked at my home. I would be happy to take you to town to buy some necessities when you're dressed and ready," he said. "You can text me; I can write down my cell number."

"We don't have cellphones."

"Oh," said Diana. "I own a beauty shop in town and we also sell cellphones."

"And movies," Ariel added.

"It's all right," you answered. "Why waste all this peace and quiet by having phones? I can just walk into town in about an hour. Would you be free at that time? I would like to get some hardware supplies and maybe a bed."

"A bed is important," Diana giggled.

You led Ariel toward the front door. Diana and I followed.

"Congratulations, again."

"Thank you both, I will see you in an hour," you said, practically pushing them out the door. And when they were gone, you swept me off the floor and lifted me up by my backside. I wrapped my legs around you, giggling as you danced around the barren house.

"Seriously?" I laughed. "You took the brand off your shorts?"

"Fuck. I hadn't thought of a last name! It caught me by surprise!"

"A Spaniard with an Irish name," I said, kissing the side of your face, my legs still tight around you. "Sexy."

"Carin." Your look changed from playful to wistful. You leaned me against the wall and brought both hands to my face. "We have to sit down and map this all out."

"I know," I answered.

"Don't regret anything. I promise to make you happy."

"I don't."

"Want to know what's really sexy?" you growled.

"What?"

"Julia," you breathed into my ear. "Julia O'Neill. That name just turns me on."

"Oh yeah?" I licked the outline of your lips, searched for you with my hand and guided you inside me. You gasped as I placed all my weight on you. "Tell me—who's more turned on, Roman O'Neill?"

Chapter Twenty-Eight
The Rules

April 2016

There were rules, and there were guidelines. The rules were quite simple: no phones, no computers, no contact with anyone outside of this island. Obviously, there were technical reasons behind the rules—no computers because IP addresses can be traced, no phones because signals can bounce off cell sites.

Now, on the other hand, the guidelines were flexible. In my head they were allowed to be broken—these were more personal things you and I discussed but really didn't place parameters around. Don't watch the news, use your new name, don't get too close to people, talk it out.

You made me promise to speak to you about anything I felt, telling me that you expected this displacement to take its toll on us one day.

I had one more that I didn't mention—kept it to myself but made every effort to comply.

Stop thinking.

There's nothing to think about.

He will know. Trish will know. I'll find a way to let them know.

All I ever wanted is right here with you.

So many times while we were together, I decided you were perfect.

I watched you build our house, make it a home, forage things together and link them to our history. That time, you were placing the finishing touches on our bed frame. You returned from a trip to the local mattress maker, vexed by the fact that these beds were made to rest firmly on the floor.

"What about the bugs and dirt?" I'd asked.

You nodded, deep in thought. There you were hours later, hammering away on uneven pieces of wood, positioning them together, determined to allay my concerns.

"So your dad was a craftsman?"

"Yup," you answered, looking cute in your eye goggles, sitting cross-legged on the floor, surrounded by a power drill, a long saw, and some guiders.

"What was his favorite thing to make?"

"Who?" you asked.

"Your father."

"He was a sculptor. Later on, he worked for a furniture maker, carving out designs. He's retired now."

"Your home must have been so beautiful."

"It was. My mother loved nice things."

"Well …" I laughed. "Our mothers would have gotten along great."

Significant progress had been made in the two weeks we'd been in our home. It had taken two days for you to paint the walls white and four for you to build us some chairs. Everything else, we found at the roadside furniture store recommended by Ariel and endorsed fully by Diana. Our glass kitchen table had bamboo legs that matched the chairs you'd built. We upholstered the sofa in green floral print and found a Spanish chandelier abandoned on the side of the road. We kept the same oven, purchased a new fridge. Of course, new is used and used is new in this place. Our money went a long way.

While you created things, I polished them, made them shine like new. Those chandeliers looked like they were fresh out of the store, the yellowed formica countertops were bleached to an immaculate white. Ariel had a friend who had helped us install some electric wires to power up the lights and support our large central air conditioner. You wanted one for the bedroom and one for the living area—we compromised on a heavy duty one in the living room, thought to leave the bedroom door open so the cool air could permeate throughout the house.

It was the middle of summer. Blistering hot, bustling with life, kids out of school, many working either in the fields or on the beach selling seashells. Summer in this country was not the summer in our country; tourists were scarce and limited to mostly locals.

For days I watched as you cut the boards to size, taught me all about pocket screws, asked me to help you with the glue, sanded, stained and applied multiple coats of varnish. You slid the scraper evenly along the length of the wood, making it look easier than it was.

"You're so dexterous," I teased. "You do good things with your hands."

You slipped your goggles up your forehead. "I do, do I?"

"Yes sir, you do." I leaned my chin on the back of the chair, wrapped my arms around it, facing you. "I will always remember this."

"Remember what?" You paused to look at me.

"This. You making me things, creating our life."

"Don't worry." You smiled. "I'll be here to keep reminding you."

I walked to the kitchen to lay out the table. You followed me with your eyes, shaking your head.

"My mom always said, it's all in the presentation," I teased. I laid out the placemats, plates, and matching napkins.

"I would've loved your mom," you said, getting up to wash your hands.

I wrapped my arms around your waist and kissed your shoulder. Touching you grounded me, reminded me why I was here and why I should remain in the present. In the newness of our life together, I refused to bring the past into our home. Except that I missed them. I missed my mother and most especially my son. For weeks I'd conditioned my mind to make me believe I was merely on vacation. Or on a long business trip.

"Let's eat."

I hadn't cooked in five years—but since we'd moved in, I willingly accepted the role of homemaker. That night, it was a chicken stir-fry. You scooped a large cup of rice onto your plate and topped it off with vegetables and oyster sauce.

"I'm starving." You smiled before gobbling down a mouthful.

"Matias?"

"Mmm, baby. You are the best cook ever."

"I've been thinking ..." I took a sip of my water. "What if I just wrote a le—"

"Not yet."

"What I've done to him, it will scar him for life."

You kept going, chewing, spooning, drinking your water. I tried to act as if everything was normal. Here we were, lovebirds in paradise, off to a new beginning. I couldn't help but wish Charlie could be a part of this new life, too. You know what they say about newlyweds—there's a honeymoon phase, a delirium that serves as an enclosure from the realities that are kept at bay. They don't go away—they surround you until you can no longer deny their existence. I had made my choice with no regret. I deserved to be with you.

You took a deep breath and blinked twice as you exhaled. I wondered what you were thinking because you stayed silent. And then you ate your food, poured yourself a glass of wine and carried on as if the conversation were over.

Except I didn't want it to be. I was moved with the same kind of pain—the pain of missing my mother—the tightness in my chest, the twisting in my stomach, the craving need to see my son.

"Don't you care about me? About him?" I burst out, tears streaming down my face. I dropped my fork and ran to the bedroom.

155

"Carin!" You knocked on the door before pushing it open. "Please, I didn't mean to upset you." You sat next to me and pulled me close. "Please, don't cry. I want to explain it to you."

I swatted my hand across my face, still distressed by your lack of empathy.

"Listen, I'm not crazy. I'm not stupid. I'm not evil, either. The pain you are feeling, I can only imagine what it may feel like. But I know that eventually, the world ..." You paused. "Real life, our old life will find us and take you away from me. All I want is a little bit more time with you. With you in this place, alone. I just want this time with you. I want you to love only me, here and now. I know it's selfish, but I can't bear to think of anything else."

"I miss him so much." I started to cry again, more out of guilt because I knew that I agreed with you. I wanted the same thing. Nothing for nothing. You give up love to get love. At least I convinced myself of this.

"I know." You held me tighter. "If you really want to do it, just know that this will be the start of the end. What we've done—has set things in motion that we can't undo."

"I don't want this to end."

You didn't encourage or discourage me. You wanted me to decide on my own. "I love you, Carin."

"Julia." I smiled, pulling you down on the mattress until your weight was on me, your face aligned with mine.

"Julia," you answered, pushing my legs apart. "I love you, Julia."

Chapter Twenty-Nine

Sarong

I learned how to tie a sarong around my chest, twist it in a way that it covered me up entirely. Every day, I tried a different way to do it, fold it in a triangle or twist it from a square. Most of the time I succeeded—sometimes, it just wouldn't stay on. I also learned how to wear a bandana. It kept my hair in place, decreased the frizz that came with the humidity. Considering I hadn't had a haircut in months, direct sunlight seemed to accelerate its growth, thickening it and lightening it at the same time.

The jeepney ride to Diana's beauty salon took fifteen minutes. In the hot wind, that's all the time needed to grow a rat's nest of matted hair on my head. I consciously tried to comb it down before entering her store, using the bandana to tie it up in a bun.

Little bells on the door announced my arrival. Diana was busy sweeping up the remains of a haircut. Soft music played in the background—the Bee Gees, actually—and water ran in a pedicure tub. The walls of her salon were plastered with magazine pictures of beautiful women with beautiful hair. There were three barbers' chairs and three pedicure chairs. The salon was sparsely decorated—a TV, a counter filled with videotapes, two bonsai trees on a makeshift desk and some silk pillows against a wooden bench.

"Hi!' she greeted. I wanted to reach out and touch her shiny, black hair. "Are you looking for Roman? He left to go with Ariel—said he needed more materials for the outside of your house."

"No, no," I said. "I do know he left to go to Looc."

She laughed.

"What?" I asked. "Did I say it wrong?"

"Well, it's pronounced LOW–OCK," she said. "Not *look*."

"Oh. Haha."

She motioned to the barber chair. "Come, sit. Did you come for a haircut?" She moved closer to me. "Your hair is beautiful, thick and light like the foam. It matches your eyes which are so blue like the ocean."

"Thank you."

She took a comb and began to part my hair.

"No, sorry." I turned the chair away from her. "I didn't come for a haircut."

"Let me do your eyebrows then," she said, touching my face and running her fingers above my eyes. "I can just shape them since it's been a while."

"Sure." I giggled. "It has been six weeks."

Diana bent down and opened up her supply cart. There were plastic bins on wheels located right under the mirror. She pulled out some tweezers and placed a drop of lotion on her fingers before smoothing it over my face. For a while, I thought she was going to pluck the hair on my cheeks. No idea why she wouldn't have just lotioned my eyebrows.

She spoke under her breath, her face close to mine, her lips almost touching my nose. "How long have you and Roman been married?"

"Not long," I muttered back, careful not to breathe on her either.

"Why did you choose to move here? Of all places, there are more accessible and developed resorts around us."

When you're living a lie, you'd better be ready to cover it up with more lies. "We came over on a private tour and just loved it here. Roman and I have had very hectic careers—our jobs had consumed our lives recently. So we went on sabbatical and decided to find a place where we could disengage from the world a little bit."

You're rambling, Carin.

"Newlyweds. Your husband is working so hard on your new home. I can see how much he loves you."

"He does. I am very lucky."

"Yes. But he's lucky too. And it's funny because the people in town call you Ken and Barbie."

"Ken and Barbie?" I laughed.

"You know—the perfect dolls."

"We are far from perfect!"

"The women have a mad crush on your husband. They think he is an actor. And the men say you look like Miss Universe."

"Hardly!"

"Are you adjusting to this place?" she asked, grabbing a tiny pair of scissors and cutting the edges around the space between my eyes.

"Yes, I am, thank you. Roman and I are so happy to be here."

"That's good," she said, putting her tweezers and scissors away. She sprayed a soothing liquid on my forehead while shielding my eyes. "We are done! Now your beautiful eyes will stand out more."

She busied herself once again, taking a towel to wipe down the chairs.

"Actually, I'm here to ask you for a favor." I kept my tone low, afraid you could walk into her salon at any time. Highly improbable but the guilt I felt made everything possible.

"Oh?" She sat on the seat next to me, her legs hanging in the air, away from the ground. Slowly, she leaned over, tilted her head, as if offering me her left ear.

I leaned back. "I would like to send a letter out, but I don't have any stamps or stationery."

"To write to your family?" she asked, standing and making her way toward the front counter. "I have some paper here. Mang Inog next door has stamps, and he goes to the post office once a week."

Diana handed me a pen and a yellow-lined pad of paper. She then placed an envelope on the counter by the mirror.

"Thank you," I said.

"I also have a cellphone. Would you like to call them instead?"

I averted her gaze and darted my eyes between the pen and the fingers that held it. "No, I …"

I paused, carefully choosing my words. People who lie always have to slow down their words, pace the stories they make up, convince themselves first before anyone else.

"I have so much to say to my sister. We weren't on good terms when I left."

"Oh, I see." And then she moved around. "I have to clean up before the children come back from helping their grandfather in the fields. Take your time to write your letter. When you are finished, we can walk next door to get some stamps."

"Thank you, Diana." I shielded the paper by hunching forward before addressing the envelope.

"You're welcome," she answered. And then, "Julia?"

No one but you called me by that name. It was still unfamiliar to me, a stranger's name. I missed the cue to answer.

"Julia?" she stressed, this time louder.

Julia. That's me. I'm Julia. "Oh, yes! Yes!" I responded, kicking myself for not paying more attention.

"If you need anything else, let me know."

Chapter Thirty

Short

Two weeks turned to six weeks and six weeks turned to two months. We led an idyllic kind of life. The repairs on our home had settled, and we had time on our hands. We finally made it outside of the island to the neighboring province. They had shops; they had stores; they had groceries.

Civilization was closer than we thought. When you applied for a teaching job at the small university, they accepted you right away.

"That's great!" I clapped when you told me the news. I accompanied you for an interview, shopped while you met with them for two hours.

"It's a small job, teaching business to freshmen students. It won't pay us much—just three thousand a year, which in their standards is quite a bit of money. That will go a long way in this place."

"I wonder if I can come in with you on some days, take more art classes. You know, I did have some of my work displayed at the local gallery when I was in college."

You gently stroked my arm. "Carin, baby. Too risky."

"What's risky?"

"You and I in that province. There's a direct link to the mainland. I'd rather you stayed close to our home. Maybe find a day job there?"

I shrugged, slung the shopping bag over the wooden boat and

climbed in.

For a dollar a day, we found a fisherman willing to transport you across the water to your new job. I thought of it like the daily train pass or the daily parking fee I paid in Chicago. How often did one get to cross the beautiful Pacific Ocean, let alone daily, as a job perk?

We were blessed.

Despite the pain we caused the universe, blessings continued to abound. I hoped that it wasn't at the price of something else.

The first week you started your job, I made you a list of art materials to purchase for me.

You brought them home excitedly, telling me what the lady at the bookstore recommended, carrying not one but three square canvases, your laptop bag filled to the brim with oil paints, charcoal pencils and cray-pas.

You made me an easel out of bamboo, set it up on the porch, bought a used CD player and restarted your music collection. I began to fill my days with art, drawing and painting most of the time.

I started to write about my days without you. I wanted to remember them and read them back to you. And because I lived my days in color, I drew for you the different shades I saw every day. I painted the clouds and the sky, the ocean, the seashells. I wanted you to see how deep the color gray was when you left for your job, covering the sky, peppered with stars and blurred out by the early morning mist. I wanted you to see how the sun turned bold red as you rode the Bangka back home, skating across the water, in a hurry to retire for the day.

On the first Friday of your first week, I sat on our porch with my back toward the sun, finishing up a painting I'd started on Monday. Summer was slowly fading away, and although the breezes were still hot as an oven, I noticed more shade than light. I twisted the brush in my left hand, making circles of different depths, trying to mold my strokes into churning clouds. Afterward, I took the charcoal crayon and began to introduce the different hues of the sky, always changing, reflecting back the light from the sea. My fingers were covered in paint, colors bleeding into my nails. I had an hour to clean up, soak my fingers in turpentine before getting started with dinner.

"Excuse me?" I heard you say. "What are you doing in my house? Where is my wife?"

I turned around to face you. You continued to stare, eyes squinted but unblinking.

"Matias, it's me." I looked to the ground, apprehensive about what I'd done. I rifled my fingers through my hair over and over, nervous and unsure.

Slowly, you walked up the steps until you stood inches away from me. "Your hair, it's brown."

"Yes."

"You dyed it? And cut it short." You towered above me and I remained seated. You touched my hair, tracing the strands until you reached my neck. It felt cold and exposed.

"Diana did. I went to see her today."

You offered me your hand. "Come."

You sat on the stoop, the top step of our porch and placed me on your lap. I left a palm print on the wooden floor as I leaned down for balance and swung a leg over your knees to face you. The paint was still on my hands.

"You hate it."

"No, on the contrary, I love it. It suits your face, this short hair. Shows off your cheekbones." You grazed your fingers across my face.

"Did you have a good day?" I asked. "You're early."

"Fridays are apparently half days," you answered. "And I'm having a great day now. What made you do it? Cut your hair."

"Well," I said, smiling, "everything is so new for us. I wanted to have new hair, too."

"Carin—"

"Julia," I countered, swiping a trail of blue paint down your nose, across your cheek, leaving a trail of blue lines on your face.

"Julia," you whispered.

"Do you know what Julia likes to do?" I pulled the hem of your shirt up and over your head then trailed kisses down your neck to your chest, to your abdomen. I unbuttoned your jeans with my other hand, paint getting all over your skin.

You laughed. "These were my only clean pair of jeans."

I grinned when you leaned back on your elbows and arched your body upward, allowing me to slip them off.

"What does Julia—" You gasped as I enclosed my mouth around you.

"You."

You held my head down with both hands, keeping a cadence with the movement of my mouth. You were too large, too thick, my hands made up for what my mouth could not cover.

"Julia, Julia," you moaned. "I'm going to come. Sit on me."

Not that day. That day, I craved your taste. I desired to drink you in, quench my thirst for you.

"Come, Matias," I said, moving my hand up and down, keeping my mouth on you, taking you all the way in. You shook and shuddered as you met your release. It took a few seconds for you to recover, and I held you until you did.

A loud, rickety truck stopped right in front of our home. You were at work. I stood outside on the porch, a water can in hand. Music played in the

background and I sang along.

"Delivery, miss." An elderly gentleman shuffled slowly from the driver's seat to the back of the truck.

"What is it?" I asked happily, so sure it was something you had purchased from the village.

I followed him to the truck and peered in the flatbed, excited to find another piece of furniture, some groceries, something from the world outside of ours.

Instead, I fell back in horror.

"Mom! I found you!"

"Charlie!" I screamed. "Charlie!"

"Carin!" you exclaimed, holding me down as I thrashed my arms and rolled around the bed. "Baby, it's okay. Carin!"

"Charlie!" I cried. "He was here! I saw him!" I was hysterical, out of breath. Sounds emerged from me, piercing and painful shrieks I'd never heard before. "Matias, Charlie was here!"

"No, no," you said, enclosing me in your arms, holding my head firmly against you. "You had a bad dream. No one is here, but me."

I sobbed into your chest. "Oh, Matias. I miss him so much. I miss my Charlie!"

You didn't say a word. I felt you tighten your hold on me, but you stayed silent. You gave me time to process it all. You knew this would eventually come. That the guilt I felt over what I'd done would inevitably catch up with me.

In time, you released me and ran from the room, just as my sobs subsided into hiccups. I sat on the bed with my arms wrapped around my knees.

"Here," you said, handing me a glass of water.

"I don't know how long I can take it."

"So you've been feeling this way for a while? How long?"

"I've missed him since the day I left."

"Of course, I knew that. But this bad?"

I gulped down a mouthful of water. "What could you have done?"

You fluttered your eyes, opened your mouth to say something, and then changed your mind.

I placed the glass on the night table and stood.

"Where are you going?" you asked, your eyes still laden with sleep, your voice weary. You watched me pull on a sweatshirt and slip on a pair of shorts.

"I'm sorry," I said. "Just need some time alone."

Chapter Thirty-One
Breakfast

I walked for miles, starting out along the shore, illuminated only by the lightweight flashlight I held. The sand looked gold, touched by the water and packed tightly like cement. Flying fish and silvery crabs sparkled in the moonlight—the tide was still high, leaving only a nick of room between the upper bank and the water.

You were right. Once we returned, I would devote my life to making it right with those I'd hurt. There would be no room for you in my life. I finally understood why we were both desperate to buy some time.

Pretty soon, the path led me into town, curving to the right, the softness under my feet turning into rubble and stone. It was 4:00 in the morning and the lone lamppost was working overtime. In the dimness, I could see candles in the windows, clotheslines, bicycles parked along the road.

I walked on, lost in the sound of the crunching gravel. I knew my way around. Five hundred feet away was the rotunda that led to the plaza that led to the church. Shanties and storefronts lined the perimeter, their windows shuttered with metal bars affixed to the ground. Diana's beauty shop stuck out like a sore thumb. It was the only one with a neon sign and a door. Even the post office looked like a wooden box. Electric lines hung lazily along crooked, wobbly wooden posts like unstrung Christmas lights.

As I reached the rotunda, someone called out to me. "Julia!"

I turned around and saw a little figure standing in the alley next to Diana's store.

"Psst. Julia!" she hissed. "It's me! Diana."

I traced my steps backward and approached her. She wore a duster with a cat print on it, loose and flowing. Next to her was an open window with candles on the sill. "What are you doing all the way here?" she asked.

"I couldn't sleep," I answered, a sheepish grin on my face. "I'm going back home now."

She eyed the top of my head. "Did Roman like your hair?"

"Yes, he loved it."

A little boy appeared from under her nightgown while a little girl peered from behind the door.

"We're about to have breakfast. Come! Join us."

"No, thank you," I declined. "I don't want to bother you."

"No bother!" She swatted a hand in the air. "Ariel left for the mainland. The kids and I are heading out for errands soon."

I smiled and allowed her to lead me inside. It was a tiny home, cozy, neat but scarcely furnished. Full of warmth and welcome. I felt it. Like a soft blanket that wrapped you in safety and security. There were no pretenses, no hidden agendas. A couch was for sitting, the table was for eating. Every function served without pretension. Hardly the kind of living I was used to. Our home in Chicago had furniture we couldn't even use, antique benches so brittle we couldn't sit on them. I liked this simplicity. It felt like the home we had, you and I, and I was comforted by it.

Diana carried the little boy on her hip and held the little girl by the hand.

"Sit."

I guessed that was directed at the children. They obeyed willingly, climbing into two booster seats while she walked to the stove, pulled out some cups and saucers and turned on the burner to heat up a kettle.

A younger woman, probably in her twenties, stood with her hand on the handle of a frying pan. She hurried around Diana, taking over the cooking while her employer peeled fruit for the children. I played with the little boy, gave him my flashlight, turned it on and off while he broke into fits of laughter.

In a few minutes, we sat at the table laden with rice and sweet meat and fried eggs. The woman had taken the children upstairs. Diana ate with her fingers, while I politely declined anything more than a hot, steaming cup of dark brewed coffee.

You loved our weekend breakfasts, and I wanted to be able to have a meal with you.

"Are you okay, Julia?" Diana began.

"Uh-huh," I mumbled, taking a sip of my coffee. "I really just couldn't sleep."

"That's a pretty far walk. What is it, five miles?"

"Something like that." I laughed. "Now I'm actually exhausted. I should get going soon."

"Julia? I hope we can find more time to get to know each other," she said. "I'm not sure if you know this, but Ariel and I have only been here for a year."

"Oh? Where did you used to live?"

"Long story." She grinned. "Maybe too long for this breakfast." She grabbed my gaze as I lifted my eyes from the table. "You have a long story too, huh?"

I nodded. No words for strangers at this point.

"We do the craziest things for love, don't we?"

I stood, making sure my eyes never left the floor. "I really have to get going. Thank you so much for the coffee and the hospitality. Your home is so welcoming, your children are beautiful."

I couldn't wait to get home to you, tell you how much I loved you, how perfect life was with you.

169

"I'll see you soon, Julia. Enjoy the sunrise on your way back."

"My sunrise is keeping my bed warm for me," I answered with a smile.

I paused to look around the living room before rushing back to bed. Through the curtains, a burst of sunshine spread itself like tiny floodlights. I stopped to absorb the feeling. The same one I'd had when I walked into Diana's home. I took a deep breath, filled with a rush of energy, removed my shoes and tiptoed into the bedroom.

There you were, staring at the ceiling, arms across your chest, fingers clasped.

"Hi," I greeted, undressing and slipping under the covers next to you.

"Hi."

"Have you been up this whole time?"

"Yes," you answered.

I scooted until half my shoulder was underneath yours and half your body was on top of mine. We both kept our eyes on the ceiling. And then slowly, you turned to me.

"I know I'm not enough and I don't know what to do about it."

"You are," I answered, skimming my thumb across your jaw, feeling the rough growth of your beard. "You are enough. I just wished I could have both of you." You didn't answer, so I went on. "Do you ever think of that, Matias? Do you ever miss your home?"

"Never," you whispered.

"Not even the life you had before? The parties, the people, the challenges, career?"

You wrapped a leg around mine and pulled me in by the small of my back. "We dance on the water in the moonlight, that's our party. The

170

people in the village are our friends. I love teaching at the university. We don't need much money. And I get to do this all with you. What's there to miss?"

You waited for me to react. When I didn't, you looked into my eyes. "You could. If that will make you happier, you could." You paused. "Leave. You can go home."

I couldn't imagine my life without my son. But I couldn't imagine my heart, my soul, my being, without you. "No!" I exclaimed. "No, my love, I won't leave you. You are my sunrise, my home. You are enough."

Chapter Thirty-Two

The Monsoon

Writing that letter helped me survive the next two weeks. Communicating with someone outside of our world assuaged my guilt, gave me comfort to think I had at least appeased those who thought they'd lost us.

The friendship we've had, the love we've shared as sisters, lean on that for now. You know me, you know my heart. The past six months haven't been me. He is fixing my heart. He is bringing me back to life. For now, this has to be enough for you. Please Trish, save me in Charlie's eyes. I know it isn't fair, but he has you and Jack and Liam and Paul. Give me this time. But know that I love you and that I'll be back.

Night and day, you worked on projects around our home. You painted our porch in blue and white, repaired the rails surrounding it and installed a hammock which faced the sun and the limitless horizon. I noticed everything about our surroundings, tried to bookmark them into memory.

I settled into domesticity, cooking, cleaning, washing our three sets of clothes. Diana and I found some blue and white jars to scatter by the entrance. Every empty space was filled with plants and flowers. You grew tomatoes and fertilized your eggplants. We found one more chandelier for our bedroom, bought a street painting for twenty dollars and hung it up on the living room wall. Our home possessed a character born out of a combination of stuff that had filled people's lives and that now filled ours.

The ocean always scared me. I feared it so much that it intrigued me to no end. I studied its creatures, its demographics, its science. I read extensively about whales and sharks, how they behaved and how they lived.

You, on the other hand, were like a dolphin, swimming long distances, surfing the waves and battling against the tide.

On some nights, I would sit a few feet from the shore, deep enough so that the water reached my knees, and watch you frolic in the water under the bright light of the moon. I would close my eyes and mark that vision indelibly in my mind. They were happy times, peaceful times I never wanted to forget.

"Tonight, you come in with me," you said, taking both my hands and pulling me upward, making my green notebook fall onto the sand. "What are you writing, anyway?"

"Just stuff," I answered. "Stuff I want to remember."

A cold, hard object touched my toes under the sand. "Wait a minute," I said as I pulled it out of the water. It was a blue bottle, shorter and stubbier than a wine bottle. Its translucence reflected the moonlight so perfectly I could see the tiny gas bubbles that formed within the glass. There was a cork attached to its mouth, keeping the sand inside it intact.

I let go of your hands and laid the bottle next to my notebook.

'We should slip a message in it and send it out to sea," you teased. "Save me from this man who's about to ravage me!"

I took my place back with you, missing my hands in yours even for those few seconds. "I think I'd say—Help! I am hopelessly in love with this man."

Your face lit up, and you squeezed my hands tight. "Come," you said, walking backward, leading me deeper in the water.

"No, thanks!" I screeched. "I'll stay here and watch you like always."

"Why are you so afraid of the sea?"

"Because you never know what's in it. I'm not good with unknowns."

You continued to pull me in.

"No, Matias!"

"I got you, baby." We were chest-deep. Well, I was. You were more torso-deep. Tiny waves rippled the water, causing it to swish.

"What if," you whispered, "I fucked you right here and now. Would you get over your fear of the ocean?"

"You're kidding, right?"

You lifted me up, held my legs with each hand and wrapped them around your waist. "No, actually, I'm not."

"I've never done it in the water. Let alone in an open space where people could see." I giggled, not doing a single thing to stop you.

"It's the best."

I scrunched my nose.

"I mean, I've heard it's the best. Never done it before either."

"Liar."

I felt you grow against me. You tilted your head down and licked my ear before moving on to my lips, engaging me in the deepest, most surrendering kiss I had ever experienced. I moaned when your fingers found me. There was no fear there. Just love. And ambivalence about anything that had existed before you held me that night. I was ready.

"Always ready," you echoed, pulling on my top until it flopped and floated in the water.

"Matias."

"Carin, you don't have to fear anything when I'm with you."

"I will always remember this," I hushed in your ear, tightening my legs around you at the same time. When you thrust yourself inside me and when I screamed your name, I knew heaven was listening. I deserved that night, earned the right to this happiness. Now if only the moon and the stars could share their peace with me.

Chapter Thirty-Three

Art

I kept on, wrote about our days and our times together. In my mind, Charlie was away at summer camp, and I wrote to let him know how things were going at home. I used to send him pictures of Brutus, of his fish, and of Paul and his antics. I did that too, painted pictures of the images that were part of my day-to-day life.

Do you remember how easy it was to communicate via text and phone just months ago?

What existed now was a new normal. We had no way of communicating while you were across the water, on another island. And because of that, waiting until the end of the day to see you filled me with unabashed anticipation every single day.

Those days went by so quickly. I guess it was because when you live in love, it consumes your entire being. There was no sense of time or space. We lived in the tiniest of homes, but our living room was a porch on the beach, facing the endless horizon.

For two weeks I had been working on a project for you. It was going to be a gift. A self portrait—something I'd never painted before, and a part of my quest to make sure you remembered. I took the image from the corkboard in the kitchen, filled with Polaroids of us. You had found the camera at one of the roadside tents, and Ariel brought us boxes of film whenever he went to the mainland. I'd chosen an image of me that you had taken in the bedroom, when I was pensive, unguarded, and in deep thought. Sometimes, I would get confused when I looked at the woman in the pictures. She looked so different, so at peace. There was nothing to clamor for, nothing to fight for anymore. She had earned her right to happiness.

One sunny day at the end of May, I looked up from my canvas to see a beautiful furry creature running toward the house, kicking sand everywhere and being chased by a woman in a navy blue dress. It took a while for me to recognize Diana.

"Julia! I'm so sorry!" she yelled.

Before I could wave back, I realized what she was apologizing for. The puppy came charging toward me, running directly into the easel, which toppled onto the floor, paints, canvas, and all. It was a tiny, furry little thing, wrinkly like a Bulldog but with a smaller head and a skinnier body. It sat on its hind legs and looked at me while I gathered the mess it had just made. The canvas on the easel fell on top of all the others, leaving the pile of artwork like a shuffled deck of cards.

"Julia!" Diana gasped, out of breath. "Oh my god, I'm so sorry. I'm not sure why she ran like that. The kids had put a little leash on her but it broke in two when we were walking here."

"It's okay," I said, gathering up the paints and tearing off a piece of the buffing cloth to wipe up the drops. The puppy sat still even as I approached it. "Who's this?" I held its tiny face in my hands and stroked its ear.

"No name. We've had her for three months, and I thought it was a good time to take her over. Give you some company."

"I didn't know about this," I said. "You're giving him to us?"

"Her."

"Her."

I stood to straighten the paintings strewn across the deck. One by one, I leaned them against the far end of the railing.

"What is she, exactly?" I asked, turning around to take another look at her. "She's adorable!"

That was the puppy's cue to walk toward me. She took a few steps and sat right by my feet. My heart sank for a second as I remembered Brutus. And Charlie.

"Boston Terrier and Bulldog mix."

The puppy had the right combination of golden brown and white. A green patch of skin encircled her right eye.

"What is this?" I asked, bending to trace my finger around it, surprised that she allowed me to touch her face. "A birthmark?"

"We think it is. But it could also be a mole or something. The vet said it was just a skin discoloration. Nothing wrong internally."

I sat on the ground and took the puppy in my arms. Diana walked around, hands clasped behind her back, studying the pictures against the wall.

"Julia, these are beautiful. I never knew you were a painter."

"I'm not," I said shyly. "I just recently picked it up again. Need more practice."

"Oh, come on!" Diana replied. "These are painted by an experienced artist. They are simply exquisite! Are you sure you didn't have any formal education in art?"

"When I was young, I wanted to be a painter. 'Artists don't make money,' my dad used to say. Hence the business school."

"Sounds like my parents." She pointed to my work in progress. "This one … This is you, isn't it? Look at the expression on your face. So real."

"Thank you." I lifted the painting, blew on the leaves that stuck to it, and settled it gently on the bamboo stand. "I'm only halfway done. It's my surprise for Roman."

She smiled at me, her eyes crinkling. I could tell that she was bursting with questions, the way she blinked rapidly, her thoughts moving faster than she could filter her words.

"The church is looking for an art teacher for grades one to five. Is it okay if I recommend you? You know—the one right at the plaza. They don't pay much, but you get a stipend for supplies."

I clapped my hands in glee. "Oh my god. I would be so honored!"

"How about we go now?" She glanced at her watch. "It's only three o'clock. Roman can cook his own dinner."

"He doesn't get home until six," I said, walking toward the front door. "Let me put out what I need to cook so it will be ready when I get back."

We stepped out of the heat into the air-conditioned room. "What about her?" Diana asked.

I tilted my head at the puppy. "I have to check with Roman—he's been working so much, I'm not sure he'll want to take care of a puppy at this point. But she is so precious!" I bent down and snapped my fingers. The puppy came running to me. "Can you leave her with me so I can get to know her? I want him to meet her tonight."

"Yes, let's take her with us now so we can get some supplies. She is yours if you want her," Diana said. "Any names for her, Julia?"

"I have some in mind but I'm excited to see what Roman will come up with."

She told me of a short-cut into town, through a thick grove of coconut trees, across a manmade bridge and along a winding path in the middle of a pasture. It was private land, Diana told me, but everyone who lived on the water was allowed to go through. Oddly enough, we didn't take that route.

"Let's walk along the water today," she said. "It's so calm and beautiful."

I nodded and allowed her to hook her arm in mine. The puppy followed happily. Once in a while, Diana would pause to make sure she was right behind.

"You are in love," she said, looking at me. I kept my eyes ahead of us, fixed them on the blue sky and a lush green hill that sprung out of the sand.

"Yes."

"He is your world." She was here for the count, ready to dig her heels in.

I blushed, feeling the warmth rush through my body. "Yes, you can say that."

"I would say it is quite literal."

A giant wave barreled toward us, knocking me down on the sand as we squealed. She held out her hand to me, and I pulled on it. I was drenched from the waist down, her dress dripped heavily.

"Let's walk further up," she instructed. "Anyway, as I was saying— was your life very busy before that you just had to get away?"

"Something like that," I answered. The air was so hot my clothes were dry almost immediately. It reminded me of the times I'd used a blow-dryer to get out wrinkles.

"I'm intrigued by you," Diana announced. Still, I felt no uneasiness. When she held my hand or hooked her arm in mine, I delighted in it, welcomed the friendship we were building.

"Why? We're just normal people, trying to start a life together."

"Hmm," she said with upturned lips. "It doesn't seem as normal as you think. A couple like you, modern, smart, sophisticated—wanting to hole up in a nowhere place such as this."

"How do you know I'm sophisticated when this is all I wear?" I said, gesturing to my shirt and shorts.

"Elegance comes from within," she said. "It can't be bought, it can't be copied, and it can't be imitated." ·

"Thank you. That's very nice of you to think. But believe me"—I laughed—"there is nothing special about us! And this place is paradise! What are you talking about?"

The puppy yelped loudly at a nearby group of ducklings that gathered around a puddle. I scooped it up as we crossed the street into town.

Our conversation was halted for now. But I always knew I'd have to find the answers one way or another. Everything was just a matter of time.

I chose not to respond. We both kept our eyes on the puppy as she trotted along, paw-prints hardly making a mark on the sand. Diana tugged on my arm as she steered me toward town, chatting aimlessly and pointing at different landmarks along the way.

There was the meat packer, the town doctor, the woman with three husbands. Did I know that Mang Inog, the guy at the post office, had just lost his wife? We took a turn, left this time, and found the battered, gray school building.

"We're here," Diana said. "I'm excited for you to meet Sister Pilar."

"Me too," I answered, taking the puppy in my arms before stepping under the tall archway that led to the courtyard.

"Julia?" Diana stopped to address me before leading me down the open corridor. "One day soon, we're going to have to tell each other's stories."

Chapter Thirty-Four

What You See

Fifteen feet from the last step of our porch sat two giant tree trunks, buried in the sand and cut down to perfectly flat stumps. You and I would sit outside on balmy nights, waiting for the tide to come in. That night, I laid some wine and a tray of cheese on one of them and sat on the sand, anxious for you to come home.

You hopped out of the bangka and waded in the water. I jumped up and waved with the biggest smile on my face. I rushed toward the shore, impatient for those arms of yours to encircle me. You looked worried, tilted your head and searched my eyes for answers.

"Hi!" I gasped, wrapping my arms around your neck.

"What happened?" you asked. "Is everything all right?"

I pulled you toward our house, toward the wine and the cheese and the re-purposed tree stumps. You saw them and smiled, relaxed.

"I got a job!" I giggled.

"That's great! Where?"

"At the grade school in town. Teaching art to first and second graders! Diana saw my work and took me in to meet the principal."

You gently held my face and kissed me. "You are awesome. Simply awesome. Congratulations, baby."

"Mmm," I answered, pulling you down toward the ground. My lips had missed yours; they didn't want to separate from you just yet. When we pulled apart, we sat side by side on the sand, knees up, yours between mine and mine between yours.

"So, tell me all about it," you said. "I want details."

"Wait. I want to show you something first."

I didn't have to. You stiffened when you felt something nudging you from behind. The puppy was sniffing your shirt, breathing in your scent.

"Who's this?" you asked, turning to take it in your arms. It sat very still, stared at your face. I could tell that it was love at first sight for both of you.

"It's a her. No name. I've been calling her Puppy all day. Diana brought her this morning. Did you know about this?"

"I may have mentioned to Ariel that you might enjoy some company." You laughed. "That guy seems to be into everything."

"He's great," I refuted.

"He is," you agreed, still holding her but diverting your attention to nuzzling my neck. The puppy followed you and began to lick my face. We both hooted loudly.

"What happened to his eye?" you asked, doing what I had done—tracing a finger around the green spot surrounding the left side of her head.

"Something about how she was born, bruising," I said. "That's why the buyer rejected her. She's a mutt with a facial flaw."

"I have the perfect name for her."

I looked at you. *Spill it.*

"Olive."

I wanted to cry right then. I wanted to thank you, tell you it was one of the countless moments I memorized about you, one of the times I knew I loved you—because you remembered. You wanted to make sure Brutus was never forgotten.

"Olive," I choked, "it's perfect. She looks just like—"

You turned to me. "Go on."

"She looks just like Brutus when he was a puppy. Do you know who he loved the most?"

You shook your head.

"My mom. She spent the most time with him while I was at work and Charlie was at school."

You didn't say anything. For a minute, you allowed me to get lost in my thoughts. I stared out into the ocean. How much had changed since I met you. I wanted to talk about them without the overwhelming tightness in my chest. "Thank you," I whispered.

"For what?"

"For allowing me to hold him close by keeping him in our conversations."

"You can always tell me anything." You released Olive and turned your attention to me. I leaned on your shoulder, encouraged your embrace. "Now, tell me how you got this job, you wonderful artist, you."

The stars emerged from the darkness. They lit up the sky and created colorful rainbows all over the water. I reached for the wine and poured our glasses.

"Cheers," I said.

"Cheers." You clinked your glass on mine. "Now tell me!"

"Well," I started. "Diana showed up this morning while I was working on the porch. She saw my paintings and raved about them. She offered to have me meet the principal to see if I could fill the open position for an art teacher. I met with her for an hour. She had many questions, some I couldn't answer, some I made up on the fly. I was so sure I wouldn't get the job but when it was over, she shook my hand and asked me to start next Monday!"

"What kind of questions did she ask?"

"The one everyone wants to ask. Diana had the same questions today while walking into town."

"I'm sorry," you said.

"Why are you sorry?" I linked my arm around your legs and leaned my head on your knee. "There's nothing to be sorry about. We just need to figure out what our story is."

"It's not a story." You enunciated carefully. If I didn't know you, I would have thought you were upset. But that was just you. Always trying to be one step ahead, always making sure I understood. "It's true. We met, fell in love, moved to get away from our very hectic lives. In more ways than one, those are the facts."

"Word," I teased, wanting to lighten your mood.

In a way, I didn't have to because Olive reappeared with a bamboo stick in her mouth. You pulled on it gently until she gave it up to you. "Do we have food and toys for her? I can get some in the market during my lunch break tomorrow."

"I have a month's supply in the house. Went with Diana today after we visited the school."

You nodded and gently pulled on the stick until Olive gave it up and traded it for a piece of bread. "Carin, I've been wanting to talk to you about something." You turned to face me, taking both my hands in yours.

There had not been one single time when your eyes failed to hypnotize me. They were cold as ice, hot as coals, burning like fire, lit up with wonder. That night, they looked parched, thirsty, hungry, searching.

"What is it? You're scaring me."

"Marry me. Let's get married. Everyone knows you as my wife. Let's make it official."

I didn't mean to mock you. But I did turn my eyes sideways as if rebuking your joke with another joke. "Time out. I was already married." I paused before reminding you. "I'm still married."

"Not here. This is our fresh start, remember?"

"You can't be serious," I reasoned. "I failed miserably at that marriage. Why would I want to do that to you?"

"Because I'm not Jack."

"But you're still another human being. And besides, divorce is illegal here. Once we're married, that's it. There'll be a lot of unwinding to do, and it's not worth it," I stammered.

"Olive!" you called out before standing and brushing the sand off your legs. "I'm going to take her for a walk."

"Matias."

Olive ran toward you. This time, she had a flip-flop in her mouth. It dragged itself on the sand, too big to fit between her tiny jaws.

"Thanks for the wine. I'm so proud of you, babe. Don't wait here for me. I'll see you in the house."

"Matias, no! Wait, please. I didn't mean to hurt your feelings." I chased after you.

You stopped and turned around. I wrapped my arms around you, held you tightly. Olive stood on her hind legs, pulling on your shorts. My cheek was on your chest. I didn't want to let you go.

"Why does it always seem like you're going to leave?" you whispered, your tone sad, dejected. You were a myriad of contradictions—strong, heavy arms, soft, timid voice. Every woman should build their man up, give him the conviction to accomplish his dreams. I wanted to be that woman for you and at times I felt I was tearing you down.

"I don't know."

"Are you going to leave me, Carin?"

"No," I mumbled.

"Then why do you always say silly things like that?"

"Because everyone leaves," I answered. "Eventually, everyone leaves."

"Not me," you said, caressing my back. "I will never leave."

"We can't stay here forever. Soon, you will want your success back. Soon, you will want to feel fulfilled, productive. This is a temporary place of solitude. The problem with peace is that it can stagnate people.

185

Human beings exist to rile up the world over and over again because peace gets stale and mundane."

"Carin," you said, pulling me tightly against your chest. "Your love is my success. Your laughter is my peace. I see new things with you every single day. We have everything we need here. Why would we want anything more?"

"What do you see? You go back and forth on the boat each day. You see the same things on your way and back," I argued.

You stroked the top of my head while drawing a breath. "Ah, that's where you're wrong. Every day, the sea is a different color. The clouds show me different shapes. And then when I come home to you, you show me your love in so many different ways. Your face has expressions I haven't yet mastered, our home has so much character—every chip, every crack, I discover those each day. And when you laugh ... God when you laugh, I forget where we've come from and all I know is that we are here."

"Show me," I whispered. "Show me more of the things I can't see."

"I will, *Carina*. I will."

I looked up at you and pulled your head down toward my face. I kissed you that night—with the moon and the stars as my witness.

"Take away my fears," I asked of you. "Because I want to marry you."

Chapter Thirty-Five

Secrets

With June came the monsoon clouds and torrential rains. Everything around us was lush and thick and thriving. I worried about your boat rides when the winds caused the waves to thrash, prayed for your safety when the thunderous clouds brought gashing flashes of deadly light. On weekends, we would cuddle up inside, rested and pacified by the steady drops of rain and the droning roar of the tide. It was our sanctuary, our home, our respite from the world.

June also brought the start of the new school year. Instead of teaching two grade levels, I was teaching four. It was perfect—working in the morning hours and getting home by the early afternoon. I didn't make much—got paid at the end of each week. My monthly salary would add up to seventy-five dollars, nothing compared to yours. I showered the children with new supplies every week. In reality, I spent more than I was paid, but I was happy.

The doorbell dinged as I stepped into Diana's salon one Thursday after school. We'd fallen into this weekly routine—grabbing a quick bite after school and spending some time running errands. I walked in on something—a man with his back to the door was speaking to Diana in a reprimanding tone, as she continually wiped the tears from her face. She jerked her head back when she saw me and forced a smile.

"I'm sorry, I should—" I faltered, slowly backing up toward the door.

"Hi, Julia," Diana greeted. The man turned around to face me. It was my turn to lean back in surprise, my legs desperate to give way. I recognized him immediately. It was Vincent Fernandez, the doctor's son.

I stood frozen in place, afraid to make a move. When his face showed no acknowledgment, I was relieved to realize he didn't know who I was. I smiled to myself. Of course, I've got short, brown hair now. I was also wearing a native sarong.

"Julia," Diana repeated. "It's okay. This is my brother, Vincent."

Her brother? What was she doing in this sad, impoverished place when her brother owned the island?

I rushed toward him with an outstretched hand. "Julia O'Neill, nice to meet you."

Vincent nodded and turned back to his sister. He spoke quietly, leaned closer to Diana, concerned about my ability to hear what he was going to say. "Diana, I'm going to head home. Please consider coming over next weekend. Papa wants to see you and the children."

"I'll let you know," Diana answered, a tinge of defiance in her voice. "I'll discuss it with Ariel."

When he walked out the door, Diana exhaled loudly. "Whew. That was close."

I sat on the pedicure chair while she went to the refrigerator and pulled out two Styrofoam boxes and two bottles of water. "I thought we'd have lunch here today. I got you your favorite sweet bananas and cooked some tocino and fried rice." She handed me the box and the water. I settled into the seat and pulled the retractable table out in front of me.

"Thank you. This is perfect," I said.

She smiled and sat on the barber's chair, twisting it so we faced each other.

"So, can you tell me what that was?" I asked.

"That was the long story I told you about. My brother and my father own the island. Recently, they sold half of it to a development company that is going to make it into a resort."

I was shaken by that statement. I tried to mask a reaction by looking at my food, taking a banana and putting it into my mouth. "Why did he seem upset?" I asked.

"Ariel is the love of my life. As you can see, he is much older than me. We met while I was still in high school. He was a friend of my father's. As soon as I turned eighteen, I ran away to marry him. My father and mother disowned me. Ariel and I moved from job to job, home to home, trying to establish our life together. People knew who my father was and refused to get involved in the middle of our family drama. We finally settled on this island, far away from them. That only lasted a year. Vincent is back, begging me to make peace with my father."

"Do you miss your family? I know I would miss mine," I said, careful not to call out any similarities between our situations. There were many.

"I do, of course, I do. But Ariel is enough for me. I didn't want to choose, but they made me. And I am happy with my choice."

"What does Ariel think of all of this? The estrangement?"

"He tells me all the time that he would give me up if I wanted to go back. That he just wants me and the children to be happy."

"Roman says that too," I answered, revealing something I shouldn't have.

"What did you say?" she asked, blinking, leaning forward in earnest.

"Oh!" I giggled. "Roman always says he wants my happiness first and foremost—that's what I meant."

"Oh," she said.

"Well, are you going to see your family?" I asked, making sure we moved right along.

"I don't think so. My father is a proud man, but so is Ariel. I don't ever want to pit them against each other. Maybe if Vincent wants to take the children to see their grandparents, he can send for them here."

"Makes sense," I agreed. "But eventually, you will have to come to terms with whether you want your children to know your heritage."

"And you, yours," she said to me. "When you have them, of course. I've learned that we can't have everything we want, Julia. Life is so full of choices. Oftentimes, the choices you make for yourself will hurt someone else."

Lunch was delicious. The fried rice mixed with egg and soy sauce was the perfect complement to the sweet cured meat that Diana had made for us. We spent one hour at her salon, talking about her childhood and the family life she used to live. She'd grown up in a life of privilege and yet, never craved nor missed anything she'd had before Ariel.

I wanted to open up to her about everything. I wanted to tell her proudly that I too had given up my old heart to get a new one.

Except there was no turning back for me. I had killed myself, killed those I loved to have this new life. Would I ever get over this guilt? Would I ever be able to truly love Matias, knowing that I'd ruined lives in the process?

We ran around town, our regular routine, picking up fresh meats and vegetables and one hotdog-looking little dog toy for Olive. During our last stop for the day, Diana and I were in a jovial mood, bursting into fits of giggles about everything we saw and heard. The odd man, the odd smell, the chicken chasing the duck in circles. We walked out of there, giddy, happy, high on our day.

"Car?" I smacked right into you as I stepped off the raised stoop at the entrance, on to the muddy ground. You had Olive in your arms, your hair tucked into your favorite Real Madrid cap, your curls peeking out by the ears. You saw Diana and course corrected. "Julia?"

Diana laughed and released my arm, giving no indication that she'd noticed the slip. "Hey, Roman!"

"Hi," I greeted, standing on my toes and giving you a kiss on the cheek.

"What were you doing at the post office?"

"Oh," I paused to collect myself. "It's errand day. Deliveries."

"For Diana?" you asked.

I nodded briskly, leading you away from the doorway. "What's wrong? Why aren't you at work?"

"They called off school due to the coming typhoon. I went by the house but you weren't there."

"Errand day," I said again. "Did you need anything from here? We can walk around a bit." I waved at Diana as she approached us. "Di, thank you for lunch today. I think we're going to walk Olive around the plaza since we're already here."

"Great idea!" she said, glancing at her phone. "Ariel just texted. He's home so I gotta go."

I took Olive from you and set her on the ground. She wagged her tail happily as we tugged on her leash and walked toward the plaza. The fruit market was bustling with activity. In the middle of the square, children played, grownups sat by the fountain, music blared despite the darkening sky. I saw the young women of the town eyeing your every move, sighing, smiling at each other. It wasn't their fault. You had such a presence.

I walked away from you and Olive to buy my second sweet banana of the day—plantains rolled in brown sugar and fried in hot oil until a sweet, sugary crust formed around them.

"I could live on these," I said before offering you a bite, which you obliged.

"Oh my god, that is good," you admitted. Three little boys played with Olive. Her leash was long enough for her to circle the steps surrounding the fountain. Music blared through crackled, scratchy

191

speakers, muffled at first by a single burst of thunder.

"Hey." You smiled, pulling me close to you. I molded myself in your arms. "Do you remember this song?"

I paused to listen and then smiled back. "The Godfrey."

"Dance with me," you whispered in my ear, swaying side to side. Olive stood still and watched us, along with the rest of the town. There we stood for a few seconds, suspending time and believing that nothing else mattered. Forgetting that all the pain we had caused was for this one dance.

At first, it drizzled. And then it poured. Huge drops of golden rain washing all our cares away.

Slowly, we moved to the words of the song, side-to-side, eyes closed. I pressed my head to your shoulder at first, then lifted it when you leaned down so that our lips touched. We kissed, we swayed, we relived that night. The night I'd lost my heart and soul to you.

And when the song ended, we opened our eyes to find that we were all alone in the middle of the square. You, me, and Olive.

"I love you, Carin," you whispered.

"I love you, Matias." I caressed your face with my hand. "Dancing with you always gets us in trouble."

"Let's finish this trouble at home, okay?" you said, sealing that promise with another kiss.

"Okay."

Chapter Thirty-Six

Sudden Loss

We built a life, you and I. In four months, there we were, solid, functioning citizens of that island. The effervescence of those times still mesmerized us, bonded us together.

We even had a social life. Of course, it only consisted of Ariel and Diana, but two nights a week, we ventured into town and spent time with others in the square. Olive went everywhere with us. A few times, we caught her sitting at the dining room table, leaning back on the chair with her two hind legs. She mimicked the way you looked, back straight, hands clasped, excitedly waiting for dinner.

I still made it my mission to memorize every bright moonlit night, every cool rainy day. I learned to live in the moment. Nothing mattered but the fact that I was with you. The big things—my sins, the fact that I had left Charlie and never looked back—gnawed at me every single day. Still, I justified it. Still, I believed that I deserved this time with you.

Once in a while, when I was listless and quiet, you held me close and pressed your lips against my forehead. "You miss him," you'd say.

"Yes," I'd answer.

"A little more time," you'd request.

And I would nod.

"Tell me," Diana said, that last day in June during our normal walk home.

"Tell you what? I asked, kicking an empty can of Coke in front of me so Olive could chase it. I dropped her off each morning at Diana's while I taught. On most days, she and I would make the five-mile walk back home alone. On some days, Diana would join us and wait for Ariel to drive home from the mainland.

Olive used her nose to nudge the can forward. Diana locked arms with me as we trudged slowly through the warm sand, stopping once in a while to coax Olive to keep moving. Sometimes it would take us over an hour and a half to reach our cottage. I think we both needed these walks. We were two kindred souls who in many ways were hungry for the gift of friendship.

Diana let a few minutes pass before trying again. "Tell me why you look sad sometimes, and your eyes only light up when you see your husband."

"Of course my eyes light up," I squeaked, defensive. "He's my husband."

"So you're telling me you had no life before you met and married Roman?"

"I've told you everything," I emphasized again, ensuring that we didn't break cadence with our steps. I wanted every step to take me closer to home. This felt much like an intrusion, except I knew the inquisitor and she loved me. "Maybe you think I'm sad because this life is new to me. I'm adjusting to rural life after having lived the bustle of a major city all these years."

"And this is a good change, no?" Diana asked, changing her approach.

Olive halted in the middle of the pathway, a sign that she needed me to pick her up. I did.

"Yes, of course, it is," I answered. "We were meant to be together, Roman and I."

"Isn't it funny," she said, "Even when two people are meant to be together, it still takes a lot of hard work to make sure it happens. Sometimes, we have to move heaven and earth just to follow fate."

"Yeah." I chuckled. "Everything for one thing. One thing for everything."

"You know, when I left to elope with Ariel, I didn't even think twice about it. I knew I couldn't live without him. When I heard my father on the phone with the dean of a college in the States, the plan had been set in motion and he was going to send me there. I didn't even pack bags! I just got in the car to go to school and never came home. Ariel met me after my class and we just walked away from my old life."

I thought about that for a moment. We were nearing our home, but I wanted to learn more. She was wise beyond her years. "Do you ever regret what you did?" I asked.

She paused for quite some time. Olive wiggled in my arms when she saw our home in the distance. She shook her little body as I released her on to the sand. I turned to Diana, who bobbed her head as she spoke.

"I regret the hurt I caused. My mother got sick and passed away before meeting my children. Vincent and I were very close, and he was my best friend. We are exactly one year apart in age, so we did everything together. When I first reconnected with him, all Vincent wanted to know was why I didn't warn him. Sudden loss is ruinous, I think."

Sudden loss. I flinched. Diana looked at me with concern, catching me just as I threw my shoulders back and lost my footing.

"Are you okay, Julia?"

"You know how I lost my mom," I answered. "I'm just remembering the pain."

"I know," Diana said. "But pain is redemptive. Before my mom

195

died, she and I made peace over the phone. She told me that she understood why I did it and that she was proud of how brave I was. That I was an inspiration to her because I stood up for what I wanted in my life. And she couldn't have asked for a better husband for her daughter than Ariel."

This time, I was the one who offered her comfort, stepping toward her and wrapping my arms around her shoulders while Olive ran up the stairs and barked at the front door.

You opened the door and swept her up in your arms. You were a sight to see, reminding me why this was all worthwhile.

"You're home," I said, smiling from ear to ear.

I turned to Diana, all pain, all worry, all forgotten. "He's all I need. He is my past, my present, and my future."

Chapter Thirty-Seven

Windchimes

"What's this?" you asked when I handed you a T-shirt. You held it up and placed it against your chest. It was a peace sign in red, white and blue.

"I found it at the market the other day. I figured we would wear it for tonight's fireworks."

"Fireworks? We're having fireworks?" you asked, still not sure where this was all going.

"I found some at the market too. Some sparklers and a few bottle rockets. I'm not sure how Olive will feel about all the noise, but I thought we should test it," I said with a chuckle. "Of course we're having fireworks! It's the fourth of July."

"Oh, you mean the market next to your favorite hang out."

"What?"

"The post office!" you teased.

"Stop." I gently slapped your arm. "Diana ships things for her business all the time."

You took one step toward me and I wrapped my arms around your neck.

"After I run some errands with Ariel," you said, your tone regretful.

"I know."

"Sorry, babe, but it's my only day off and I want to finish the backsplash today. Ariel will be here shortly to take me across the river to get some of the Spanish tiles you wanted."

I caressed your face before kissing you. "Hmm," I said. "You are the best. I'll be home waiting for you, Mr. O'Neill."

"Mmm." You kissed me back, playfully nipping at my top lip. "We'll have our own fireworks." Your kiss deepened, your right hand slowly creeping into my t-shirt. "How about we start—"

Beep. Beep. Beep.

"Your ride is here." I gently pushed you back. "Don't worry. I'll be home waiting."

"I love you, Car."

"Love you, Matty boy. Hurry back home."

Diana got out of the truck as soon as I stepped onto the porch. "Hi!" she said. You waved at her and ran down the steps to the passenger seat. "I brought something for Julia."

You blew me a kiss and got into Ariel's truck.

Diana stood at the bottom stoop with a paper bag in hand. "I hope you don't mind," she said, looking sheepish, her eyes searching mine. "Ariel said they'd only be gone for an hour, so I asked if I could come along and deliver this to you."

She shoved the bag in front of me.

"Thank you," I said, reaching for it, holding it stiffly between three fingers. "What is it?"

"I thought we could hang it by the door," she gushed. "A wind chime!"

I held it up, allowing the brown bag to drop. Olive seized the opportunity to crumple it with her paws. The word L-O-V-E, spelled out in red, held three tiers of crystal hearts, which cast back the sunlight and turned it into little diamonds on the wooden floor. Layers of metal tubes and glass cylinders gave out a crisp, tinkling sound as they swayed with the wind.

the year i *left*

"It's beautiful," I gasped. "I can't wait for Roman to put it up." I walked toward our front door and placed my finger next to the wooden frame that enclosed the outdoor lamp. "Right here."

"Are you familiar with the legend of the wind chimes?"

"I mean, we have them in the states too, but I never really paid attention to their meaning," I said.

"Here, we believe that wind chimes bring good luck. But more importantly, its melodious sounds are so beautiful that they are believed to carry with the wind to every part of the world. I believe it calls out to the ones you love, Julia. Whoever it is you've left behind, they will hear you calling out to them."

She knows, I thought. *How does she know?*

What she said, what I'd been feeling that day, led to my undoing. Fourth of July parades, candies scattered along the street, fireworks, bottle rockets, sparklers. My mom decked out in red, white, and blue, sporting her Uncle Sam hat. All those things made up who I used to be. You made up who I was now.

"I left my family behind for Roman. I had to choose between him and the rest of them! I chose him! I don't regret it," I cried, tears flowing freely. Diana took both my hands in hers. "I have a son named Charlie, who just turned eleven. I left him and my husband and my sister because this was the only way I could come back to life. I've been dealing with it for months. The pain of missing Charlie kills me, but Roman brings me back to life."

"You're not married," she stated as if she'd known all along.

"No."

She didn't say a word, but kept her eyes on me, urging me to go on and assuring me that she understood all at the same time. Briefly, she left my sight, and I realized it was to hang the wind chimes on the nail that stuck out by the outside lamp. She led me to the top of the stairs and we both sat.

"Will you be going back, eventually?"

199

"Yes, eventually." I sniffed. "Roman doesn't say anything, but I know he senses that this is just temporary. I want both of them, Di. I want Roman, I want Charlie. Why can't I have both?"

"I don't think anyone made you choose," she said. "Just like no one told me to leave my family for Ariel."

"In the months that have passed, I think I've been able to figure out why I did it. I was under such a deep depression that I felt no hope until Roman came along. But I'm not saying I have no fault in this at all. I'm saying that no matter how this started, I was a willing participant in everything we did. I love him so much that I accept all consequences for my actions."

"Do you tell Roman about these thoughts? Missing Charlie?" she asked, hands still on mine, our bodies facing each other. I noticed she wasn't in her usual summer dress. She wore fashionable jeans and a pair of Gucci loafers. Maybe she was beginning to accept her identity, where she came from. Maybe Ariel was helping her to make peace with her roots.

"He knows. I have recurring nightmares. When we talk about Charlie, all he does is ask for more time with me. But every second, every minute serves to worsen the situation at home. Them not knowing where I am or where I've gone," I said.

Diana nodded, staying silent, absorbing it all. Finally, a smile lit up her face and she squeezed my hand. "What we do for love. It's gallant, actually."

I smiled back, a weak, half-smile, partial agreement, partial acknowledgment that the gravity of what I'd done would in no way lessen just because it was done out of love.

"Why are you so kind to me?"

"Because I see you struggling every day. I can tell that you're beating yourself over the choices you've made," Diana answered.

"How so?"

"You're always lost in your thoughts."

I nodded wistfully. My eyes fixed on the wind chimes, watching them swirl. "I have to make it right."

"What does that mean?"

"Simply that I will have to leave," I choked, holding back more tears.

She draped an arm around my shoulder and pulled me toward her, allowing me to lean my head against hers. This time, pain and relief mixed in equal parts. The pain was so great because I had verbalized my thoughts, my feelings, the ones I'd held back for so many months. The relief bequeathed to me by this woman knew no bounds. Someone else knew my story. If anything, she could help me convince you that I had the right intentions.

I cried for both these reasons. I didn't hold back. I slumped into her and sobbed uncontrollably while she stroked my hair. She knew I needed to run out of tears. Only then can the veil of sadness be lifted to let in some of the light.

There was a light to all this—it was the love I had for you. I wondered then if you knew this. If the only way I could make you believe was to give in to what you wanted.

"Diana?" I whispered, afraid that our time together would soon be cut short.

"Yes, Julia?"

"Will you help me plan a wedding? I know I can't be married in the church, but maybe a ceremony where I give him my vows, to love him forever, to show him that this is the only love I want in my life?"

Chapter Thirty-Eight

Love

"How do I look?" you asked. You stood in front of me, wearing a pair of white linen slacks paired with a crisp white linen blazer. "Should I wear something else? I feel like this makes me look like the groom."

"Diana picked that out for you. You're the best man, after all," I said, smoothing my hands over your shoulders, admiring your beauty. "And just for the record, you look amazing."

"Thank you," you whispered, leaning over to give me a kiss.

"What time is the ceremony?" you asked. "If I had known earlier, I could've taken Ariel out for a bachelor party of some sort."

I scrunched my nose in response. "He has three kids."

"All the more reason to have given him an excuse to go out!" you joked. "And how come you're not getting ready? Aren't we going together?"

"I promised Diana I'd follow with the kids. I didn't want her to have to worry about them."

"Okay," you said, kissing my forehead. "Hurry over, though. I want to stand in front with you."

"You bet," I said, smiling.

the year i *left*

On the 29th day of July, I carried out my promise to you, on the island, in front of strangers and our two closest friends. The plan we hatched, Diana and I, went without a hitch. There you were, standing with Ariel at the foot of the bridge, believing all along that you were a part of their vow renewal ceremony. I owed Diana so much for this day. She went all out, planned every detail. From the white orchids and hydrangeas that lined the makeshift bamboo rails on the bridge to the string of lights that illuminated our path. The heavens helped too, bringing on the most exquisite afternoon sun that slowly descended upon the water as the ceremony began.

They shipped our outfits from the mainland. Your linen white suit and my off-white dress. Diana insisted on me wearing white, but I've always lived my truth and I wasn't about to change that. And so we settled on ivory, a dress that made me feel like a siren—long and sleek with a halter neck and bodice made out of lace. As for my something old, I wore my mother's pearl white earrings—something I'd taken with me when we first made the trip out here. Diana's pearl bracelet was my borrowed, and Olive's collar was all decked out in blue.

I was more nervous than I'd ever been. I knew it was because I wanted to get this right, say the right words to you, make you see what was in my heart that day, make you believe that I had only started living after I met you.

Three of our students began to play their violins, a song that was familiar to both of us. Our song from the Godfrey, our late night dance at the plaza. You couldn't see me yet, but I saw you, standing in your resplendence, hands clasped, smiling and making Ariel laugh. When the music played, you turned to Ariel. This was *our* song, not theirs. And then their children began to walk slowly toward you. You saw Toto in a white satin suit, looking like a little man at four years old. Chiqui followed in a white satin dress, carrying a basket of white rose petals. And then Gabby in the identical dress, except that she led Olive wearing a collar filled with blue hydrangeas, visibly irritated by the weight of the flowers.

And when you saw me, you stumbled backward. Ariel held out his arms to steady you. You looked at me searchingly. I held your gaze and tipped my head in a slight nod. You swayed from side to side, Ariel with arms at the ready, until you buried your face in your hands and sobbed. I paused, not knowing what to do but seconds after that, you were smiling, cheeks glistening with tears, holding out your arms to me as Chiqui, Toto, Gabby, and Olive made their way to stand next to you.

"A vow is validated when you make it in front of witnesses," Diana said *during this moment's planning stages.*

"We can't do it in front of a priest or a minister," I said, speaking openly now that she knew my story. "I can't bring religion into this. I was married in a church."

"No, I didn't mean those witnesses. I meant people. Normal people," she said, rolling her eyes.

"That's going to be a little bit difficult," I laughed, reminding her that our world was a little limited those days.

"Leave it to me," she said, tapping her fingers on my lap.

If anything, I knew our vows were valid. Diana had invited the entire town. Seventy people, all dressed in their finest attire stood respectfully around the bridge, some standing in the water, the others with their shoes digging into the sand. There was Mang Inog, the postman, the doctor, Olive's veterinarian, twenty students from the school, the principal, the dean of your university, some teachers, and some bystanders too. They clapped when I reached you, finally safe, finally home. I weaved my fingers through yours. Diana motioned for the music to stop and there we were in perfect silence.

"Hi," you said, beaming from ear to ear. "You are breathtaking. So beautiful."

"Thank you."

Diana and Ariel stood by our side, like proud parents, guardians, cohorts in a world where love's sacrifices have set us free. After a minute of silence, Diana signaled for me to begin.

I cleared my throat and squeezed your hands tight. "Roman," I began. I found that I wasn't speaking loud enough and so I started again. "The poet Rumi has written: 'If you will find me not within you, you will never find me. For I have been with you from the beginning of me.' Roman, I am here to declare to this congregation, to this town, to the people in this village that today I pledge my love for you. I want you to know that my life only began when I met you, that I'd been waiting all my life for you and that finding you, loving you, has given me purpose, made me whole. I want you to know that no matter what happens, no matter what life throws at us, I was meant to be with you. You have my heart now and forever. I promise to love you all my life. I take you as my life's partner, my lover, and my best friend. And will hold you as the most precious gift I have ever received for the rest of my days. And..." I paused to reach my hand to your face and gently wipe away your tears. "If you would one day, ask me again, to take another chance on you, I will not think twice. Because I would rather have a life of not knowing with you by my side, than a life of knowing without you."

Your shoulders shook, your eyes were closed, tears continued to stream down your face. And yet, you held on to my hands, brought them to your chest and kept them there. "I wasn't prepared for this," you said.

The congregation laughed. "Surprise!" Ariel hushed and the three children giggled.

"But here goes," you continued. "God, you take my breath away." The crowd clapped. "Julia, I loved you from the first day that I met you. And to be blessed by your presence, your love, your goodness is something I never imagined I deserved. I promise to take care of you, to honor you and to make sure that you never ever regret falling in love with me. You are my heart, my soul, my reason for living. This is the only life I want. I love you more than words can say, and with the heavens and the earth and the sun and the sky as witnesses, I promise to love and cherish you more and more each day."

Gabby pushed Chiqui, who pushed Toto out in front of us. "The rings!" they squeaked as Toto held up the little white pillow that held them.

It was more a pin cushion, actually, with two rings made out of tiny metallic beads, coiled together on thin pieces of metal. I noticed right away that they weren't identical. There was a mixture of colors. Different shades mixed within every layer.

"I made them, *Tito* Roman," Chiqui whispered, her chest puffed out in pride.

"They're perfect, *mi amor*."

Slowly, I slipped the band around your finger while you followed my lead and did the same.

"What happened," you whispered. "What happened after he climbed up the tower and rescued her?" A line we both knew too well.

"She rescues him right back," I answered, my voice strong and confident.

"Can I kiss her now?" you asked, while pulling me to your chest.

"Wait!" Ariel instructed before turning to the crowd. "This congregation has been witness to the declaration of love by these two people, Roman and Julia. In our eyes and by your words and actions and your giving of self to this community, we bestow upon you the grace of being husband and wife." He turned back to you. "Now, you can kiss her."

And you did.

Chapter Thirty-Nine
We are one

You and I sat in the midst of the merriment, finally taking the time to appreciate everything happening around us. The bridal table, set on a makeshift stage, was flanked on all sides by wooden tables with their feet anchored into the sand. The starlit sky and a string of bright lights provided the perfect evening glow. Electric fans powered by a heavy generator kept the humid air and mosquitoes away.

We celebrated with seventy people. Some we knew, most we didn't, but it was a celebration all the same. We feasted on lobster, fish, and shrimp and hefty trays of their local paella. I didn't want a wedding cake because it wasn't a wedding, so we served little pastry dishes of coconut pies and lemon meringue. Olive, exhausted by the afternoon's festivities, lay on the sand by your feet, fast asleep.

"I love you," you whispered as you kissed my shoulder. "This is the best day of my life."

"Good," I teased. "Because it will be a long time before we do this again."

"When can we leave?" you asked, slipping your finger into the tiny lace openings on the back of my dress. "Because I want to play peek-a-boo."

I laughed just as Diana and Ariel approached us.

"The woman of the hour!" you exclaimed. "Diana! I don't know how to thank you for this!"

"Thank this one," she answered, laying both hands on my shoulders. "She really wanted this to be perfect for you."

"Well, it was," you said, taking my hand and bringing it to your lips. "Perfect day."

"Guys, are you sure you don't want to do the first dance? Our surprise band is getting ready to play!" Ariel said, breathless from excitement. "You'll love them."

I shook my head before you could respond.

You got my drift and smiled at me with your sparkling eyes. Because we lived our lives in secret, we learned to communicate without words. It was amazing to see how we'd morphed into our disguises in five short months. It was the life I'd always wanted to live.

"Actually, Ariel…" You motioned for him to come close until your mouth was next to his ear. "I'd love to sneak out of here and take my wife home."

Ariel smiled. "Go on, man. You're free to leave."

The guests cheered and focused on the bridge where a band was getting ready to play. They looked like the Village People—a policeman, a fireman, a Native American, a biker, and a cowboy.

"Dude!" you exclaimed. "Are those the—"

"Village People!" Ariel answered. "They are so good! Not the real ones, of course."

I giggled. "Of course."

You stood, took Olive in your arms and turned to me. "Race you home?"

Running through the sand in a floor-length gown wasn't exactly a good getaway plan. We breezed into our home, breathless and winded. Olive went straight for her bed right by the night lamp. We stood facing each other by the foot of our bed. When I reached back to unzip my dress, you stopped me.

"No. Not yet."

I stepped forward and touched your face.

"I still want to have that first dance with you," you said.

"Here?"

"On our dance floor."

A moment later, I was in your arms, on the sand, under the moon, by the two tree stumps across from our front porch. The music in our hearts played loudly, the wind chimes calling out our celebration to those who couldn't be with us.

Can you hear me, Charlie? I'm calling out to you. I want you to know that I miss you so much and that I wished you could have the chance to fall in love with him too.

"Hold your gaze," I whispered.

"Or she may get lost," you whispered back.

We swayed back and forth; you hummed in my ear while your hands roamed all over me. I welcomed your touch, the feel of you, the fact that you were there, wanting me.

"You miss him, I know."

"I do," I admitted. "I wish he was here."

"I'm sorry."

"Don't be. One day, I will make him understand how you saved me." I kissed you with all the wantonness and abandon, opened myself up to you with my lips, my tongue, while you slowly unzipped my dress. With frenzied urgency, I ripped off your jacket and lifted your shirt over your head, breaking away only to allow you to slip your pants down your hips. I sank to my knees, placed you between my breasts and teased you until you lifted my head up and guided me to you.

We were both naked now, our clothes in a rumpled heap on the ground. I smiled, a mischievous, impish grin before pulling you down on the sand and straddling you.

"Tell me what you want, baby," you growled.

"You," I moaned, placing my full weight on you.

You held me by my hips and guided me up and down, slowly at first and then increasing in intensity until I screamed out your name when I came. And then without warning, you separated yourself from me and flung me backward. Your eyes raged with intensity, brown to black, your lips pressed tight. "I want you to feel me inside you for days."

Obediently, I turned around and offered myself to you.

You entered me from behind, gently first, until you filled me. And then you made yourself known to me over and over again, touching me all over and pulling on my shoulders so that I placed all my weight on you.

"Give it to me, baby," I mumbled. "Give it all to me."

"Carin!" you bellowed, shaking violently as you found your release. I reached back to touch your face as you settled your chin on my shoulder. We always stayed this way, you inside of me for as long as I could keep you. We lost ourselves in the whisper of the wind, the melody of the wind chimes, the rustling of the palm trees, the plopping sound of coconuts.

"I know you love me," you muttered. "If you want me to, I think I can let you go."

Chapter Forty
CXN

"**B**abe? What's eating you?" I took your hand before leaning back on the marble chaise. We were on the terrace that overlooked the pristine blue water and the lush green mountains. Everything in the room was yellow and white. Yellow pillows, white couches, yellow and white patterned tiles. I turned to admire the oversized Ming Dynasty vases scattered around the deck. Blue and white contrasting decor.

Your face was clouded with worry, eyes crossed, lips in a straight line. You chose your words carefully.

"It's just that ..." You paused, trying to shift gears. "How did you pull this off, anyway?"

"What, booking this honeymoon?"

You nodded.

"You mean how I did it?" I asked, needing clarification. It was a long story, and I didn't want to bore you with the details.

"Everything." You squeezed my hand. I could tell you were trying so hard to make light of the conversation. But still, you looked worried, your eyebrows coming together in a knot.

"I wanted to go somewhere really special. Get pampered for once. Spoil you. So I thought we could sneak off to a resort on the mainland.

Just a quick trip."

"It's kind of out there, Car. We are in the best resort in the world. Better than the Ritz Carlton. How are we paying for this? We don't have credit cards."

"Diana. I paid her cash, and she went ahead and prepaid for everything."

I watched you tap your fingers on the coffee table before straightening your back. Still seated, but neck tense, locked in place. "You withdrew from your account?"

"No! No, of course not! I know how that can be traced. I used the money we had left!"

This time, you inched toward the edge of your seat and stared out into the distance. It made me nervous, seeing you in such deep thought. You looked like you were having a debate with yourself—one eyebrow raised and then the other, followed by a heavy sigh. I moved to the ottoman so I could face you directly, placing your feet on my lap. I brushed my fingers lightly on your leg.

I felt you stiffen, but maybe I misread it. "Come back to me," I whispered. "Please, there's nothing to worry about. Look!" I picked up the booklet from the side table. "They have caviar! And Moscato. And they have boutiques downstairs with the brands we both love! Let's just have fun. It's two days. And then we can go back home."

"I just think it's a bit risky."

"What?" I said lightheartedly, running my fingers up and down your leg. "This? Come on, baby. Two days. We deserve this. I promise you, I was discreet. Diana registered us in our new names. No one knows us here."

"And you trust her to keep this in confidence?"

"If we can't trust Ariel and Diana, we're screwed. They're the only other human beings we interact with. Olive, maybe, I don't trust." I forced a laugh, tried to elicit the same from you. Olive looked up from her pillow. "But Ariel and Diana?"

You inhaled deeply and tried to force a smile.

"Please," I said. "We don't even have to leave our suite. We have everything we need right here." I leaned in and planted kisses on your face, your ears, your nose.

You closed your eyes and smiled. "Convince me some more."

"Well," I whispered, exposing myself to you, "there are strawberries on the tray in the room that would really go well with this."

I would have loved to take credit for thwarting your initial freak out. But as soon as I turned on the television, I knew that you were back. Your eyes were glued to that screen as you flipped channels all day long. First sports, then news, then sports again. We stayed in all that afternoon, alternating between ESPN and CNN. The larger-than-life screen brought us back to what we left behind five months before, caught us up on what was happening around the world. We were like children seeing Disneyland for the first time.

"Anderson Cooper still looks great."

"Wait. What happened in Vegas?"

"Justin Bieber is back with Selena Gomez?"

"Who's Selena Gomez?"

"Are you kidding me? Matias? You don't know who Selena Gomez is?"

You found a Cubs game streaming in through a sports channel, and I found CNN on the bathroom television. There you were, on the sitting couch, transfixed on Jake Arrieta pitching a no-hitter and whooping in between cheers. I saw the old you, the guy's guy, the sports addict, come back to life. And I loved you all the more. I saw the light come back in your eyes for the first time in months, saw remnants of the man I'd first fallen in love with. Each day of living in seclusion had brought me closer to you, made me love a different side of you, the cautious, often serious, deliberative side. But that weekend, you were back to the way you had been—insisting on nothing but the best. We had Cristal for our champagne, caviar and truffles to feast on while we stayed in.

"Hey, look what I found!"

You unglued your eyes from the television to watch me hold up my hands. "What is it?"

"An iPAD," I said, pressing down the power button.

You paused the game and turned to me. "No, Carin. Don't."

I ignored you—double clicked on the Google icon and started to type.

You turned off the television. "Stop, please. Don't go any further."

I shook my head and squinted at you with no intention of heeding your instructions. "Oh god, do you think if I ordered a book or two today, they can send it to this hotel? I'm dying to read something other than those old Fabio books. Meggy and Ralph have both passed on. Hold on—search. Oh, here it—"

You grabbed the tablet and threw it on the floor. The force of your pull scared me. I shrank back and moved to the opposite end of the couch.

"Get dressed," you said, standing and heading toward the bathroom. "You want a fucking book? Let's go buy you an actual fucking book."

Chapter Forty-One
The Beginning

"Carin, please, wait up!"

We weaved our way through crowds, shuffling through the narrow aisles at a high-end mall. It was filled with lookie-loos. No one was buying anything, just walking aimlessly back and forth, in large droves of people. I was many steps in front of you, carrying a bag of books. You went against the traffic and pushed your way between two couples and a woman in a wheelchair.

"Baby, please, slow down. I'm sorry," you said, grabbing my hand.

"It's okay," I mumbled.

"Can we stop, please?"

"Not really," I said. "I just want to get back to the hotel and go home tomorrow."

You stopped in the middle of the stream, causing the unsuspecting mass of people to pile up behind us.

"Matias, come on."

"No, please, let's stop for a second." You pulled me to the side. We leaned against a glass barrier in front of a jewelry store. "Listen, baby. I'm sorry I lost my head. I freaked out as soon as you started typing on the search bar. Those things can be traced, you know."

"I know. But I was just so excited to catch up on everything we missed."

"So you're telling me that you weren't going to eventually try to look Charlie up."

You stumped me. It still hurt to hear his name. I wrote his name a lot, but hardly ever said it. Maybe I would have. No, I think I would have.

You knew not to wait for an answer. Instead, you cradled my face in your hands and kissed my nose. "I just need more time with you. A little bit more time."

"Okay." I nodded.

"The thought of losing you makes me crazy."

"I'm sorry I upset you," I said. "Let's just go back now. I've got my books."

"Are you kidding?" you said, smiling. "We're at a real mall. We have so many things to check out."

Once again, you cut crosswise through the crowd, annoying the people who stopped to let us through. There we stood, in front of a display case with Cartier watches and diamonds.

"Like this store."

There are beaches and there are beaches. For the past five months, we had our own slice of paradise. We dipped our toes in sugar white sand every single day, heard the rush of crystalline blue water right outside our door. Spending time at a resort on the mainland was nothing compared to the home that we had. Their beach just wasn't of interest to us.

Instead, we took advantage of the material comforts that were hard to come by—like wine and food and a whole slew of kitchen gadgets. We walked for miles, checking out the mall and the surrounding stalls, the fresh market, and the buildings around the city. We entered the office buildings and took the local transportation around town. We were frugal, conscious of the remaining funds we had, but a dollar went a long way in that place and so we ended up with a few things to take home with us. We were constantly surrounded by all sorts of people, oftentimes engaging them, asking questions, getting opinions.

That day, the thought crossed my mind more than once. Were we as good together when we were in our element? When we weren't hiding?

I thought we were.

You constantly reminded me that we were on our honeymoon, which meant we holed up in our room most of the day before we left. When we finally emerged from the room, we felt obligated to take a walk along the beach.

"Feels different, doesn't it?" I asked while walking along the shore with you.

"Yeah," you said, squeezing my hand. "Even the sand feels manufactured, more compact."

"And the crowd of people. It makes me appreciate where we live. Most days, you and I have a one-mile radius all to ourselves."

"I can't wait to get home."

I looked up and smiled at you. Such simple words with so much meaning. I felt a tingling in my stomach, a swell in my chest. If only I could stop missing Charlie, my life would be so serene, so complete.

We stopped to watch two children, a boy and a girl, chasing each other in ankle-deep water, the froth of the surf wrapping itself around their legs. They giggled every time one of them got knocked down by the waves. The boy had sandy blond hair like Charlie's, same lanky build, same freckled nose. The girl had her hair in French braids. They looked like twins. Same height, same build, same face.

"Are you twins?" you asked as they got on their boogie boards and prepared to swim farther out.

"Yes," said the boy.

"How old are you guys?"

"Seven," said the girl.

"Okay, well be careful out there. Don't go out too far," you said, waving to them. You held on to my elbow and led me away, laughing as the boogie board slid out of the boy's arms into the air.

We hadn't taken too many steps forward when the young girl chased after us. "Mister, please," she said in a very heavy Spanish accent. "My brother!"

"What happened?" you asked. "Where is he?"

"I don't know! He disappeared in the water!"

"Stay here," you said, running back toward their original location. I took the girl's hand watched you run into the water and disappear from sight.

The girl started to cry. I knelt down to give her a hug, my eyes still fixed on the water. I couldn't see you. The waves were so high I couldn't make anything out over or under their crests. "What's your name?"

"E-mi-lia," she said in between hiccups. Her braids had come undone, wiry tufts of hair cascading down her small face.

"Emilia, don't worry. Do you know that my husband, Roman, is a great swimmer? He'll find your brother."

"Emilia!" An older man darted toward us, followed by a frantic woman wearing a large brim hat.

"Emilia," screamed the woman. "Where is Enrique?"

"In the water, Mama!" she answered. "The man went after him, trying to find him."

"Call the police!" the woman yelled to her husband, who had his phone to his ear.

"Please stay with your mother," I said, running toward the water, desperate for any sign of you. I wanted to swim out, but my fear was so strong, my legs felt like lead. They refused to carry me forward. Instead, I stood knee-deep in the water, aware of every single sound and movement around me.

The mother wailed on the shore, falling to her knees while her husband tried desperately to comfort her. Emilia stared out in front of her, alternating between wringing her hands and biting her nails. I heard the shrill cawing of seagulls in the air, saw a dolphin vault above the waves, felt the chill in the air.

That wasn't going to be the day, Matias. I always knew it would come. But not like that.

It seemed like forever before the blaring of sirens and flashing lights appeared. Three policemen in khaki uniforms approached while a news truck barreled toward me. A loud boom and then jet skis starting out from the shore. A woman in a blue dress followed by photographers jumped out of the truck.

"There they are!"

The father ran into the water. I saw you then, swimming sideways but moving very slowly. You held the boy's head up in one arm, the other arm paddling swiftly. "Matias!" I screamed, louder than I ever had before. I knew you couldn't hear me, but I had to say your name. I sank to the ground amid the glaring, flashing lights. The jet skis bobbed up and down in the water as you handed them the boy. He was limp, unconscious. I could tell because it took two men to lift him out of the water.

By the time you got back to the shore, an ambulance was waiting to tend to the boy. The drove of people surrounding me had now focused on you.

"Sir!" said the pretty reporter in a dress, tripping over the camera wires that were trenched in the sand.

"Matias!" I ran to you, elbowing those in my way.

You stopped when you heard me call your name, frantically moving your head from side to side. We were desperate to find each other. And when we did, I wrapped my arms around you so tightly, feeling every part of your wet skin, tasting the salt on your face, tears of relief streaming down my cheeks.

"I'm okay," you said.

219

"Sir!" The reporter shoved a microphone right in your face.

You batted your arm in the air, causing the reporter to step back. Right then, someone called out her name.

Quickly, you tucked my head under your arm, shielding my face from the cameras.

"Let's get out of here," you said. "On the count of three, we run as fast as we can. One. Two—"

You gripped my hand and pulled me across the steep sandy hill. We ran as fast as our legs would take us. Until the scene at the beach was as distant as the boats on the water, the flashing lights merely sequins in the sky.

Chapter Forty-Two

Gratitude

"How long have I been asleep?" you asked, rubbing your eyes before stretching your arms in the air.

"Fourteen hours," I answered, nuzzling your neck, inhaling the life out of you. "You smell good." I leaned my head on your chest as you wrapped your arms around me.

"Are you okay?"

"Yeah. I'm feeling rested now. Yesterday it felt like I had just run three marathons."

"I was terrified. I knew you were doing the right thing. But in my head, I kept thinking—'who would I blame for this if I lost him'?"

"You weren't going to lose me," you whispered into my hair. "I'm a great swimmer."

"Tell me what happened."

"He got pulled out by a rip current. By the time I found him, he was so tired from thrashing in the water. Luckily I got to him before the undertow pulled him down. He was conscious when I reached him. He wrapped his arms around my neck and then passed out. The boogie board was nowhere to be found. I tried to keep his head up while swimming. In fact, my ears still don't feel right. Feels like I still have some water in them or something."

I reached out and caressed them. Your ears. "We should see a doctor in town when you're up to it."

"Not today. I just want to stay home with you."

"Ariel told the university you'd be out for a few days."

"Good old Ariel," you said, shifting as if trying to sit up. "Today is good enough. I'll be fine tomorrow."

I pushed two pillows up for you to rest your head on. "You hungry?"

"Starving."

"I figured. Be right back."

You were sitting up, leaning against the headboard, ready for the tray I brought into our room. I smiled when I saw the blanket draped neatly across your waist. You pointed to the pillow next to you. "Come back to bed."

Instead, I sat at the edge of the bed. "Coffee, French toast, strawberries. Eat up."

"Mmm, Mrs. O'Neill. You spoil me."

"You're a hero, babe. You deserve to be spoiled." I poured you some coffee, watched as you spread some butter on the French toast. "Hey, I have another surprise for you."

"Really?"

"Uh-huh." I fished the neatly wrapped painting out from under the bed. "I finished it!" I tore the wrapping paper up and set it nicely on the bed, right in front of you.

"Oh baby," you said, pushing the tray of food to the side so you could get closer. You touched it with your fingertips, traced the outline of my face with a big smile. "It's beautiful. It really looks like you. Your eyes, your mouth. It's a remarkable self-portrait."

"So you like it?"

"I love it," you answered, pulling me in for a kiss.

"Good. I want you to remember me always."

"There you go again," you said with an exaggerated frown. You rolled your eyes and puckered your lips. "Stop saying that."

I laid the painting flat on the ground, moved the tray to the night table and crawled under the covers next to you.

"My turn," you said, reaching inside the drawer next to you. "I have a surprise too."

You handed me a little red box, wrapped in a giant black ribbon. "A real wedding ring."

I gently tugged on its ends, careful not to unravel its perfect bow. And when I saw what was in it, I gasped. "Oh my god. What did you do?"

"I bought you a ring," he answered. "The one you deserve."

I was speechless. It was a gesture that meant the world to me, but I had a sick feeling in my gut that this would sink us. "This was the one we looked at the other day—the two-carat solitaire, Matias. This must have cost at least fifteen thousand dollars."

"Relax, Carin. It's okay. Spending the weekend in civilization reminded me—you and I—we're millionaires."

"How did you pay for it?"

"I memorized my credit card. They took it down, and it went through."

"Credit card," I said, shaking my head. "You just freaked out when I went online. You said you didn't want to be traced."

You had guilt written all over you—eyes darting from side to side, hands waving all over the place. "I know, but I saw how much you loved it and wanted to get it for you. I used our married name, gave the home address in Chicago. I figured if it did set a trail, it would be a fake one." You waited for me to say something. When I didn't, you went on. "If they trace us to this resort, what does it matter? We're no longer there."

"Please don't think I don't love it. It is the most beautiful thing I've ever seen. I'm just overwhelmed by the cost."

You prompted me to slip it on my finger, and I did. It fit perfectly.

"God, Matias. It's gorgeous."

"You're gorgeous," you said, smiling.

"But I don't need this. I'm completely fine with the band Chiqui made for us."

"You've given up so much for me. For a life with me. You deserve this and more, Carin. I want to give you everything. Besides ..." You reached out to tap my nose with your finger. "Your birthday's coming up. It's also an anniversary gift. We met on your birthday."

I held my hand in the air and watched the diamond reflect the light from the window, specks of white bouncing all over the wall. "I remember."

"Will you wear it all the time?" you asked quietly.

"Of course I will, baby. Thank you."

"Thank you," you responded. "I'll make sure and pick up some materials to hang the painting up on the wall right here." You pointed behind us.

I slid down under the blanket until I was neck-deep in it. "Hey, handsome," I cooed, pulling you on top of me. "You said you'd give it all to me. Pay up."

Chapter Forty-Three

Temporary

*E*very beginning has an end. And every end starts with a beginning. I figured that out in seventh grade, and when that thought dawned on me I never let it go. I would lay awake at night, anxious and afraid. Thinking about how once you're born, once you begin to exist, there is no way out of this world but to die. I spent that entire year in morbid fear of death. It was also the year that my father walked out on my mother. The year all those fears became a fixture in my life.

This time, I was totally unprepared.

Two days after we returned home, you were raring to get back to work. We got up at the crack of dawn. I remember checking the skies like I always did, just to make sure I knew what to expect. You crossed the ocean every day, and the skies told me whether or not to worry. They were so clear that day, like a matted photograph, unmarred and unblemished. I made you a mushroom omelet. You were so excited to try the hot sauces we'd brought in from the mainland.

"Mmm. I think I like this the best." You held up the skinny bottle of piri piri. "I can really taste the garlic."

"You and your spices." I leaned over to kiss you. Our faces stayed close together. "Are you sure you're feeling good enough to go?"

"I feel great."

Death started with a knock on the door.

"Good morning!" I pulled the door open to find Diana and Ariel standing timidly outside. They crouched behind the doorframe, reluctant to walk in. There was the strangest shift in the air. It turned cold. They turned cold. The only friends we had in that foreign land looked terrified, sad, disenchanted. Eyes downcast, bodies stiff and guarded, miles and miles between us and them.

Everything that happens when friends feel betrayed.

"Why are you standing outside?" I said, pulling Diana by the hand. She stumbled in, Ariel following right behind her.

You stood in greeting, walked over to kiss Diana on both cheeks while I held onto her hand and led her to the kitchen table.

"What's up, guys?" I asked. "My hero is ready to go back to work."

"Well," Ariel said, pausing to look at his wife. "I don't know if you want to do that today."

We stole a glance at each other. "What's wrong?" I asked. "Please, both of you, sit. You're making me nervous."

Diana fished a newspaper out of her plastic tote and laid it on the table. "This came out today. My brother dropped it off."

The couple seemed to ease off on the tension, taking a seat next to us. On the front page of the local paper was a large picture of you, emerging from the water, your eyes staring directly into the camera, your arm raised in a delayed attempt to cover your face.

WE JUST WANT TO THANK HIM. Emblazoned across the page was that headline.

"They are hoping Roman comes forward so they can reward him for saving their son," Ariel said.

"Who are they?" you asked. "I don't need their reward. I just want to be left alone."

"You saved the son of the Spanish ambassador," Diana piped in. "They are a high profile family. Enrique and Emilia go to the international school on the mainland."

"Shit! Of course, it had to be them," you hissed.

"Roman," I whispered. "It's okay."

"It's not okay," you said, looking straight at me.

Diana and Ariel turned to each other. And as if on cue, Diana turned to the next page. "And here you are."

There I was, on my knees, looking out at the water. I thought about all the hearts we had broken and all the deception now blown wide open by those pictures.

Ariel addressed you. "Vincent told Diana your names are not real. That you're Matias Torres."

"And I'm Carin Frost," I said.

Diana grabbed my hand. Hers was warm, light, full of understanding. "We know."

"Roman," Ariel said, his tone soft. "They're looking for you. You can't go back to the university."

You stared at your hands laid out on the table. "The ambassador knows my father," you muttered.

I jerked my head toward you.

"My father owns the largest furniture business in Madrid. He's friends with that man."

"You said he was a craftsman," I countered.

You didn't answer.

A few seconds passed before you pushed back, the ear-piercing screech of the wooden chair against the floor startling the three of us. Olive ran out of the bedroom and leaped into my lap.

"Fuck!" you yelled, standing and pacing around our little house. In a few steps, you went from the living room to the dining room to the kitchen and back around the dining table. You sat on the couch with your head buried in your hands.

No one said a word. We sat and waited. I wanted to be close to you, touch your skin, calm you down, but I thought it best to leave you alone.

When you finally spoke, I walked over and sat next to you. "Ariel, we will need your help. Can we close up this house and keep everything here until we send for our things at a later date? We don't have much to take with us, but I'd like to keep the paintings and some other things Julia—I mean, Carin decides she wants. I can—"

"No," I uttered silently. The one word that would bring us back our peace.

You leaned away, confounded. "No?"

I knew I had to pull you back in. "Matias, we can't keep hiding. This isn't us."

"But this is us," you argued. "This is our life." Your face went slack, your eyes wet and dull.

"They'll find us wherever we go."

"Not if we're smart about it," you pleaded.

"This was temporary."

"Temporary?" you howled, your eyes bulging. When you stood, you did so with such force that it smacked the couch hard against the wall. You ran to the kitchen, picked up the vase we'd purchased at the flea market and flung it against the tile wall.

"Like this?" You picked up a plate and did the same thing. "Temporary like this?"

You moved on to the glass-blown bowl sitting on the coffee table. "What about this?"

Crash.

I saw your eyes linger on the picture of us on the wall. You lunged at it, pulled back for a second and then threw it on the ground. "And this?"

Crash.

"There you are, Carin! Pieces of our temporary life on the floor!"

I was wracked with sobs, covering my face in my hands, desperate to answer but out of words. "No, no!"

Olive ran in circles, stressed out and upset. I scooped her up and held her tight.

Diana ran to me. Ariel did the same to you. He placed both arms on your shoulders and shook you. "Roman, buddy, it's okay. Let's take a minute to calm down, okay? Come on," he said, leading you to the door. "Let's take a walk and talk this over."

You twisted your neck, turned to look at me before allowing Ariel to push you forward.

And when I heard the door slam shut, I folded myself in Diana's arms.

"What have I done?" I cried.

"Shh. It's okay," Diana cooed. "You have to understand him. All these months, you've been preparing yourself for this day. He didn't see it coming. Or he didn't want to see it."

"How could he not!" I cried. "We've been playing house all these months! How could he not?"

"People believe what they want to believe. Maybe he thought there'd be a way, somehow—"

I cut her short. "What way? What other way could make this a permanent thing?"

She shook her head, lost for words.

"It doesn't matter. I've hurt him. I didn't mean to hurt him. I love him so much."

I knelt on the floor and began to pick up the pieces of glass, remembering that in my old life, I'd be besieged with thoughts of hurting myself. Not then. I wanted to see this life through, live it so I could have another chance of living with you. And Charlie.

"Julia, don't. Let me get the broom and we can sweep it."

Diana ran to the pantry to pull it out. I stood and grabbed both her hands. "Please believe me. This is me, Carin, Julia—the person you know, your friend. Please don't think there was any pretense in what I showed you, what I told you. Please don't think that our friendship was anything but genuine and real. I love you, Diana. You're my friend."

"I know, I know," she whispered, tears running down her face. "You think it was me who took care of you. But the truth is, I needed you too."

Chapter Forty-Four
Death and Dying

*D*iana helped me clean up for the next few minutes. Without a word, we began to pack up the things I wanted her to keep. We wrapped the paintings in plastic garbage bags and folded our bedding neatly for her to put away.

I was grasping at anything you'd touched, holding those things close to my face to remember the feel of you. The furniture you'd built for me, the things we'd picked up on the side of the dirt road, the books I'd read to you late at night. I wanted to hold on to all of them. I offered to send her money to place them in storage but she refused to accept anything from me.

When I'd done enough to get our home in order, I wanted to look for you.

We found you on the beach, sitting with your feet in the water, Ariel with his pants rolled up to his knees. He smiled when he saw his wife, lovingly took her hand when she offered it. We didn't exchange any words. Ariel squeezed your shoulder while Diana blew me a kiss. And then they quietly disappeared in the dark.

I sat next to you, brought my knees to my chest and wrapped my arms around them. You turned to me with the same tears you'd taken with you when you left. "I'm sorry, Carin. You didn't deserve that."

"It's not your fault," I answered. "To be loved like this. No one will love me like this but you."

"I'm going to die without you."

"You only die without love. Our love for each other—it will keep us alive," I said.

"Were you waiting for this all along? For the day we'd be found? Did you want to be found?" you asked. I could feel the pain in your voice. Once these words are uttered, they become tangible. They confirm our truth.

The tide began to rise. Still, we sat. You held on to me protectively, making sure I stayed anchored on the sand.

"I knew this time would come. I just didn't know how or when," I replied. "The thing is, I don't think I wasted a single second of our time together. All this time, through all these months, I loved you with all of me. There was never a moment when I could have loved you more, touched you more, laughed with you more. I did it all to the fullest, Matias."

You nodded. "Those vows you said to me—"

"I didn't exist before you. I was meant to love you."

We were now waist-deep in the water. You made a move backward, closer to the shore. "Let's go," you said. "It's getting deeper."

"I'm not afraid anymore. You took away all my fears. We can stay," I said. "It's a gorgeous night and we're never going to see the stars like this again." I took a deep breath, filling my lungs with the salty sea air. "Mmm. Can you smell that? I'm going to miss everything about our home."

My voice broke. I set my tears free. Every word I said that night, I said because I had to. I had to show you that we could both make it out of there alive.

"What are we going to do?" you whispered, trying to stop the flow of my tears with your thumbs.

"I don't know. I suppose we have to go back, make amends for the hurt we caused. I have to make it up to Charlie."

"And Jack?"

"And Jack, and Trish. And you, your mom, and dad and your family. Isabella."

You shook your head. "I'll die without you," you said again.

"No, you can't."

You rolled your eyes. "How can you say that? You wanted to die so many times."

"But that was before you!" I held up my right hand. "Look! No more pain, no more scars. You've healed me."

You spread my palm across your face and kissed it.

I continued. "We have to make these months count for something. We celebrated love and life! This has to be enough. Many people don't even get this privilege, ever."

"Privilege, my ass. Why couldn't we just fight to be together? Plain and simple. Fate, faith, whatever else fuck is at play here, I can't go on."

"That's the point of all this. You can't skip steps. If I didn't lose my mother, if I didn't go through all that pain, my heart would not have met you. This is all part of our story. This time with you," I looked at you and smiled. "I've had a lot of time to think. I'm here because I came from there. The scars on my hand had healed because I wanted them to."

You faced me with pleading eyes. "Please, Carin. We have to find a way. Let's go tomorrow. Leave everyone, start over."

"I can't leave Charlie any longer than I have. I have to go back to him."

You looked away. Stared straight into the ebony sky. "I know."

The water was now up to our chests. I knew we had to go. "Let's go home, my love. We'll figure things out together, okay?"

You stood and offered me your hand.

I looked up at you and said, "Six months ago, we threw our lives into this water. Tonight, we're taking them back. We're taking them with us wherever we go."

There we stood, soaked to the bone, our clothes weighing us down against the waves. We held each other, arms tightly locked in an embrace, my head resting on your chest, your lips on my hair. I felt your chest rise and fall, heard your jagged breaths in my ear, felt your tears slip slowly against my back. I didn't know whether to cry for us or to cry for those we'd hurt. The only thing I was sure of that night was that the moon and the stars would hear us.

And because we'd done what we did out of love, the world would forgive us.

Chapter Forty-Five

The End

When we entered our home, you didn't question what you saw. Instead, you stood in the middle of the living room with your eyes closed, still holding tightly to my hand. To the side of the house by the kitchen counter were all the things I wanted Diana to keep. Olive was asleep on the floor instead of her bed—as if she knew that she'd have to be ready to leave at any time.

"Diana will come for our things," I said in an almost-whisper.

You looked around once, twice, before burying your face in your hands while slowly sinking to the floor on your knees. You clutched at your chest as if trying to pull your heart out.

"Please! No!" I cried. I dropped down to the ground with you, cocooning you in my arms. I tried to absorb the shocks that wracked your body, tried to remain steadfast, to keep us alive.

"Carin, please, don't leave me. We can figure this out," you begged. "I'll give you time to make your amends with Charlie, but promise me you'll find me."

"I promise. I promise."

I took your face in my hands and kissed you. It was a soul-rendering kiss, urgent, demanding. We tasted each other, blood and sweat and tears. Touched every inch of our skin, memorized every mark, every mole, every scar. And when you came, you lifted my legs up, laid them on both shoulders so you could thrust as deep as you could. Give me all you had to give.

"I love you, Carin," you gasped. "Without you, I am nothing."

I don't even remember when we fell asleep. We talked until dawn, made love three more times, made plans to purchase our tickets home in the morning.

It took them one day to find us.

It was Olive with her supersonic ears who stirred us from sleep by barking in my ear.

"Shh," I whispered, careful not to rouse you from your peace. Our bodies, our legs, our arms were intertwined, twisted around one another on the bare wooden floor. Olive perked her ears and sat up on her hind legs, her head snapping upward in full attention. And then I heard it. The low drone of a motor, maybe an airplane or a boat. As seconds passed, the noise seemed to fade. But then it returned—this time it sounded like a plane was about to crash into our home.

"Matias."

We held each other, calmed each other down with a lingering kiss.

Calmly, we got dressed, moving around the house to wash our faces, take our wallets and our keys. I placed Olive's collar on her before you opened the front door.

We walked out, holding hands, standing at the stoop of our porch. In the distance, a helicopter was trying to land a few feet from the shore.

The waters were angry, waves slapping along the shore, the tide bringing with it rocks and sediment. The force of the propeller created a sandstorm that uprooted our flowers, caused the wind chime to fly off its post. We stood, keeping watch, our fingers locked tight, both our stances steady—not rigid, but accepting. As the propeller slowed, it sliced through the air first with loud thumps and then a hiss.

The sun was so high I had to shield my eyes.

I saw them disembark—first Jack, then Trish, then Charlie. He'd grown so much in the six months since I last saw him. Taller, I think. He'd let his hair grow out. His bangs were down to his nose, the length of his hair down to his chin.

"Mom!" he shrieked, running toward me.

I let go of your hand. When you tightened your grip on my arm, I yanked until you let go.

"Charlie!" I ran faster than I ever had before. Faster than when we'd tried to get away from the reporters on the beach. Or the day of the earthquake. Or the day of our vows.

You walked slowly behind me with Olive by your side.

"Olive!" Charlie shouted. "Hi, Olive! Is that Olive?"

I stopped dead in my tracks, turned to face you. You stopped too— shaking your head, shoulders stooped, your mouth hanging open. Your eyes flickered back and forth, and your face began to crumple, folding in evident pain.

"Carin? Why does he know Olive?"

I stepped backward, not knowing what to do. And then I kept on running.

When I finally reached Charlie, I held him in my arms and cried. "I'm sorry, baby," I sobbed. "I missed you so much."

"It's okay, Mom. You had to get better."

I looked up to find you standing in the same spot, watching as Trish and Jack and Charlie surrounded me, built a wall around me. They stood guard, their arms locked around me as if protecting me from you.

Another sound, a deep grumble, came from the water. Not loud— subtle, subdued. A speed boat approached, long and slim, driven by a man in a suit and sunglasses with another man in shorts and a T-shirt standing next to him. A thought flashed in my mind—one of you telling some coworkers about the beauty of an Aston Martin speedboat. Right then, I knew who the man in the boat had to be. He was assisted off the boat by the other man, who painstakingly laid out a ladder, lifted him up and carried him on his back, careful not to get the older man wet.

"Papa." You walked toward him and folded yourself in his arms.

That was it, I guess. The moment we had both feared was upon us. Little did we know a few months ago, that every day we'd spent together was really a long, drawn-out goodbye. We walked towards the helicopter. The pilot started the engine—sputtering once and twice, and then those bothersome blades began slicing into the air once again. The noise blared but the pounding in my heart was all I heard. I turned around to see you walking toward the water.

"Wait!" I screamed at the top of my lungs, making sure my family heard me.

I ran for you. I ran to you. Stumbled on the sand, my feet digging in with each step like it was quicksand, waiting to swallow me whole. You didn't run to me. You waited, tears in your eyes, your father already in the boat, the man turning the key to start the engine. They weren't tears of sadness or pain. The hollow in your eyes, the glazed look, the lack of expression showed me that you were gone.

"Live, Matias. Take my love with you. Live for us."

The irony of your fears and your worries about my being the first to leave. That day, you made sure it was you. You were the first to leave.

Part III: YOU, ONE YEAR LATER

"How can our love die
If it's written
In these pages"

Rupi Kaur

Chapter Forty-Six
Back At Home

$\mathcal{G}$ can feel her presence as if she's still here. Everywhere I look, during the one-mile walk closer to the shore—I see her. This was the refuge we'd made together. A home built out of one big lie, one horrible deception. And yet, I want to be here. I feel no guilt, no regret. This past year, I've considered myself lucky to have had her in my world. The thing is I'd always known it was temporary. She just wasn't the type of person who would do that sort of thing. But I thought that if I denied it long enough, we would find a way to make things right. Together.

My thoughts are all of her as I walk along the water, my feet sinking with every step into the warm, soft sand.

I stand in front of it, in all its little glory—our one-bedroom bungalow repainted and refurbished but now falling apart. We'd used our hands to make it our home. It remains unoccupied; Ariel had been waiting for further instructions from one of us and I guess neither of us have had the heart to think about it.

It hasn't even been that long. Sure, it's taken me a year to make this trip. A year since I'd last seen her, touched her, begged her to assure me that we were making the right decision. It has taken me twelve months to accept the fact that the past is a closed door and there's nothing one can do to change that. Still, I think this is the perfect place to lay it all to rest. It had been, after all, our home for many months—and the times I had with her were still the happiest times in my life.

That sounds so wrong, considering I am going to be married in two weeks.

Which is why I had to come.

It tears me up to see our home this way, but the salty sea air held no shame when it penetrated the wooden walls and allowed the mold to cultivate and flourish. Without life and its fierce protection, death always seeps in. I slowly make my way toward the front deck. It stretches out along the length of the house—dead plants and cracked Chinese jars still fill all four corners; our blue hammock has twisted itself into a knot. The crashing waves, the soft gentle breeze, the squeaking floor, the silent melody of the rusted wind chimes—these are the sounds of life that envelope me, and yet, I am dead.

I refuse to enter the house just yet, thinking it best to settle myself on the top step overlooking the sand and the sea. In my right hand is a brown envelope containing a tiny green notebook. When I'd first received it from Diana, I couldn't imagine why she'd sent it to me.

"She wants you to know," was all Diana had said.

I'd never even known she kept a diary while we were together. I imagined when she would have had the time to work on it and realize that there were many occasions. This was how she had filled her days, maybe. Until she couldn't take the silence any longer

Now, here it is.

It has to be a hundred pages. Written and addressed to me. I'd tucked it away in the same box that contained all my memories of her, knowing full well that one day I'd be ready.

This day is it. The travel agent suggested I stay at a resort, but the only place on this island that has any meaning for me is right here.

I take a deep breath before unlatching the leather-bound book, its button flapping loose. Coming apart after being opened and closed for a million times. It is so her, this book, this letter full of memories. I wonder right away whether she'd kept the tiny notes she used to leave for me all over our house. She reveled in words. Thought they were important. As if she had thought that I, too, would need something to help me remember one day.

She couldn't have been more wrong. Since the day she left me on that island, I start and end my days with thoughts of her.

"Will you remember this?" she'd asked me often enough. "What about this?"

She had chronicled our time together. One only does that for things that are not meant to be taken for granted.

At that thought, I am filled with anger. It had been her plan all along? To leave me eventually, carry on with life?

That's water under the bridge now. I'm here to live inside her for two days. I deserve this before I walk away. I deserve to breathe her in one more time. Before she becomes just a memory.

Upon seeing her handwriting, tears fill my eyes. Tucked inside the tiny pocket is a picture of us. It was taken during our first month together, a selfie she'd insisted on while we sat on the sand watching the moon sweep over the sky. Her eyes sparkled blue, brighter than the ocean. Her hair, sun-kissed and light, her lips, her skin, her cheeks, smooth and perfect like a porcelain treasure. In my head, she speaks the words she had written:

With gratitude and love to the one who brought me back to life.
Because of you, I have heard the colors of the sky,
Seen the rushing of the wind
And tasted the sound of love's sweet words.
To you, I give all my life, all my love, my present and my past
Whether together or apart. The one truth I will always have is you.
Matias, whoever it is you become, whatever the future holds for you, know that it was, it is, it will always be—you.

I cry.

But it's not enough.

I pound my fists on the ground, but the physical pain won't release my agony.

My words, my actions, the fact that I begged for every minute, every second with her. In the end, they still led to this one big loss. What does it matter now that she's gone?

This book is my only link to the truth. Her words have comforted me, made me believe in what we had. But all that was erased in an instant when she turned her back to me and returned to her family.

For a while I allow myself to get lost in my memories, associating every broken, dilapidated object on the porch to the days and months we'd called this our home. Before I know it, I've been there for four hours. The heat of the afternoon sun is slowly fading and the winds begin to grow colder. I'm in a debate with myself about staying the night. I have yet to enter the house, knowing there'd be nothing there but memories and empty promises.

I look up to find a truck zigzagging its way toward our home. I don't recognize it at first—a huge, black Ford 150 truck with an enclosed cabin in the back. The driver waves at me and I wave right back. Somehow, Diana looks different. Her hair is dyed a deep red-brown. It is now long and cascading down her shoulders. She is wearing makeup—I know this because her lips are red and her eyes look wide and awake. But her smile remains the same—warm, genuine and sincere.

It takes a while for her to alight from the truck. Instead of stepping off it, she carefully slides down, sits on the end of the car floor before laying her feet on the sand.

I see why as soon as she turns to me.

"Hi!" I greet her, stepping toward her as she dusts the sand off her skirt. She is heavy with child, surely in her third trimester.

Diana takes my arm with her left hand and keeps her right one on her stomach.

"Congratulations!" I say, kissing her cheek.

"Thank you." She smiles. "Our fourth and fifth. Twins!"

"Oh my! That is great."

She shuffles slowly across the sand and steps up onto the porch. I watch as she reaches into her pocket to pull out our keys. She unlocks the door and huffs loudly while pushing it open. A pocket of air escapes from the room.

"It's because I locked up all the windows," she says, motioning me to come in. She steps in first, places the keys on the counter and settles on one of the dining room chairs. I make my way to the bedroom, eager to remember how we'd left it that day. I turn to Diana, who looks at me with pity, head bent, one hand on her chest.

Since then, the sheets have been removed and folded neatly in the closet. But although the bed was empty, a few of our personal items still linger in their regular place. Carin's alarm clock, her comb, her old, frayed copy of *The Thornbirds* laying neatly on her night table. My sneakers and my hiking boots are still leaning against the wall on the opposite end of the room.

"Come to the kitchen," Diana calls. "The things she wanted you to take home are here."

I leave the bedroom and take a seat on the couch. Its cushions had been wrapped in a tarp and tied neatly like a package. I have so many questions and I can no longer wait for her answers.

"Have you heard from her?" I ask, looking directly at Diana while she looks right back at me. Her shyness is gone. It's been replaced with conviction. The way she sits, the way she conducts herself. There is a shift in her attitude. Not toward me, but maybe toward what happened to me.

"No, not directly. About three months after you both left, Trish, her sister, called me to let me know that she was slowly getting better."

"Better?"

"Trish said that they confined her to a wellness facility, afraid she would try to hurt herself. When her sister called, Julia was already settled back at home with her family."

"With Jack?" I ask.

"She didn't say. It was mostly to assure me that Julia was recovering."

"Carin," I reminded.

"Julia, Carin. It's the same person to me." Diana keeps her gaze on me. We sit in silence, our eyes moving around the room and then resting on each other. "You look good, Roman. How has it been?"

"You mean, how have I been since I went back home to Madrid?"

"Yes."

I avoid it for as long as I can. "How are you, Diana? How is Ariel and the family?"

"We are fine," she answers. "I've made peace with my father. In fact, he is building us a home next to his so that the children can get to know him. We are moving off this island in a few months. Ariel would have loved to be here too, had he not needed to visit the construction site today."

I shake my head.

She continues. "Julia taught me—"

I raise my hand to correct her. "Her name is Carin."

She gives in, knowing she won't be winning this fight. "Carin taught me that every moment in life needs to have meaning. She had enough courage to make sure that she lived her life that way. We were like two peas in a pod—we chose similar paths in the name of love."

"But you have it all."

"She needs time to get it all back," Diana says. Her tone is defiant, unapologetic. She's taking sides.

I don't hear her words. From the corner of my eye, I see another reminder, another ploy of hers to get me to remember the vivid details of what I'd lost. I reach for it. The blue bottle, its cork still in place, lay on the ground underneath the sink. I bring it up to my face to take a closer look. She'd placed a few more things inside it since I'd last seen it. Our rings were in there, some sand, a few shells. "It didn't break—" I blurt out, devoid of all interaction with Diana. I remember throwing it during our fight. I turn selfish because I want my answers today. "Why did she do it, Diana? Why did she betray me like that?"

"Matias, why do you call it a betrayal?"

"Because all along, I thought she was here on this island with just me. That her time, her love, her attention was focused on flourishing what we had."

"She loved you. More than you will ever know. You wanted too much from her."

"Is she with Jack?"

"I never asked."

There used to be days when that was all I believed. They're gone now, those days. They've been dismissed as a foolish phase. "She knew this would eventually end. How could she not, when she was feeding information to her family the whole time!"

"She had a son! A son! No matter how much she wanted to deny that, she had a life she was responsible for. No matter how much she wanted it to be just you, Charlie deserved to know his mother didn't die."

When I don't answer, she finishes her thought. "One day when you have a child of your own, you will know exactly why she did what she did." And then it dawns on her. The newspaper articles after we were found, the accolades for saving the young boy's life, the press releases about how Isabella stood her ground and welcomed me back home despite my six-month falsehood. "And you? What's next for you? I heard you may be getting married."

"Once you've lived the greatest love in your life, everything else is a practical choice."

"I don't think you answered me."

"Yes, we are engaged. I'm making amends for my sin to my family by giving my parents their grandchildren."

"Huh." Diana gets up from the chair and slowly waddles behind the kitchen counter. "I've done that before. Don't try to make it right by making the wrong choices." For a brief second, I can't see her head. "Here," she says, lifting up a frame and holding it above her head. "It was very important for Carin that you take this with you. She spent many weeks perfecting this portrait."

"Yes, because she was leaving me and wanted me to remember her." I take it from her. It's facing me, those big blue eyes full of promise and love. They stare right into me, extricating every beautiful memory I have of her. This painting epitomizes the love she so boldly gave me. Did I really expect a mother to abandon her child? My responsible, honorable Carin.

No, I don't think so.

Clutching the canvas in both hands, I lean over to give Diana a kiss on her head. "You have been the best friend to both of us. I don't ever want to lose touch with you."

"You won't." She smiles. We both walk back into the living room. "Listen—there's a flight that leaves at eight tonight for the mainland. I'd be happy to take you to the airport from here."

I turn around and nod in understanding.

"There are many more things I think you need to hear from her."

Chapter Forty-Seven
Why Not?

"**E**xcuse me, who are you waiting for?"

Funny how much things have changed in the past year and a half. The office, although still in the sprawling grounds of a downtown Chicago location, looks completely different. Completely changed. Gone are the shelves laden with trophies and accomplishments displayed for the public to see. Also missing is the ostentatious receptionists' bar that spanned from one end of the floor to the other. The executive offices have also disappeared. Everywhere you look there are rows and rows of rectangular picnic-like tables with benches and unassigned seats. In the middle of the common area are pod-like sofas and coffee tables where what seems like a younger generation of employees is congregated on their phones and laptops.

"Carin Frost? The Chief Client Officer?"

She gives me a blank look. Her eyes register nothing.

"Who?" asks the floor coordinator. I see her ID and that's exactly what her title says on the badge. "No one with that name works here."

"Is Jane around?" I ask. "Jane Wobler? She was her secretary."

The floor coordinator walks noiselessly across the brand new glass floor, picks up the phone and begins to converse with someone on the other line. She walks back toward me, noiselessly once again, to give me the news. "Jane is on her way up to see you."

I wait for ten minutes, listen in on the conversations of some of the young account executives. One of them complains of nonstop traveling to Asia for the new expansion project. The other one is asking to be assigned there since her fiancé works in Hong Kong. I also see what the floor coordinator has been waiting for.

"Mr. Torres?" Jane is cautious at first, greeting me with barely a whisper. A smile breaks on her face once I stand to give her a stiff hug.

"Jane, hi."

"Hi." She rubs my back as if comforting me in a motherly fashion.

"The woman over there, she has no idea who Carin is." I pull back but remain standing. We are face-to-face. There is a ruckus going on in the other corner of the room. I see now what the coordinator had been waiting for. There is a young man, a famous actor, being escorted around by a group of men in black suits. He looks like me, dark hair, dark eyes, bearded. Only much younger. At least in years of experience. And suffering.

"Carin never came back here after—"

"Oh." I am disappointed. She sees it in my face because she reaches out to touch my shoulder.

"But if you asked for her using her other name, they would have known who she was. She's made a name for herself in the city doing other things."

The irony of the world hasn't been lost on me in the year that's gone by. I'm living it again today, sitting in another reception area that is the antithesis of the one I'd just been in. Jane told me where to go and well, here I am, waiting to see her. This time, I'm sitting in a plastic chair, one of three leaning against a cold brick wall in the basement of a two-story building in the East Pilsen neighborhood. When I walked in, I was greeted by three kindly men who called her Miss Carin. The first floor was an open gymnasium where adults and children were playing basketball. Directly across from it was a cafeteria full of people, women in hairnets and a long line of people with metal trays and paper utensils.

I see her walking in my direction and that familiar rush courses through me. She looks exactly the same as the first day I met her. She's got her natural hair color back and it's longer than I remember, tied back neatly in a ponytail. The image I have of her in a suit is replaced by a long-sleeved blouse and jeans. And sneakers.

She sees me and skids to a stop; her eyes grow wide, her lips pull apart. But then she collects herself, squares her shoulders, and continues on toward me. I stand right as she approaches me.

"Matias," she says. We don't touch. I nod before following her into her office. It's the door right next to me with a large window looking out into the hallway. She takes a seat at her desk and gestures at the chair across from her.

"Please, sit."

Sit? Just like that. Sit.

I resist the urge to touch her. Any part of her.

I see the nameplate right away. She's using her maiden name. Carin Miller.

"How long have you been in Chicago?"

"Landed at eight this morning. Jane told me where to find you."

"Jane," she says with a smile. "She always tells you where to find me."

"So, you're here now? This is your job?"

"No. I volunteer here. I run it. This homeless shelter. I'm the director."

"You mean it's not a job. So you don't work."

She leans back in her chair. "We don't have to work, you and I."

The way she says it angers me. Not because of its arrogance, but because I sense a benevolence that I have yet to find in myself.

She keeps smiling. Why am I not seeing any pain? Why isn't she sharing my pain?

I decide to go for it. I've got a flight to catch at ten this evening, and my mother thinks I'm on an out of town business trip. It was the only way for my family to accept my leaving two weeks before the big day.

"You're using your maiden name."

"That is my name, yes." I notice her fingers clasped together as they rest under the desk. I can't make out a ring since I can't see anything.

"You're not with Jack anymore?"

"Would you forgive me, if I'd done that to you? Can you blame him? Of course not. I'm divorced."

"And Charlie?"

"He's doing really well. He and I are in therapy together. He tells me he understands why I did what I did, but he's a child. He has unconditional love for his parents."

I can't take my eyes off her. It feels like I'm noticing things for the first time. Like I'm falling in love all over again. Did I even know that her one front tooth was slightly crooked and that her dimples were that deep? That her eyes light up the room, any room. Even in this dark and abysmal place, we didn't need any light.

When I stay silent, she continues. "There are days when all hell breaks loose and things look hopeless. He screams at me, reminds me about what I had done. But those days are slowly dissipating. Most times, he forgives." She smiles weakly, her eyes misting with tears. As if in disbelief, she shakes her head and smiles to herself. "Do you know he told me on that helicopter that he knew I was alive? Such a smart kid. Even before Trish heard from me, he knew. He wrote me letters, every Friday after school. Even if Trish didn't know where I was, he wrote them and kept them for me." Her chin trembles and her jaw tightens. "He said—" She tries her best to stop from weeping, but her face is crumpled up in pain. "He said he didn't want me to miss a single thing during the year I left!"

God help me. I want to hold her more than anything in the world. But she has quickly composed herself, lightly dabbing her eyes and taking a deep breath.

"Did the therapy help you too?" I ask.

"They said I had severe clinical depression. You know, suicidal thoughts and all that. But I don't even see a psychiatrist anymore. I'm doing well."

"At least one of us is," I say. "So if you had sought professional help before we met, it would have saved you the trouble." I puff up my chest, try to ease the pain.

She leans in toward me and locks me in a stare. "That's not true." *I still get lost in them. I still see my dreams through her eyes.* "It was more than that. Even before I got so sad." We both feel the tension cut through the air. I think she can still see right through me because she puts her happy face back on and lightens her tone. "I would have gone to the end of the earth with you. Sickness or no sickness."

"Bullshit," I say through gritted teeth.

"Matias."

"I'm not here for a social call," I declare loudly. "If I wanted to catch up with you, I would have called."

Her lips begin to tremble. She's trying to stay composed.

I go on. "I'm here for some answers. You may have moved on, but I haven't."

"This isn't fair."

"I'll tell you what isn't fair," I say. "Why did you lie to me, Carin? Why did you keep writing home when I thought you and I had something real, something permanent? All along, I was the butt of your joke. All along, you knew you would leave."

"Please, no. That wasn't it. I—"

"What else? What else didn't you tell me when I was foolishly thinking we were making a life together? Huh?" I challenged, standing

251

and leaning over the table so that I hovered above her.

"What about you? You never told me that your father was one of the richest men in Madrid! Was that something that you just conveniently forgot to tell me?"

"What does that have to do with anything between you and me?"

"It tells me who you are, Matias. It's where you're from. It's part of your story. We couldn't just pick up and start over like blank slates, blank pieces of paper!"

"Why"—I bang my fist on her desk—"not?"

She just shakes her head over and over again. Looks at me as if I've grown a third head.

"And then you send me back the ring. Oh, no. Correction. You returned the fucking ring to the fucking store and sent me back the fucking money I paid. As if you were trying to erase every single trace of me from you."

"That is not true!" she shrieked. "You paid so much money for it! It was only fair."

"What else didn't you tell me, huh? Were you making plans to go back to Jack too?"

She looks incensed, closes her eyes as if I caused her physical pain. "What?"

"You fucked me over, Carin."

"I have a son! What did you want me to do? Really make him believe his mother had died? Scar him for life, which I did anyway—dead or alive—because his mother wanted to run off and start over with some guy she met at work?"

I laugh out loud. "Ha. Some guy!" I stand and fling the chair with so much force, it hits the brick wall and ricochets back to its original place. She flinches for a brief second and then moves toward me with resolve. "While you've found yourself and your altruistic atonement, I've been drifting, not knowing how to survive another year without you. But now I see it. Now I see it. I'm done here. Goodbye, Carin."

Chapter Forty-Eight
The Letters

9 dash out of there without looking back. I hear her screaming after me but I don't pause. All of a sudden, that dark, dank basement is suffocating me. I need to get some air. I climb the steps, three at a time, bolt past the staff standing by the entrance. And then I am outside, running my hands through my hair, pacing in a circle.

My mind is a kaleidoscope of images, but there is one that is first and foremost.

I know that I am not going to marry Isabella. I am not going to settle.

I want to leave, but I know that I'll never see her again. I didn't want it to turn out this way. I didn't even get to touch her. Say goodbye. Tell her that life from here on will be a compromise.

That life with her was the only thing I'd ever done for myself.

"Matias!" she screams from behind me, out of breath and red in the face. She proceeds to throw a bunch of envelopes at me. They hit me in the back and fall to the ground.

I scramble to collect them before the wind blows them away. I'm on my knees, in the middle of a busy sidewalk. Cars are zooming by on Canal Street, commuters with backpacks are running to the train station. The sun is out in full force, a beautiful summer day. I hold the letters as

I stand up to face her.

"They were letters I sent," she heaves. "Yes."

"How many?"

"Once a month. So, five."

"I see."

Her arms swing back and forth and she can't stay still. Tears are streaming down her face. I want to hold her but I know she won't let me. She won't come near. She keeps her distance. "But they were to Trish. Just to tell her I was fine. To tell her—them—not to worry. That I'd just gone on a break, followed my heart for once—but that I'd be back once you and I figured everything out. That I'd be back for Charlie. Losing a mother is devastating! Loss ruins you. I was not going to do that to my son!"

I look down at the letters and flip through each one. Each graying, linen envelope has no return address. I play with the dates in my head—the first one is dated one month after we settled in our home. The next time I hear her voice, it comes in spurts because she is crying profusely.

"And yes! I knew we'd have to leave. Our lives. They're made up of our families—these are the people who have molded us. Even Isabella and Jack. No matter how much I wanted to, I couldn't just walk out on that. They came back to me in my dreams, in my thoughts. Every wonderful moment with you felt incomplete, felt like a farce."

"A farce," I repeat. "I loved you."

"I've paid the price. You went back to your comfortable little life while I paid for my sins. So, go back. Just go back," she says, turning away from me.

I rush to her. She tries to fight me off, pounding her fists on my chest and grimacing as she pushes me away. But I don't let go. I hold her tightly, her chest against mine, muffling her sobs on my shoulder. I feel the weight of her body on me and it brings me back to the days when that had been all I needed to live. I fed off that touch, that body. I've never felt emptier in my life.

People stop to watch us. I don't care. She mumbles through her tears. "I wanted all three of you. Why was it so wrong to want all of you?"

"Three of us?"

"I didn't know I was pregnant!" she squeaked. "I lost our baby eight weeks after I left the island."

With that, she collapses, her knees hitting the pavement. I want to fall on the ground too, but I know I have to hold her up.

"Let's go somewhere we can talk," I say, guiding her directly toward a Starbucks on the corner. She shakes her head and points to a metal bench on the edge of what looks like a small playground. There are colored benches adjacent to us, filled with parents, their voices reverberating in nonstop chatter. This time, we sit close to each other— side by side, but not touching. The sun is still out. It reminds me of the perennial summers I'd thought we'd have forever.

She is facing me, speaking quietly in my ear, conscious of the fact that there are people all around us. Before I say another word, she launches into her story, making sure to leave no detail, no question.

"I loved you," she says, self-consciously wiping a tear. She looks to the side, wanting to see if anyone is watching us. Everyone is so engrossed in their own little ramblings, we are fine. "You were my life. I wanted to give up everything I had, everything I'd known, for you. But I have a son. I have a beautiful son with a bright future, who has no one else but me. I couldn't abandon him forever. I am his mother. I didn't even know I was pregnant until the miscarriage started. So you see, Matias. I died too."

I gasp. I try to breathe but my lungs are locked up. It's a physical sickness—the feeling of dying because there is no air left in the world to sustain you.

She sees the pain in my face, takes my hand and squeezes it. "We've lost so much because of what we did. Our credibility, our loved ones. It was reckless, random. In a way, I am happy you're going to be married soon. You'll have the family, the stability you've always wanted. You love so much, you give so much, you deserve someone who will love you with all her heart again."

"And you? You don't deserve to be happy?"

"I am happy. I was never at peace without Charlie, and now I am. We're repairing our relationship. I'm reconnecting the pieces I've severed."

"I died without you."

"Soon, you will be married and have your very own family."

"It's not too late," I cry too, pulling her to me. "I want that with you. We can still have that, Carin."

She rattles her head, goes limp like a rag doll.

I want to explain. "I did it to appease my parents. I've hurt them so much. But I can't hurt myself again. Why can't we give this another chance?"

"We have so much to atone for. We can only move forward. There is no going back. Do you remember the vow I made to you? I loved you. More than life itself. I gave up my world for you. We had a life. We had a child. That's the end of our story."

"No," I answer. "I won't accept that."

She stands before letting go of me. Slowly, she backs away, inch by inch until we are standing a few feet apart. There is a life-sucking vacuum that emerges out of nowhere. We are tired. Spent. I want to fight but she is right.

"For a while," she says, "Olive refused to settle into her new life. She refused to eat, hardly slept, was overwhelmed by the sudden change in her environment. She would circle the house over and over again, as if trying to find something. It was you she was looking for. It took her three months, but now she is fine and well adjusted. Time heals all wounds, Matias. Pretty soon, the pain we feel will succumb to the travails of daily life. We will be fine. I promise."

"You and I, we've made a mess, haven't we?"

She laughs. "Understatement."

"But we can fix it. Let me fix it. I'll fix everything, okay? You deserve your peace, Car."

"And so do you." Her eyes glisten with tears.

We sit in silence for a few seconds, watch as a blond-haired little boy runs to his mother for a juice box. Another little girl is rolling around on the grass in what looks like a major tantrum. The colors of the summer are muted in this place. The metal bars and swing-set links are tarnished, the grass is brown and discolored. We all allow our feelings to mask the real view of the world. We see it all through different colored lenses. I saw mine in Technicolor. I don't see that anymore.

"Carin! There you are!" A man in a blue suit dashes toward us, out of breath but smiling. "I was on my way to the Starbucks to look for you there."

"What's wrong, Josh?" she asks. I wonder if she's relieved to have the perfect exit. She's wanted to walk away ever since she got here.

"The Mayor is on the premises doing a surprise tour right this minute."

"But," she argues, looking at her watch. "We didn't have an appointment today! We're not ready!"

"I'm so sorry." Josh turns to me with a slight bow of his head before getting back to her. "So sorry but you have to come back."

We're replacing every single selfish act we committed with this newfound selflessness. Helping others, sacrificing for our families. I get it. It's our penance.

"I have to go," she says, stepping in and wrapping her arms around me. I close my eyes and run my fingers through her hair for one last time.

"I'm not giving up on you, Juliet," I whisper to her.

She flinches, squeezing her eyes shut and drawing a deep breath. "Goodbye, Matias," she whispers back, her lips skimming the tip of my ear. Her breath is warm against my skin. "Please, if you want me to get better. Don't come back."

Epilogue –
Three Months Later

I can see her sitting in her favorite place, the booth facing out the window. Today, like most days, she has her sketchpad with her. She's a creature of habit, it seems. Taking a break from three to four in the afternoon, ordering a tall, nonfat, toasted white chocolate mocha and drawing. I can't see what she draws. I can't imagine what she's thinking. But she's always alone. Sometimes, she'll be approached by different people. Men, mostly. But she's always more interested in what's on that piece of paper.

It's been three months since she told me never to come back.

Instead, I did the opposite.

I repented for my sins. Made everything right back home. My parents were consoled by the truth I finally told them. That I could never be the son they wanted. My mother cried and said that all along, I'd misunderstood their intentions. They never wanted me to be someone I wasn't. All they wanted was for me to have a stable future. Something that my father had worked so hard all his life to give to his family.

Isabella's heart broke a second time, but she told me that she'd met someone during the time I disappeared. Like me, she felt it was her duty to her parents to rekindle what we'd had in the hopes of setting the universe on its original course.

Our duty. Our parents. The people we love. We're wired to please, to compensate. We forget most times that the thread that follows one act is often indestructible. That's life, you know. Finding that balance between being selfish, taking care of your happiness without upsetting the ties that are intricately wound around every single decision you make. In making amends with my loved ones, I realized how truly selfish I'd been with my love for Carin.

Starting over.

That's what I did.

I may not be running my father's business in Spain, but I set up an import/export company right here in town. My office is a two-room flat in the Lincoln Park neighborhood. My father is my partner. Our business, Casa Olivia, grossed three million dollars in three months. I'm beginning to believe that my parents' days of disappointment are over.

I live in a three-bedroom penthouse on the 21st floor in a building in the North Shore area. I know I'm by myself right now, but who knows what can happen in the near future. I have so much hope. Love does that for you, gives you hope. I believe with all my heart that she loved me before. If I show her I've righted all wrongs as best as I could, then maybe she can love me again.

Today is finally that day. I've worked my way, prepared myself, set a new life in motion. I want her in it. I want to try. This time, no lies, no false pretenses, and no living on islands away from the people we love.

Christmas is in the air. All the heavy promotions about pumpkin spiced lattes and gingerbread cookies line the counters. The barista is humming to "O Holy Night" by Alicia Keys. There's a Christmas tree in the corner all decked out in red, peppermint sticks hanging like ornaments, free for the taking.

I take a deep breath before approaching her table. Today, she sits by the front door on a raised two-top, her legs are dangling above the floor, one furry brown boot hooked around the leg of the chair. She's drawing furiously and there are colors today. I watch her vigorously shade her pad with a green crayon.

"Hi," I say, hands in pockets, tone subtle and quiet.

She looks up to find me there, her eyes wide with surprise. I see her lean forward as if wanting to greet me with a hug, but she pulls back just as quickly. Her eyes light up for a second, and then she looks away. I can tell she has many questions, but she doesn't say a word.

"Is this seat taken?" I ask.

"No, it isn't," she answers with a smile.

It's a sunny day on the island. The breeze is blowing softly and we are making love on the sand.

"Thank you," I say, pulling the chair back and taking a seat. "My name is Matias Torres." I offer my hand.

She plays along.

"I'm Carin Miller. So nice to meet you." Her hand is warm, her thumb brushes lightly against my wrist.

I lean in to see what she's drawing. I finally see it, and it brings me to tears. Of course, I try my best not to show any emotion. It was the intensity of my love, the greediness of my need that separated us and I don't want to drive her away.

"Love those palm trees," I say. "What beautiful scenery. The ocean is so blue and the clouds are luminous. How does one translate such a vivid image on paper?"

"I still see it clearly, you know," she whispers timidly, her eyes remain fixed on her pad. "The happiest time of my life."

"I've had those times too," I answer.

She puts down the crayon and takes a sip of her coffee. "So, Matias Torres—what is it that you do and what brings you all the way to this neighborhood?"

"I own a furniture store. We import handcrafted furniture from Spain. My father is my business partner, and we just opened in Lincoln Park two months ago. You should come visit it sometime," I say, afraid I've overdone it. "We're online, you can look us up. Casa Olivia is the name."

"Oh! That's not going to be difficult to remember. I have a dog named Olive."

"You do?" I laugh. "What a coincidence."

"What kind of furniture do you make or import?"

"All kinds," I answer. "Most of them, we custom make."

"I bet you make really beautiful tables," she says.

"Yes, tables." I smile back. Our eyes meet. I'm careful not to take it there today. "Carin Miller, aside from having a dog named Olive, what else should I know about you?"

"I'm a divorced mother of a wonderful boy named Charlie. He just turned twelve! He goes to the Catholic school right in this neighborhood."

I nod. "Sounds like he brings you so much joy. You two must be very close."

"He does. And we are." She smiles with her eyes this time. They curve down to touch the corners of her mouth. She glances at her watch and hurriedly begins to pack up her crayons, placing them in a zippered pouch together with some charcoal pencils. "I'm so sorry to have to run but I have a staff meeting in ten minutes. I loved meeting you, Mr. Torres. I hope I see you again."

"Maybe we could have dinner sometime?" I ask nervously. As if this was my first date with the woman I am going to love all my life.

"I would love that," she answers. "Have a good evening."

And when she walks away, she takes with her every trace of a former life. And I let her. Because in its place, she's left a part of her behind with me.

The part that has given me the hope I need.

The promise of a new beginning.

Acknowledgements

This book delves into a subject that most of us don't recognize until it's too late. Depression is a serious illness. It tricks our minds into hopelessness. My goal was to bring it to the forefront so that we all get to the help we need to overcome it.

If you're reading this, it means you've reached the end of my journey.

I am truly indebted to each and every single one of you for giving my books a chance. You have given me my words, you have shared with me your lives, you are the reason for this second life, this passion, the inspiration. **Thank you**, from the bottom of my heart.

There are too many of you to name, but you know who you are. Thank you, **Brae's Butterflies** for your years of friendship and support.

My agent and friend, **Italia Gandolfo** and my publishers, **Vesuvian Media Group and Spark Books** for your unwavering faith in me. **Liana Gardner**, for keeping me sane most of the time. **Jim Thomas**, my editor, who for the past four years has been my teacher and guide; **Holly Atkinson and Katie Harder Schauer** for your tireless efforts to make sure the book is just perfect. **Hang Le**, you created my favorite cover.

Ashley Baker, Trisha Rai, Michelle Kannan for being the best PAs in the whole world. Once upon a time.

Tarryn Fisher, you are always here.

Willow Aster, you too.

To all the **authors and bloggers** who have supported me over the years, I am truly grateful to you for this experience. To **G. Celasco and E. Chriqui**, for that incredible time.

And to my family, who loves the two sides of me every single minute of every single day. You make it all worthwhile.

My books have always been about strong women who do the dumbest things for love. Keep doing dumb things because LOVE will always win. If it is meant for you, you will find it.

Believe in yourself. Know that you are not alone.

And NEVER, ever say NEVER.

xo

.

About the Author

Christine Brae was born and raised in the city of Makati, Philippines before she met and married her best friend who whisked her away to Chicago over twenty years ago. Since then, Christine has established herself as a full time career woman, holding a senior executive position in one of the largest global advertising agencies in the world. She is the author of six novels, has an established fan base and a dedicated following. Her titles have consistently ranked in the Top 100 months following their release.

www.christinebrae.com